STONE COLD

Marilyn Todd

This first world edition published in Great Britain 2005 by
SEVERN HOUSE PUBLISHERS LTD of
9–15 High Street, Sutton, Surrey SM1 1DF.
This first world edition published in the USA 2005 by
SEVERN HOUSE PUBLISHERS INC of
595 Madison Avenue, New York, N.Y. 10022.

British Library Cataloguing in Publication Data

Todd, Marilyn
    Stone cold
    1.   Claudia Seferius (Fictitious character) - Fiction
    2.   Private investigators - Rome - Fiction
    3.   Rome - History - Empire, 30 B.C. – 284 A.D. - Fiction
    4.   Detective and mystery stories
    I.   Title
    823.9'14 [F]

    ISBN 0-7278-6187-5 (cased)
    ISBN 0-7278-9140-5 (paper)

Typeset by Palimpsest Book Production Ltd.,
Polmont, Stirlingshire, Scotland.
Printed and bound in Great Britain by
MPG Books Ltd., Bodmin, Cornwall.

Prologue

*D*eep in the dense, dark forests of south-west Gaul, a young woman gathers berries in the afternoon. From time to time she pauses to nibble on brambles that shine like ravens' wings, or clusters of ripe red raspberries that scent the air and show the teeth marks of mice. There is no wind in the forest, and what little sunshine manages to penetrate the aromatic canopy is sprinkled with butterflies and powdered with fine particles that float in the stillness.

Passing slender rowans, their branches heavy with ripening fruits, the girl is reminded that her father uses this bark in his tannery, just like he uses the bark from holm oak and the young branches of sumach. She smiles, revealing dimples in both cheeks. Soon she will be married, and then (praise the Hammer God!) there will be an end to the stench of stale urine that every tanner uses to loosen the wool and hair from the hides.

Brigetia had never grown used to it.

Even though she was born here, she has never grown used to scraping the slime off the skins then shunting the sludge into the river, but, come the next quarter of the moon, she'll be free of all that, and for ever. Her sister can jolly well take over the task of collecting piss pots from the homesteads and emptying them into cisterns that are sited far too close to the house for her liking. Brigetia will be moving into her husband's house in the village! Then his widowed mother will have to give up her place by the hearth and Brigetia can start raising chickens and children, her hams hanging from the rafters, her stews bubbling in cauldrons without taint from any damn tannery.

Brigetia smiles again, and the dimples in her cheeks turn to pits. Ah, but what a strapping fellow Orix is, with thighs

1

like tree trunks to sire lusty sons and a strong back to make the siring a pleasure! As she tucks rosehips into her basket, she pictures him preparing for their wedding, first looping his long hair into the traditional Santon war knot before donning the tribal Virility Helmet adorned with stout prodding horns. What feasts and celebrations are in store! Stretching on tiptoes to reach an overhang of elderberries, she sees drinking cups brimming over with foaming ale and can almost smell the ox roasting on the spit as the pipes and drums of the marriage dance echo round the forest. The sun begins to sink, and as Brigetia tosses her gold braids over her shoulder, flycatchers trill in the ancient gnarled oaks, turtle doves coo and, in the distance, a woodcutter's axe chops with rhythmic regularity.

Behind a holly bush, eyes monitor Brigetia's every move.

They follow the curve of her ripening breasts, the sway of her pubescent hips, the velvety plumpness of her dimpled cheeks. For a split second, the eyes flicker back towards the village, where coils of grey smoke spiral up from the treetops, testimony that food is being prepared over cooking fires by the womenfolk for men who will not cease labouring until the sun has sunk a lot lower yet. Not that it makes a jot of difference. Nobody walks this woodland path, for it ends at the tannery and there are better – and more fragrant – routes to the river for those who live in the village.

The Watcher's attention reverts to Brigetia.

To the clearness of her complexion and the brightness of her blue eyes.

Every now and again she stops to hold up her left hand and admire the betrothal ring that gleams on her third finger. That the ring has been exquisitely crafted the Watcher can tell from here. The intricacy of the whorls etched in the bronze reflect the skill of the engraver, which in turn reflects the esteem in which her young bridegroom holds her. Quite right, too. The girl is perfect. Perfect in every way.

The Watcher waits until Brigetia bends down to gather a handful of bilberries.

The woodland floor is soft and springy.

The Watcher's feet make no sound.

2

One

'Make way! Make way for the Governor!'

It was a testament to the soldier's vocal chords, Claudia decided, that he was able to make himself heard above the jangle of breastplates and the tramp of hobnail boots crunching over the bridge.

'Come on, you lot!' he shouted. 'Move aside, move aside!'

An old peasant foolish enough not to have learned Latin in his own country suddenly found himself in the gutter as the chariot trotted past, a triumph in imperial purple and gold, the heads of the pure white horses held appropriately high as their braided tails bobbed and their hooves clip-clopped in perfect harmony over the cobblestones. No sooner had the Governor and his escort passed, however, than the gap was immediately filled again with riders, carters, donkeys and pack mules vying for space amid the swarms of pedestrians entering and exiting the city.

Standing in the middle of the bridge, resting her arms on the warm stonework as she leaned over the side, Claudia watched the bob of traffic in the slow-moving waters of the Carent. As was to be expected, most were Gauls, the women clad in jaunty fringed skirts that fell to mid-calf, their menfolk with long hair whitened with lime and sporting such luxuriant moustaches that they overhung their top lips like the willows that lined this twisting river. But not all the traffic on the bridge was local, nor was Santon the only tongue spoken. Claudia cast her eyes across to the skyline reflected in the shimmering current and drummed her fingers.

Nestling beneath the high wide skies that were so typical of this part of Gaul and surrounded by gentle rolling hills and wooded river valleys, lush water meadows and forests rich in game, Santonum should have been the answer to Claudia's

3

prayers. She watched trout swimming lazily in the shadows of the bridge's pillars and swallows dipping and diving on the water, and thought that, dammit, this is the capital of Aquitania. The authorities should have turned somersaults to help one of their own who'd trekked halfway across the bloody Empire just for this. Instead, what did she get?

'Terribly sorry, milady. The files were destroyed in a fire.'

'Our records were shipped back to Rome.'

'There was a flood . . .'

'. . . mould . . .'

'. . . mice . . .'

She'd tried the barracks, the State Records Office, the temples, the tribunals. She'd done the full tour of scribes, secretaries, lawyers and civil servants. She'd bribed and gossiped her way round the basilicas and bath houses that were springing up in this new town like weeds and yet – what a coincidence – every person she spoke to would really have *liked* to have helped, were it not for the Fates conspiring against them. You wouldn't credit so many natural disasters could have befallen one city, but it seemed there was no limit to the excuses she'd encountered, much less the inventiveness of the excusers. Quite why these people hadn't taken up careers as playwrights she had no idea, but if Offialdom was hoping Claudia Seferius would give up and go home, it might as well wait for the moon to drop out of the sky.

'Stay here,' she instructed her bodyguard.

'But—'

'Butts are for archers, Junius, and whilst they might equally apply to jokes and billygoats, they are not, however, for you.'

The young Gaul's mouth opened and closed as he fumbled for a suitable response, but by the time he'd come up with one, it was too late. He was being skewered by a glare that would make a cheesemaker proud, since it could separate curds from whey in less than ten seconds.

'Here,' she insisted.

There were many reasons why a wealthy young widow might need a bodyguard – protection from bandits, rapists and thieves to name but a few – but there are certain aspects of one's private life that a girl is obliged to keep private and, on those occasions, compromises to safety must be weighed up.

4

'Jupiter, Juno and Mars! Are you deaf, man?'

She'd barely reached the end of the bridge and he was behind her.

'I cannot leave you unaccompanied, my lady. Who knows what danger might—'

'Junius,' she hissed, 'if you move so much as one inch from this spot, I'll guzzle your gizzards with gravy.'

You couldn't fault him as a bodyguard, she supposed, sweeping beyond the elegant limestone buildings fronted by shops that sold everything from potions to padlocks to peas into an unstructured tumble of thatched roundhouses and wooden shacks along the river. The boy had muscles of steel, was a dab hand with the sword and his knowledge of this guttural tongue was proving invaluable on this trip. It was just that Claudia's own shadow rarely stuck that close, and every time she turned his gaze was clinging tighter than limpets to a rock in a storm. At the corner, where a coppersmith in red check pantaloons was attempting to hammer flat a large sheet of twisted metal, Claudia glanced over her shoulder. Good. Junius might be fidgeting with his dagger and looking for all the world like he'd swallowed a wasp, but it was more than his life was worth to move from that bridge. Turning away from the river, she ducked down an alley fragrant with cooking smells. Here, women sang lilting songs as they draped laundry over wickerwork frames while others chopped herbs with their babies strapped to their backs.

'Ze lady would take a leetle 'oney cake, yes?'

'Certainly,' she told the vendor, whisking it out of his hand.

Vaguely, she was aware of someone being cursed loudly in the Gaulish language and thought she heard the words 'theeving beetch' shouted in her direction, but the honey cake was warm and distracting, and, besides, there were more pressing things on Claudia's mind.

Her father, for one.

Wiping the soft yellow crumbs from her mouth, her mind travelled back to the last time she'd seen him. Even though she was just ten years old the memory was vivid, and, although his features had blurred with the passage of time, she could, when she closed her eyes at night, still feel his whiskery cheeks against hers, and smell the masculine scent of his clothes.

5

Each year it was the same. At the start of the campaign season, he'd march off behind the legions with the rest of the camp followers, and she would wave and wave until her little arms ached and the army was reduced to a dusty dot on the horizon. Then, in October, he'd trudge home again, tired and weary, but not so exhausted that he and her mother wouldn't spend the whole winter fighting, before he packed his bags again the following spring.

Every year, except the year when Claudia turned ten. That March, her father set off – to Aquitania, as it happened – only this time he never came home.

Perhaps it was plunging from sunshine to shade in the wooded enclave that was the leatherworkers' quarter, but suddenly her step faltered and the honey cake turned to ash on her tongue. Darker memories flooded back. Of her mother, drunk as usual, reeling from one office in Rome to another, trying to find out why her man hadn't returned with the legion and what compensation they were going to pay her. The soldiers' jeers echoed for years in Claudia's head and, young as she was then, the implication had been obvious.

But had her father really had it to here with the nagging, the insults and the flying crockery and opted for a fresh start in the newly created town of Santonum? He hadn't been killed in combat, that's for sure, because Claudia remembered with humiliating clarity her mother's slurred screeching outside the tribune's office about how her man's name had still been on the lists for rations until the legion moved out, so why the eff couldn't the effing bureaucrats keep track of their own effing people?

Sadly, she realized, he could have gone missing for any number of reasons. He might have died from injuries that, as he was a lowly orderly, would not have been recorded in military logs. He could have caught a fever, picked up dysentery, fallen victim to snakebite, even sustained something like a head injury from a fall which had blanked out his memory. It happens. But for Claudia the itch of uncertainty needed a scratch that was long overdue. She had to know whether he was alive or dead to fill in the missing gaps of her childhood – except the past was proving hard to dig, and for reasons she could not have imagined.

Mice, mould, floods indeed! Rome, dammit, was covering something up, but it only needed a quick skim through the history books to remember that Rome had erected a stone wall once before! On that particular occasion, they walled off the entire toe of Italy in an attempt to starve Spartacus and his rebel slaves into submission. Unfortunately, in doing so, they'd overlooked the little matter of Spartacus being a gladiator whose very training encouraged him to think laterally and play dirty, rather than a soldier who employed the more traditional rules of combat. As Spartacus had marched his rebel army north in triumph, Rome had been left with an awful lot of egg on its face.

All Claudia needed to do was visit the chicken house while the hens were still laying . . .!

At midday, the tavern was bursting with men clad in plaid pantaloons tucked into soft ankle boots knocking back goblets of ale that spilled over with foam and wolfing down bowls of steaming dark stew that reflected the bountiful forests which encircled this town. To their welcoming grins, she slipped into a seat by the door, while in the corner a boy whistled a tune on a cheap wooden flute and his friend beat time on a coney skin stretched over a hoop. But even as Claudia's toe began to tap to the jig, she was aware that whilst the majority of Santons had adapted to life under the eagle with cheerful enthusiasm there were plenty about who had not.

Old memories die hard.

Grudges linger from one generation to the next.

Today the tribes might be allies, indebted to the troops who patrolled their borders and kept the roads and waterways free of bandits, and delighted that another army was daft enough to fight their wars for them, leaving foreign sons, not their own, mourned. But, forty years earlier, these same people had resisted invasion with a ferocity that Rome had not envisaged. First they slaughtered the men sent to conquer them – a whole army including their legate – then they routed the legionaries sent by Julius Caesar to avenge them. Oh, yes. The Santons were a force to be reckoned with.

But times change. Leaders change. Politics invariably follow.

One of the first acts instigated by the young Augustus

7

after being crowned Emperor was to expand the trade links between Lyons and the town of Burdigala, on the Jirond estuary. Being expert potters, stonemasons and metalworkers in their own right, the Santons suddenly found huge markets opening up – and at profits they'd never dreamed of. Loyalties switched in a flash, and when the Emperor finally declared Santonum the capital of the new Province of Aquitania, the resulting rash of aqueducts, theatres, bath houses and temples bestowed on them such a sense of superiority over their fellow Aquitans that they actually saw this as liberty rather than conquest.

On the other hand, there are always those who relish the taste of sour grapes. Maybe someone who begrudged the ten per cent tax he was forced to pay Rome (and never mind that he recouped more than that in his profits). Or the bigot who felt Gauls oughtn't to trade with outsiders and were diluting the pedigree by intermarriage. But before Claudia had a chance to identify a suitably embittered tribesman among the tavern's patrons, the proprietor came bustling in.

Of a certain age, well-rounded and with merry green eyes, she had a bosom that could balance a tray of sweetmeats without spillage, and she was followed inside by a man whose purple striped tunic proclaimed him a Roman of equestrian rank. Right now, the Roman was attempting to sell her his horse.

'Twenty gold pieces?' His rich, fruity tones assumed an air of mock outrage. 'I can assure you, dear lady, this beast is good for another ten years, possibly, dare I suggest, even twelve.'

The landlady's laugh was flirtatious, but genuine. 'Are we talking about you or the horse, Hannibal?'

'Both, may your gods and mine will it.' Tall, tanned and leathery, he was the same age as his adversary and had the same playful glint in his eye. 'The only difference, dear lady, is that you will find my worth higher than this poor brute's.' He leaned rakishly towards her, and Claudia thought, dear me, ships could be sunk in that cleavage. 'So what do you say, then? Forty?'

Dancing eyes assessed the snickering horse tied to the post. It was no Arab stallion, but even Claudia, whose knowledge of horseflesh extended no further than the bookies' tables, could see it was a fine, solid mount.

'I'll give you twenty-five, Hannibal, and no more.'

One eyebrow rose slowly. 'Surely you can stretch a bit further for such a, ahem, strong, handsome creature?'

The landlady chuckled. 'Well, I suppose I could manage thirty, if you press me.' She winked. 'Which I can see you're dying to.'

'You would not be wrong,' he drawled back, stroking the bunch of feathers pinned into his cloakpin. 'Suppose we say midnight, and you leave the side door unlocked?'

'Rogue,' she laughed, shaking her head. 'Now sit down, will you, before I forget I'm a grandmother. I'll bring you your money when I've finished serving this lady.'

Hannibal bowed. 'It is a pleasure doing business with you on all, er, fronts, and as for the little matter of age, I say again. Midnight! And be sure to leave the door ajar, dear lady. I have no desire to waken the whole district with my knocking, for it is my intention to inflame you, not your neighbours.'

'Men,' she tutted to Claudia, although it was obvious from the shine in her eyes and the bloom on her cheeks that the landlady was not altogether unimpressed with the horse-seller's attentions.

'Now then.' She glanced across to where Hannibal was in the process of hooking a stool from under a table with one leisurely foot and it seemed her breath grew that little bit shorter. 'What can I get you, my lovely?'

'Information,' Claudia replied, laying a kidskin pouch on the table, which chinked when the contents settled.

'Indeed.' The merry green eyes were suddenly serious as the tavern-keeper settled herself at the table and leaned forward. 'And what kind of information might a lady of quality like yourself be after, exactly?'

'Not that kind,' Claudia told her, although she was willing to bet that if she'd wanted a backstreet abortion, the woman would recommend a physician oozing compassion and skill. 'I'm trying to trace a man who disappeared from here fifteen years ago and—'

The landlady couldn't have jumped higher if she'd been stuck with a pin. Her face turned as white as birch bark.

9

'F-fifteen?' Her laugh was unconvincing. 'My, my, that's an awful long time to be going back.'

On the contrary. Judging from her reaction, it could have been yesterday they were talking about. The hairs on Claudia's scalp started to prickle.

'Why?' she asked bluntly. 'What happened fifteen years ago?'

'Nothing!'

But the answer came too fast for Claudia's liking, and the woman's blinking was too rapid.

'Nothing happened. Why should it? No, it's . . . it was, well . . . why, that was the year I married my second husband, so it was. The memory caught me by surprise, that was all.'

Claudia nudged the purse across the table. 'You're an awful liar, do you know that?'

'Aye.' The tavern-keeper nodded glumly. 'Reckon I do, but I will say this. You won't find anyone around these parts willing to talk to about what happened back then, not a soul, so my advice is don't waste your time trying.' She pushed the purse back across the table with a gesture of finality and stood up. 'I'm sorry for you, honest I am, because you wouldn't have come all this way if it wasn't important to you, but there are some things that are best left in the past and that's one of them.'

First Rome, now the locals . . .

'Look, I'm not interested in politics,' Claudia assured her. 'It's just one man—'

'No, it isn't. It's never just one man,' the woman retorted. 'It's always somebody's father and somebody's son, a brother, a lover, a friend. Let it go.' She drew a deep breath, and the next time she spoke it was gently. 'Because the way I see it, love, if the man you're looking for's dead, then he's dead, and if he's alive – well, I reckon he don't want to be found. Now if you'll excuse me, I need to see a man about a horse.'

The twinkle returned to her eye as though nothing had passed between them.

'Might slip him a plate of food while I'm at it.' She adjusted a finely dyed curl, then patted her awesome embonpoint. 'Many a good man's been lost to my veal and ham pies – and a few bad 'uns, as well.'

10

The speed with which she bounced back left goose pimples crawling over Claudia's skin. The woman hadn't been faking. Her reaction had been a hundred per cent genuine, which meant something was going on in Santonum – something dating back to the time of her father's disappearance – and if one thing was guaranteed, it was that the smell of fish in the air wasn't rising up from the river.

Let it go, she had said.

Let it go . . .? This was only the beginning, goddammit, not the end! Claudia hadn't come all this way to give up now, and the woman was right. It *was* somebody's father they were talking about. Hers! And whilst she had no idea whether he was involved in whatever funny business both sides were determined to paint over, she had no intention of leaving without knowing the truth.

The only question was, if Rome wasn't talking and neither were the Gauls, how on earth was she going to find out what happened?

Two

The air throbbed with late-summer heat and cicadas rasped in the long grass as Claudia returned to the villa. Set north and east of the town in a landscape of soft rolling hills, gentle rivers and wooded valleys dappled with light, it was an imposing edifice two storeys high set round a central courtyard that had been designed to capture every last drop of winter sunshine. As Junius helped her down from the cart and grooms bustled over to unharness the horses, Claudia was at least able to console herself that one of the few saving graces about this frustrating investigation was that she'd landed on her feet in terms of accommodation.

Dwarfed by the soaring marble columns that flanked its portico and soothed by the fountains that rippled, danced and sang in every corner of its peristyle, she reflected that she had not, in truth, been unhappy in Santonum. Just off the Forum but nevertheless right at the heart of the basilicas, the Public Assembly and all the other institutions crucial to her enquiries, she'd found the Lyre Street Inn comfortable, clean and able to serve up good honest wholesome food. But then, two mornings ago and quite without warning, her chamber door was flung open and a woman marched in, dismissing Claudia's maidservant with one wave of her manicured hand.

'I gather you are also a widow in trade,' she said, helping herself to a stuffed date.

Pointed, painted, and with her beauty long faded, only a faint trace of accent remained in her deep, almost masculine voice, and, frankly, if you didn't know, you would have taken her to be Roman through to her marrow. But Claudia had both seen and heard about the legendary Marcia. Many times during her treks around town, she'd caught glimpses of the distinctive gold and green drapes of her litter as liveried bearers carried it shoulder high through the streets, and on one occasion she'd even been close enough to catch a whiff of the balm of Gilead in which Marcia's cushions had been drenched. Rumour had it Marcia was the richest woman in Aquitania. That was probably stretching it a bit, but her wealth was renowned and, in the male-dominated, dog-eat-dog world of commerce, this was no mean feat. Especially for a Gaul.

'Wine,' Claudia had told her. 'I'm in the wine trade.' Then, noting the cut of her visitor's gown and the twinkling gems that adorned it, added, 'Vintage, of course.'

'Plonk, vintage, who cares?' Marcia retorted. 'There's no embarrassing way to get rich.'

Claudia thought about the tax she had fiddled in order to fund this expedition and smoothed the pleats of her robe. Praise be to Juno, Santonum was the one place where the Security Police wouldn't be able to ferret her out and, with luck, by the time she returned home that dear little goddess Discord would have cooked up enough assassination plots, murder and heaven-knows-what to put her petty fraud in the shade. Because if there was one thing you could guarantee about Rome, it was its obsession with conspiracies and revolt.

'Well, you know my motto,' she'd quipped airily. 'Make money first, then make it last!'

'Hm.' Marcia rolled her tongue over her teeth in a manner that suggested humour was on a par with rotting fish in her book. 'I'll send my people up to pack your belongings. This is no place for a woman like you.'

And with that she swept out again, leaving Claudia dashing down to the Temple of Fortune to donate a bracelet for her good luck.

Actually, that wasn't strictly true. Originally she'd draped a gold pendant round the goddess's neck, the one shaped like an owl and inlaid with lapis lazuli and mother-of-pearl. Then she remembered that that particular pendant matched a pair of earrings that went perfectly with that new midnight robe with the embroidered hem, so she went back and swapped it for an old silver bracelet engraved with two swans that was sadly starting to tarnish.

Actually, that wasn't strictly true, either. She'd had to pin the priest against the wall by his throat before he handed the bloody pendant back, but the main thing was, Fortune had been placated, and Claudia was damned sure that a successful businesswoman like Marcia had much to teach her.

Such as holding on to her money, for one thing!

Good grief, you wouldn't think it could be so difficult, inheriting a swathe of vineyards that covered half of Tuscany plus an assortment of properties and businesses in Rome. Yet no matter how much money Claudia made, there seemed to be twice as much going out as came in, and, dear me, it wasn't as though she hadn't made sweeping economies. For instance, she could easily have bought another pair of sandals from that cobbler's shop up on the Esquiline, a green pair to match her new emerald robe, but she'd deliberately restricted herself to six pairs on that visit and was proud of her resolve. Which, incidentally, had held equally firm at the goldsmith's, ditto the dressmaker's, the perfumer's, the hairdresser's and the beautician's, although she could hardly be expected to make a trip to Gaul in last year's fashions, now could she, and it stood to reason that she'd need matching accessories and a decent supply of cosmetics and creams.

'You're back.'

Not a woman to use three words when none would do, Marcia came marching down the portico, hotly pursued by a flurry of slaves and liveried lackeys. Heading this retinue was a man who looked like he'd been hewn out of an ancient oak. Broad at the shoulder, narrow at the hip and with his dark hair cropped in a neat Caesar cut, it was the same man Claudia had seen stationed outside the Lyre Street Inn during Marcia's visit. His name was Tarbel, he wore the same highly polished leather armour, and his eyes were every bit as alert to danger today as they had been two days ago.

'Come,' Marcia said, linking her arm firmly with Claudia's. 'I'll show you my tomb.'

Since it wasn't an invitation, there was no point in declining. Guest or servant, friend or relative, purchaser or vendor, every single person in Marcia's orbit was expected to jump when she clicked her fingers and thus, swept up in the avalanche of attendants and flunkies, Claudia could only marvel at the overheads wasted in running such an overstaffed household. And feel her skin tinge with green . . .

14

'I make no bones about it,' Marcia announced, leading her human snake past topiaried laurels and the giant white trumpets of lilies. 'This tomb will outshine every other civil monument in Aquitania.'

(Not so much a question of adapting to life under the eagle, then. More ego, in Marcia's case.)

'Surrounded by its own park, it— I say, you! Yes, you over there!'

The slave upending a bucket over an arching rose bush jumped as though he'd been scalded. His pail clattered into a bed of heliotrope, knocking them flat.

'How many times do I have to tell you people?' Marcia barked. 'You pour wine over those roots, not water!'

The slave reddened to the base of his neck. 'I – I – '

'Ah, but thees iss wine, your Graciousness.'

The creature whose immaculately oiled black curls emerged from the hedge bowed deeply. Clad in only a loincloth, and a tight one at that, his olive skin glistened almost as brightly as the bangles round his ankles and wrists and the plethora of beads braided into his hair.

'White wine, all the way from the island of Lesbos.' He flashed Marcia a broad, white smile. 'It iss better for rosses than red, being sweeter and not so harsh.'

Marcia's long, pointed nose twitched in what Claudia took to be pleasure. 'Thank you, Semir.' She turned back to the slave. 'Well, don't just stand there, boy! Get on with it.'

The slave looked like he'd just been spared execution, and his hands were shaking like aspens in a gale as he reached for his empty leather bucket. Claudia gulped.

'You . . . water your gardens with wine?' she asked, as the entourage swept onwards through the gate.

Still. Marcia said it herself, there was no embarrassing way to get rich, and who cared whether Seferius wine went down throats or down thistles? A sale is a sale is a sale.

'Semir is from Babylon,' Marcia said, ignoring the obvious. 'Next year, once my tomb is complete, he will recreate the famous hanging gardens, though right now he is busy landscaping the park, part of which is to house a menagerie the likes of which has never been seen in these parts. I tell you, my collection will be the envy of western Gaul.'

15

'Don't tell me, you have your own trapper.'

'Four,' Marcia said without irony. 'One hunting lions in Syria, another fetching me something called an elephant and two more are touring the Orient, seeking out exotic beasts for me to exhibit in crates.'

Claudia wasn't sure that a collection of half-starved, ill-treated creatures would be the envy of anywhere, much less western Gaul, and plucked an apple from the tree as she passed. Beyond the garden, vast herb beds buzzing with bees stretched away into vegetable plots, and, beyond them, lush meadows of grazing cattle, but it was down the hill to the valley that Marcia led her human snake, where the sound of babbling water competed with birdsong in the mellowing sunlight. So. The old bat had a soft centre, after all.

'This is a beautiful place to spend eternity,' Claudia breathed.

Bathed in warm sunshine and brushed by soft breezes redolent with the scent of willow and alder, tall heads of hollyhocks nodded gently on the river bank and the leaves of the poplars rustled like parchment. As a lizard scuttled over the path, a pair of blue butterflies danced down the glade and a frog croaked in the reeds.

'Obviously, the trees have to go,' Marcia said. 'You can't see my tomb for the damned things, but I'll wait a month before chopping them down. Then I can sell the wood on.'

Oh, yes. All heart, this girl.

'You don't think that might spoil the effect?' Claudia ventured.

'Exactly what the Gauls said when I started clearing the site.' Marcia snorted. 'Told me this was a holy site, a sacred place, and that I shouldn't touch it or I would be cursed. Absolute bollocks. It's my land, I can do what I like with it, and if I choose to divert this stream to feed my fountains, they will have to bloody well lump it. Also, my soothsayer tells me that this river is blessed. Padi?'

A plump Indian, who had been hidden by his taller counterparts in the crowd, stepped out of the squeeze, placed his little fat palms together and bowed. Arguably it was the most obsequious bow Claudia had ever seen.

'Mistress Marcia?'

His voice was soft and lisping, reminding Claudia of a snake slithering through the long grass.

'This stream is blessed, is it not?'

'Exceedingly blessed, Mistress. The rods speak of the long-lasting happiness it brings to all those who drink it and the stones-that-talk assure me good fortune runs through it.'

'See?' With a dismissive wave, Padi was relegated back to the ranks of liveried lackies.

Claudia looked into this babbling bringer of luck and contentment, gurgling blessedly over the rocks, and said, 'Doesn't this stream supply that hamlet over there with water?'

'So?' One finely plucked eyebrow twitched in disdain.

'Well, I thought it might bother you that the villagers will be forced to abandon their homes, now that their water supply's been cut off.'

'Bother me? My dear girl, it's time these people realized they have to take responsibility for their *own* lives. Complacency is not a virtue, not by a long chalk, so instead of grousing about what they haven't got, they ought to be looking at this as an opportunity to make a new start.'

Charity might begin at home, but only in Marcia's home, it would seem.

'Anyway, there are hundreds of these little streams for them to live by. They all feed the Carent, that's what makes it so wide and so navigable; who knows what prospects are in store for them?'

Claudia considered the prospects of poverty and family upheaval.

'When you talk about "these people",' she said, 'aren't you a Santon yourself?'

'One must move with the times or risk getting left behind with the dross,' Marcia snapped in her deep, masculine voice. 'In marrying a Roman, I acquired full Roman citizenship. Even gave myself a new Roman name.'

Her thin mouth twisted sideways.

'In fact, I make it a rule never to look back.'

Not entirely true, Claudia mused. This powerful woman was constantly looking over her shoulder. Witness Tarbel. For heaven's sake, Marcia was only taking a walk through her own grounds, yet she was shadowed by the big, Basc bodyguard, whose hand permanently hovered over his dagger. But

17

then you don't grow this rich without making enemies and, gossip had it, she'd made more than most.

'There!'

Marcia pulled up abruptly and Claudia realized they had reached the edge of the clearing.

'My tomb! Built entirely of Numidian marble. I intend to have a gilded chariot winched on to the apex, with a statue of myself at the reins.'

She didn't ask what Claudia thought.

She knew exactly what her reaction would be, long before they approached the clearing.

That was the point of the exercise.

That was the reason she'd spent a million sesterces – and what a way to spend them! For a start, the word tomb was misleading. Far from being a larger version of the stone slabs that lined the main roads into Rome (or any other city for that matter), this was a temple by any other name. Rectangular in shape and sited on a platform approached by a flight of steep marble steps, the columns were for decoration rather than support, and the interesting thing about them was that they ran all round the building in a Greek-style portico, instead of just at the front, in the way Roman architects favoured.

'It's incredible,' Claudia said. 'Truly incredible.'

'Wait till you see the front,' Marcia replied.

Here, fluted columns gave way to an exquisite line of sculpted nymphs that supported the entablature with their heads and, although only half of them had been carved into like-nesses to date, the sculptor's skill stood out a mile.

'Paris! Paris, come here, will you.'

A blond head bleached almost white by the sun nodded acknowledgement from the top of his ladder, but made no effort to lay down his chisel.

'Not *the* Paris?' Claudia whispered.

'Yes, of course *the* Paris,' Marcia retorted, as he continued to chip away. 'My dear girl, if this monument is to outshine every other, then one has no choice but to commission the best. It's the same with the interior.'

She led her inside, where frescoes of the most astonishing colours had already covered two-thirds of the walls in scenes of breathtaking authenticity, though it came as little surprise

18

to note that Marcia featured in every one . . . or that the artist had knocked twenty years off! There was Marcia greeting – not meeting – the Governor. Merchants lining up to do business with her. Marcia on her own boat. (Did that make her barque worse than her bite?) And Marcia throwing banquets at which the most exotic delicacies were being served.

'As you can see, I've combined the very best of international styles in this tomb,' she said. 'Doubtless you've heard of Hor?'

An airy hand indicated the young man dressed in a linen kilt mixing paint on a palette, but, before Claudia could come up with an answer that belied the fact that she hadn't a clue, Marcia was sweeping on, intent on showing her visitor every last detail of his work.

'Hor's famous throughout the whole of Alexandria and, frankly, I consider myself lucky to have him. Mind you, I did have to compromise.'

From his kneeling position, the young Egyptian shot his visitors a wholesome, if rather toothy, smile. Not bad looking in a sanctimonious sort of way and, although his skin was pale from working indoors, his muscles were manly enough.

'Not on the artistry, you understand.' Marcia was quick to make that clear, as the two women returned to the sunshine. 'But Hor was adamant. He would only accept this commission on the strict understanding that his older brother came too, and whilst Qeb wouldn't be my first choice for equipping a menagerie, he does come from a long line of Royal Keepers. The job's handed down father to son, you know. It's not as though he has no experience. Paris! Paris, can you *please* spare us a moment!'

Again the blond head nodded diligently, and again he made no move to descend from his ladder, but continued to chip at the nymph's pretty snub nose, pausing only to blow the dust away.

'Oh, that boy! Still, I wanted a perfectionist.' Marcia sighed, running her hand down the stylus-sharp pleats of the latest Roman fashions immortalized in stone. 'Can't complain now I've got one! Tomorrow, if I have time, I'll take you to the menagerie, and then I'll show you how Semir's landscaping is coming along, but right now I have correspondence to see to. Come.'

19

She clapped her hands and the slaves sprang into line as she set a cracking pace back along the riverside path.

'See here,' she told Claudia, coming to an abrupt halt. 'This is the spot where I intend to build a bridge over the river. There'll be arches on both banks, marble of course, and a marble path leading up to my tomb—'

The arrow came out of nowhere.

A soft hiss. A strangely musical twang. Then a dull thwack as it embedded.

'*Get down!*' Fast as quicksilver, the chiselled bodyguard threw himself over his mistress. 'You too,' he growled, pulling Claudia on to the path beside him and somehow contriving to cover her body with his, as well.

The leather of his breastplate was warm on her back, and he smelled of dense, cedary forests while his eyes, she noticed, were the colour of chestnuts.

'And stay down,' he rasped. 'Both of you.'

His sword was drawn before he'd even stood up, while, behind him, screaming slaves were scattering in every direction, though no one, thank Hades, was hit. Twisting her head, Claudia could see the arrow protruding harmlessly from the trunk of a silver birch, its feathers quivering with menacing grace.

'Padi predicted today would be a day for vigilance,' Marcia said, as though it was commonplace to be lying with her nose pressed against the forest floor. 'But don't worry. If the bastard's still out there, Tarbel will get him. He's from the Pyrenees, and Bascs have a reputation for not giving up.' A deep, almost feral growl came from the base of her throat. 'How I despise cowards who take potshots from a distance, instead of fighting in the open like men!'

'Who's trying to kill you?'

'How the hell should I know?'

Marcia seemed surprised by the question, and the rumours about the number of enemies she'd made through business replayed in Claudia's head. She thought about the villagers forced out of their homes after their water supply had been diverted. The sacred site that had been desecrated for the sake of vanity. And decided that Tarbel was one member of Marcia's staff who wasn't an extravagance!

'It might even be that creep who makes his home in these woods,' Marcia sneered. 'Who can tell what goes on in such minds? My slaves call him the Scarecrow, because the only way they know he's around is when the birds fly out of the trees.'

If that was meant to reassure her guest, it didn't work. Every time a jay squawked or a woodpecker drummed, Claudia's stomach clenched and her palms turned clammy, and it didn't help that the passage of time was marked by the arrow shaft, acting as a macabre sundial on the forest floor. Finally, there was a rustle in the undergrowth. A yelp, followed by a louder yelp, and suddenly Tarbel was propelling a youth through the bushes by an arm pushed up his back.

'*You!*' The contempt in Marcia's voice was colder than ice as she brushed the debris from her robe.

Hardly the Scarecrow. This boy could not have been more than seventeen, well kempt and clean in his plaid shirt and breeches, and he'd probably have been quite handsome, were his face not twisted in pain.

'Why not me?' he yelled. 'Zink you can treat me like dirt, just because you 'ave money? I am a man! I have feelings! I have – aargh!'

'And I'd have you by the balls, if only I could find them.' Marcia's voice was barely a rasp as she squeezed his testicles. 'You're not a man, Garro. You were never a man—'

'Zat's not what you said when I was in your bed!'

'Why do you think I turned you out? You weren't up to it then and you're not up to it now. You need to hide behind trees before you can kill and even then you miss! Take him away, Tarbel. Take this contemptible worm out of my sight!'

'You will be sorry,' Garro screamed, as Tarbel hauled him up the hill at knifepoint. 'You will be sorry for zis, you beetch!'

'I doubt that,' Marcia murmured under her breath as she linked her arm with Claudia's once again. 'It's down to Druid Law now, and that's no picnic, believe me. Oh, don't look so surprised, darling! I can revert to my roots when it suits me, and since he comes from the village it's best these things remain local. Now where were we? Yes, of course. I was telling you about the bridge I intend to span the river down there. As I said, there'll be an arch on each bank—'

21

Claudia ceased to listen. Instead, she was thinking that, all things considered, a year might be too long a wait for that tomb's completion.

Marcia had been wise to plan in advance.

High in the hills, inside the cave from which the Spring of Prophecy bubbled from the rocks, the Arch Druid Vincentrix sat cross-legged on the floor and watched the moon climb ever higher in the sky. ˙

Far in the distance, foxes barked to one another, while outside the entrance to the cave voles and mice scuttled through the bracken, safe from the deadly hooks of sharp-eyed owls, and bats caught moths on silent wing.

With his hands laced together and his steepled forefingers pressed against his lips, the Head of the Collegiate remained motionless as the stars tramped round the heavens, moving only from time to time to lean across and throw more magic herbs on to his crackling fire.

In the valley below, his fellow priests would also be sitting, communicating in the secret language of the Druids as they convened on thrones of sacred oak round a table hewn from yew on which the Keys of Wisdom had been laid out. But the issues they would be thrashing out tonight were local ones. A boundary dispute, perhaps. The setting of a dowry, when the two parties involved could not agree the terms themselves. Passing judgement on other petty issues.

The Arch Druid was above these things. It always was, and must be thus, that he is feared and revered in equal measures by his people for the powers that he alone holds in his hands, the knowledge of the future that he alone can tell, and the wisdom of the ancients that only he alone is able to impart.

Vincentrix tossed another handful of herbs on to the flames and leaned over the smoke. One by one, his gods began to appear.

First, the Horned One, who guides the souls of the newly departed from the Abode of the Dead into the Halls of Change in preparation for a rebirth in which the Arch Druid is their only conduit back to Earth. Then the Shining One, who sees everything from the golden chariot that he steers across the sky, followed by his silver consort, who assumes the mantle

22

of responsibility once darkness falls. Slowly, others joined the group. The Ancient One, bent and wrinkled, from whose tongue hang fine gold chains from which the Knowledge of the Universe falls in tiny drips. The Thunderer. The Flower Queen. Until, finally, the Gentle One, who heals the sick and brings comfort to the dying, took her seat to complete the synod.

You know why we are here.

No words were spoken. None were needed. Vincentrix nodded silently.

Our people no longer bend their knee to us, Vincentrix. They turn to other gods and foreign forces.

Vincentrix knew this to be true and made no reply.

Only you have the power to reverse this situation, Druid. With the wisdom you have learned and the power that lies within you, you must bring the people back.

One by one, they rose and left, until it was just the Horned One who remained silhouetted in the mouth of the cave.

Unless you stop the slide, Vincentrix, your people cannot be reborn.

Cannot be reborn . . .

Vincentrix kicked over the traces of the fire and sluiced his face in the icy spring water. When reincarnation ceases, the soul has no outlet. It dies. The people knew this, yet they continued to be seduced by soaring marble temples, by games, by circuses . . .

The Arch Druid drank deeply of the sweet Waters of Prophecy that gurgled from the rock, but for once no pictures formed. He drank again, and then again, and then again. Beyond the cave mouth, dawn began to tinge the eastern sky with pink.

Three

Due to its strategic importance in matters military and commercial as well as political, the Emperor had taken no chances when it came to town planning. You might think this would have been easy, all Roman towns being laid out on the same basic grid pattern, but this was Santonum, the capital of his newly created province of Aquitania, and it had to be not just good. It had to be right. So he had despatched that arch-strategist Agrippa to Gaul, and thus it was Rome's finest general who finally decreed that the town should be sited on a broad bend of the Carent (optimum defence), that the bridge should be built here (optimum impact) and that the port should be built slightly upriver (optimum profit, since merchants and sailors alike were then exposed to Santonum's temptations as they passed).

Agrippa had been in his tomb a full year now, but his name lived on in many of the public works he had undertaken, from the great baths in Rome to the thoroughfare that bore his name in Santonum, and it was down the mighty Agrippine Way that Claudia now strode.

Around her, charioteers cracked their whips as they rattled past ox carts plodding mournfully along laden with timber and hides, and mules pulling wagons piled high with barrels that were lashed together tightly with rope. Odd thing about the Gauls. They embraced so many modern techniques, yet they categorically refused to give up their oak barrels! Clumsy, heavy and cumbersome, they still preferred them to the far more manageable terracotta amphorae, and it wasn't as though these people weren't familiar with clay. No less than five separate potters' quarters were dotted round Santonum's fringes, producing some of the finest ceramics anywhere in Gaul. (Which, naturally, they exported packed in barrels!)

24

Claudia marched on, overtaken by despatch runners jogging effortlessly along the camber, by merchants cantering along on horseback with their slaves trotting at their heels like hunting hounds, and by strings of strong, Gaulish mules whose packs bulged with onions, blankets and salt.

'Are you sure I shouldn't hire a gig?' Junius asked, as he steered his mistress through a jostle of athletes heading in for the Games.

'Nonsense. The exercise will do both of us good,' she retorted, 'and besides we're nearly there. It's left at that stand of poplars.'

'You mean right.'

'I mean left.'

'The baths lead off to the right, my lady.'

'And?'

'Left leads to the Druids' village,' he said, as they approached the shade of the poplars.

'So we're agreed, then? It's left.' Claudia tossed a handful of coppers into the fountain as she passed.

The bodyguard paused. Fished the last three sesterces out of his purse.

'Junius, you're a Gaul, you don't even believe in our gods.'

'Never say never,' he muttered, 'and anyway this is for you. The Guardians of the Crossroads will be far better disposed towards your ladyship if they receive a more substantial offering.'

'And just why do you think I would need to be invoking their protection?'

Half a dozen moth-eaten dolls dangled from the lower branches of the poplars, and maybe four times as many woollen balls, offerings that dated back to last autumn's equinox, when each household hung a doll to honour the Guardians of the Crossroads, and each slave a woollen ball.

'Because you're a Roman!' he expostulated. 'You can't just go marching up to a Druid—'

'Absolutely right, Junius. I have no intention of marching up to any old Druid. I intend to speak to Vincentrix.'

The colour drained from the bodyguard's face as he made the sign of the horns to avert the evil eye. 'Vincentrix is *Head of the Guild*!'

25

'Exactly.'

If a job was worth doing, it was worth doing well, because even though Roman occupation had diluted much of the Druids' power they still held enormous local influence. Teachers, priests, advisers, judges, they were a class apart from and above their fellow Gauls, who quite unaccountably revered their priests for keeping them in intellectual subjugation.

'And now, Junius, if you have any desire whatsoever to earn the bonus I promised, you will kindly stop giving me grief.'

His sandy mop shook in puzzlement. 'I don't remember you promising me a bonus.'

'Good. Then you won't miss it. Ah, here we go!'

Give them credit, the Druids didn't sell themselves short. Downstream from Santonum, no doubt so they could keep track of the vessels that passed, a cluster of roundhouses far superior in size and materials to anything found locally nestled on a bank of lush green grass beside the river, where willows dangled lazy fingers in the slow-moving waters and ducks dabbled around in the margins. However, for a caste who purported to be at one with the universe, the flash of silver candlebra in this house and the gleam of mirror in the next showed they weren't averse to taking advantage of a few earthly pleasures while they were about it! On the far bank, a heron stalked stealthily, its crest raised in concentration, frogs croaked out a warning from the reeds and a nightingale trilled her sonata from high in an evergreen oak.

Since they were equally prosperous, there was nothing to distinguish one Druid home from another and Claudia continued along the path to where a group of small boys kicked an inflated pig's bladder back and forth as dogs snoozed in the shade and the breeze whispered through the leaves of the poplars. Considering Junius had nearly burst a blood vessel on the way in, warning her about their powers of shapeshifting and sorcery, not to mention an ability to travel different astral planes, she'd been braced for the dogs to be unleashed, at the very least, and a horde of angry Gauls coming at her, snarling with menace. The dogs didn't so much as bark. Of a Gaul, angry or otherwise, there wasn't a sign. And either the children

26

were too well bred to gawp or they preferred footing their ball to conversing with strangers.

'Where is everyone?' she asked.

'There's a council meeting in the forest,' Junius stammered. 'The whole village goes along, though the women have to wait a good distance off. But because the visions drain the priests, they need help getting home, and the older children are left behind to look after the young ones.'

'Ask them which is Vincentrix's house.'

'I don't need to, it's that one,' he whispered, pointing towards the lush green island standing at the point where three arms of the river met. 'But I really think we should leave.'

'You go. Wait for me by that dead tree down the road, that's an order.'

Not because his face had turned the sort of colour you'd expect if you mixed porridge with ash, then added mud. It was crucial that no one discovered the reason behind Claudia's business in Gaul, not even her bodyguard, and everything has its price. Even loyalty.

Access to the island was via a little wooden bridge, half hidden by the Druids' personal granary, built on greased stilts to thwart the mice, and Claudia was not remotely surprised that such a fork had been chosen as the site of the Arch Druid's house. If Vincentrix could make the river branch three ways, what other powers must the old man hold? She smiled. Whatever magic Vincentrix might con his people with, this was one old man who didn't frighten her . . .

On the bridge, she paused to watch a shoal of silver fish dart in and out of the shallows. Nearly sixteen years had slipped by since her father had marched off, but a lifetime had passed in the meanwhile and, closing her eyes, she plunged herself back to her childhood. Smelled the stench of stale piss in the hallways, the rotting cabbage stalks that clogged up the gutters, heard the bawling of babies left unattended, the howling of dogs locked inside darkened apartments, the moans of the dying, too poor to send for a physician. Even then, she'd known she had to get out of the slums and, though her little heart had been breaking when he didn't come home, part of her nevertheless wished her father luck if he'd started a new life somewhere else.

27

She opened her eyes, and the past slithered back under its stone.

It had taken several years of hardship, poverty and pain, but eventually, by adopting the identity of a woman who'd died in the plague and inveigling herself into marriage with a wealthy wine merchant, Claudia's life had been transformed.

The water beneath the bridge was so still and so pure that her reflection came back as a mirror, and in it she could see each strand of her pearl choker. The gleam of her silver bracelet. Even the cluster of emeralds in her gold ear studs. *Dammit, those gems are mine, I bloody well earned them.* She had no intention of seeing them wrenched from her grasp, just because some blabbermouth discovered her past and had her husband's will overturned. Clipping a rebellious curl back in its ivory hairpin, she continued on over the bridge, scattering sparrows from dustbaths in the path, as well as the tabby cat that lay in wait for them under a bush.

'Claudia Seferius. I am honoured.'

She spun round. She hadn't noticed him on the river bank, fishing rod in his hand, for the simple reason that his shirt was the same green as the grass and his pantaloons the same brown as the soil. Like the tabby cat, which had been equally camouflaged, he'd been content to observe and absorb, and it was only now that he decided to cast his line into the water with the gentlest of splashes.

'Where I come from, gentlemen stand up when they greet a visitor.'

'Except you're not in that place,' he replied, flicking the rod. 'What can I do for you?'

She looked at the strong, straight back. The muscles that bulged out under his sleeves. The long, barbered hair that was neither red nor brown, but somewhere in between, reminiscent of a kestrel's flight feathers.

'You?' she replied sweetly. 'Nothing.'

The rod jerked, but only slightly, and it could have been down to a bite on the end of his line.

'I'm looking for the old man. Vincentrix.'

'Then look no further. The old man is right here. I'm Vincentrix.'

She laughed. On the far bank beside the dead tree, Junius

was chewing his nails to the elbows because, even though he'd left Gaul when he was a child, his terror of the Druids remained undiluted. Magicians, sorcerers, clairvoyants and diviners, they were supposed to be able to harness the powers of the universe and guide the dead to reincarnation through wicker man sacrifice, the collecting of heads and a lot of other grisly rituals involving mistletoe, oak and castrating knives. Supernatural powers, my arse! Con artists, the lot of them, and this one – supposedly the most powerful Gaul in all Aquitaine – came right at the top of the list.

'You seriously expect me to believe you're a hundred years old?'

Now it was his turn to laugh. 'Is that what they say?' He pulled a face at his reflection in the water. 'I'm ageing worse than I thought.'

She doubted that. He could not be much more than forty, proof, were it needed, that their religion revolved round manip- ulation, rather than magic. Mixing fear with superstition, then lending an air of fake credibility to the whole hocus-pocus by sending their priests to Britain for a full twenty years on the pretext that doctrines must be learned by heart, since commit- ting their laws to writing was sacrilege.

'So I ask again, Claudia Seferius; what do you want of me?'

'I've come to give my witness statement for the events of yesterday afternoon.'

He nodded slowly. 'Of course you have. Take a seat.'

'Here?'

'Here.'

'Not overly long on hospitality, are you?'

'Interesting that we sit under a clear blue sky gazing over lush water meadows, where larks sing and the bleat of sheep is carried on a breeze fragranced with mint and wild thyme, yet you complain this is not hospitality.'

'I also assume I'm not the first person who's told you how insufferably rude you are.'

Crevices appeared in his cheeks when he smiled. 'You're the one who walked in here uninvited, remember? Do you fish?'

'No, but I'm well used to handling slippery creatures.'

29

Against the simplicity of his light woollen shirt tucked into belted pantaloons, she felt overdressed. Too many pleats, too much embroidery, and her orchid pink robe stood out every bit as much as the kingfisher that darted upriver. The silence between them stretched like worn yarn, and a water vole plopped into the shallows.

'You don't like me very much, do you?' he asked eventually.

Never confuse liking with respect, for what manner of religion deliberately instils fear into small children – and what manner of High Priest is content to allow it?

'If I say no, will you put a hex on me?'

'Do you think I would?'

'You mean, do I think you *could*.'

In response, he tipped back his head and roared. 'Are you sure that arrow was intended for Marcia?' Then his expression changed and he became instantly serious. 'My apologies. A boy attempted to commit murder without provocation and the consequences for that are severe. To joke about such a matter is in extremely poor taste, but, all the same, you did not come here to talk about the attempt on Marcia's life.'

Arrogant. But perceptive all the same.

'Why else would I come?'

He cast his line again with studied casualness. 'In that case, I ought to point out that, as much as I appreciate your commitment to justice, I have no need of your witness statement, thank you. For one thing, I do not preside over local courts and, for another, the boy, Garro, has confessed and a confession is all that is needed.'

As befits the Head of the Guild, Vincentrix's house was much larger than his fellow Druids' and it was built of stone, too, though it still retained a thatched roof. Bees buzzed in and out of the wicker hive attached to the west wall, and a pig snored against the wood pile. Through the open front door of imported, carved cedarwood, Claudia could see tables inlaid with ivory and onyx, the rich tapestries that hung on the walls, and she smelled incense and rare oils that burned from silver braziers dangling on chains from the rafters. But, for all its luxury, the eerie thing about this house was its silence. No jabber of children, no clatter of servants, no signs of another presence, full stop.

'You live alone?'

'I live alone,' he replied. 'But that is not your question.'

'No, it isn't.' Claudia skimmed a pebble across the River Carent. Took a deep breath. Let it go. 'I'm trying to find a man, who disappeared from these parts fifteen years ago—'

'Ah.' Something flickered behind his piercing green eyes, then was gone. 'As much as I would like to help you, I cannot,' he said, rising to his feet, and there was a peppery tang from his skin that was far from unpleasant. 'Druid training lasts twenty years and I was in Britain fifteen years ago. You will need to enquire of others, I'm afraid.'

Yes, and there was as much chance of them talking as Vincentrix's pig soaring over the rooftops on little white wings.

'I bid you good day, Claudia Seferius. May the Gentle Healer be with you.'

'Healer . . .?'

Vincentrix's smile did not reach his eyes. 'You *have* been suffering from insomnia since you arrived, no?'

But before she could lie and deny it, the Druid was gone. Swallowed up in the camouflage of the island. Him and his damned tabby cat.

Four

Back in Santonum, surrounded by schoolchildren tunelessly reciting their numbers and vendors hawking their wares as merchants in togas strutted back and forth and barbers clipped hair on street corners, it was easy to imagine oneself back in Rome. Caulkers, furriers, locksmiths and chandlers laboured away in workshops down side streets lined by stone porticoes. Cobblers hammered hunchbacked over lasts beneath the shade of an awning, perfumers mixed exotic unguents and lyre-makers strummed on their finished instruments, an incitement for people to buy.

Except this wasn't Rome. This was the town where her father had come fifteen seasons before, and Claudia could only imagine the impact on the tribespeople as the army came tramping over a bridge wide enough for two legions to pass six abreast. At the head of this column, the eagle. This would be flanked by standard bearers dressed in animal skins, which, in her father's unit, were of the leopard. Behind the swell of legates, tribunes, prefects and bearers, legionaries in gleaming breastplates marched with such precision that their hobnailed approach could be heard a mile distant. And, finally, the baggage train brought up the rear. Mules and wagons protected by cavalry whose mounts boasted ornate leather masks studded with silvered bronze that blinded bystanders and enemy alike. When you added in the various veterinaries, physicians, secretaries and carpenters, the engineers, orderlies and blacksmiths, the whole thing would have taken hours to pass.

Santonum was a lot different back then, very much in its infancy. Her father would not have seen any of these six-storey apartment blocks, none of the fountains, statues or other fine monuments, and certainly not the aqueduct that brought fresh water into the city. A lot of the temples were still in the throes of construction even now, though the theatre had been finished in his time, being no more than a temporary arrangement made of wood. Had her father laughed at the comedies that were being performed there? Dried a tear or two for the tragedies . . .?

Settling herself on the steps of the basilica, Claudia waited for the lump in her throat to subside. It was inevitable, she supposed, that Vincentrix closed the subject before it had opened. She'd been clutching at straws with that visit, and she had no doubt that it was the Druid Guild that silenced the Gauls in the first place. But why? What could possibly have happened that both Rome and the Santons wanted hushed up? And why – after so much time had elapsed – was it still a thorn in their sides?

Watching lawyers dash in and out of the law courts, scrolls of parchment tucked under their arms, she knew that the sensible decision would be to cut her losses and leave. The tavern-keeper was right. If her father was dead, there was nothing Claudia could do. As a mere orderly, he wouldn't have rated a tomb, so she wouldn't even know where to lay flowers, and if he was alive then the letter he *hadn't* written to her mother told her that he did not want to be found.

'Let it go,' the woman had said.

Let it go.

There was another reason to heed the landlady's advice. Biting into a spicy sausage bought from a hot food vendor, Claudia reflected how Gaius Seferius had been nearly three times her age when they married. He was fat, he was coarse and his hair was receding, but, by Croesus, was he rich! And in return for the pretty, witty young trophy he could parade before his fellow wine merchants, he'd bestowed on her a social standing she'd never known. She'd concealed her past from him – obviously – but, in the end, Gaius probably wouldn't have cared. It was the sort of thing that would have amused him.

Unfortunately, his family were not from the same mould!

Forget the extenuating circumstances. When Gaius died, he'd flouted every convention going by bequeathing his entire estate to his wife. Bitter at not inheriting so much as one copper quadran, his relatives had been desperate to overturn

33

the will ever since, and if they caught so much as a sniff of who Claudia was looking for out here she'd be back in the gutter before she could sneeze. *Let it go*, the woman had said. *Let it go*. And maybe, just maybe, Claudia would.

Had it not been for the Druid . . .

'There you are, madam!' His rich, fruity tones cut through the din of traffic and commerce. 'Hiding behind a pillar, you saucebox!'

'Hannibal.' It wasn't the sort of name you forget, and, besides, she was curious. 'So tell me. *Did* the landlady leave the side door unlocked last night?'

There was a wicked gleam in his eye as he sat down on the steps.

'The charm never fails, madam, only the stamina. Sadly, it takes me all night to do now what I used to do all night, but you will not hear the merry widow complain. I have just this moment removed myself from her bed, where she sleeps the sleep of the angels.'

'It's midday!'

'And your point?'

Claudia laughed. 'She got value for money, I'll give her that.'

'Not as much as I.' He chuckled back. 'Thirty gold pieces for that piece of horsemeat? I only paid twelve for the brute in the first place. However,' he laced his fingers together, 'forgive my poor manners, but I couldn't help overhearing in the tavern yesterday that you are in pursuit of a missing person.'

'Don't tell me *you* know what happened fifteen years ago?'

'Not a clue, madam. Not a clue. But since my current financial state renders me desirous of employment—'

'What about the thirty gold pieces you pocketed?'

'Take my advice, dear lady. Never borrow from a money-lender, especially a Cappadocian, they will follow you to the ends of the earth. Moreover,' he leaned sideways to whisper, 'they have no sense of finesse when it comes to repossessing the interest on their investment.'

'Let me guess. You borrowed twelve gold pieces to buy the horse, but it cost you thirty to repay the loan?'

'Thirty-five,' he grumbled, twiddling the bunch of feathers pinned into his cloakpin. 'Which brings us back to the issue in question. The little matter of gainful employment.'

34

'Hannibal, you're every bit as much a stranger to Aquitania as I am.'

'Impossible to deny, though you'll find me a quick learner, I assure you. A qualified surveyor of His Imperial Majesty's highways, I have lent my hand to all manner of trades over the years. Let me think! I've been a purveyor of pitch at the shipyards in Athens, a reciter of poetry for the sailors of Tyre and for a time I peddled aromatics round the Alexandrian nobility. I have worked as a skinner in Crete, a muleteer in Liguria and, albeit briefly, a tutor to two charming young boys in Helvetia. So you see, madam, there is nothing I cannot or will not turn my hand to, provided, of course, it is legal.'

'You have curiously high principles for a rover.'

'I wish 'twere so noble, but the truth, alas, is horribly base. You see, unfortunate though it is, unlawful activities run a disproportionately high risk of arrest, which invariably results in a stretch in the silver mines, anything from five to ten years. Now whilst I am not averse to hard labour, quite the reverse I might add, what you see before you is a man who cannot tie himself to any one person or place. Hence, a line must be drawn.'

Absolutely. Claudia had drawn one herself. First the Guild of Wine Merchants in Rome. Now the Druid Guild in Santonum.

Having married for money, she'd been all set to sell up when Gaius had died, because a girl can't buy new gowns with half a brickworks or smother herself in gold brooches in exchange for a few mouldy vines. Then she saw the account books, and suddenly an altogether more attractive proposition popped out of the woodwork. Far from having to marry another old duffer where she might not be so lucky and when the next one might insist on his conjugal rights, she would take over Gaius's role. I mean, how hard can it be when you have bailiffs to oversee the production process and a ready-made client list for the wine? It was that naïvety that, of course, had been her undoing. A weakness, incidentally, which had been exploited by the Guild of Wine Merchants before her husband's pyre had stopped smouldering, and slowly, by fair means or foul, they had set about driving her out. Now the Druid Guild was set to do the same. Well, sod that.

All the same, though . . .

'I'm sorry, Hannibal, but on this occasion you're out of luck.'

Desperate she might be. Stupid she was certainly not.

'You think I am incapable of finding the man that you seek?' He was totally unperturbed by her refusal. 'I beseech you to reconsider your decision, madam. You are talking to the only man who talked his way out of a fine for driving his cart through Rome during the daytime.'

Despite herself, Claudia smiled. Wheeled traffic was strictly prohibited during daylight hours. The twisty, narrow back-streets were clogged enough as it was with handcarts and pedestrian traffic, so it was only at night, once the city gates were cranked open and torches lit on every street corner, that delivery carts were permitted to enter, to a cacophony of squeaking axles, braying mules and the crack of bullwhips. Rome might be the city that never slept, she reflected, but neither could its inhabitants.

'Now this is a tale I *must* hear,' she said.

The Administration took no prisoners when it came to contraventions. The fines were punitive in the extreme.

'I was under contract to deliver a consignment of lobsters,' Hannibal said, 'and if I didn't deliver that day then I wouldn't get paid, because no aristocrat in his right mind will serve crustaceans at his banquet when they're on the turn.' He cracked his knuckles. 'The only trouble was, I had been delayed in Ostia by the aforementioned moneylender, and, since I had already bribed the gatekeeper with the last of my savings, there was nothing left in my purse with which to persuade the approaching patrol to turn down a conveniently adjacent alley.'

The Administration notwithstanding, there were times when more soldiers went blind in that city than beggars.

'So, madam, I unhooked the mule.'

'And pretended it was an enormous handcart?'

'Nothing so vulgar,' Hannibal said. 'I simply tied the old moke to the back of the cart, put myself between the shafts and started hauling.

'"Oi, you!" He mimicked the coarse rasp of the patrol. '"Don't you know the penalty for bringing wheeled traffic

36

into the city is eleven denarii?" Eleven denarii. I ask you! It would bankrupt Midas himself. "No use telling me," I called back. "You'll have to take it up with the driver." Madam, those boys fell about laughing so much, I was round the corner before they'd noticed I'd gone.'

'Impressive,' Claudia conceded, wiping her own eyes. But was a silver tongue wedged firmly in its own cheek the answer to her conundrum? What she needed on the case was a professional investigator. Someone who searched secrets out for a living. Knew which stones to overturn, and where.

Only one man fitted such a bill. Marcus Cornelius Orbilio. As the only patrician attached to the Security Police, Orbilio was more than familiar with society's underbelly, regardless of which particular society that might be, since the driving principles of crime are universal. He would certainly know where to ferret out the answers to her questions! The only trouble was, the reason Claudia knew exactly how efficient he was was because he was always one step behind her . . .

Of course, you could put that another way and argue that she was always one step ahead of the law, but, in his case, the law wasn't just tall, dark and handsome, it also took bloody long strides that were headed straight for the Senate.

She supposed that, for an ambitious young investigator with blue blood in his veins, Claudia Seferius was the perfect vessel to attach to. With the sharks circling before Gaius's body was cold, she'd lost track of the counter-tactics she'd had to resort to, although most of them, if she remembered correctly, involved forgery, fraud, tax evasion and what was that other little thing, now? Oh, yes, embezzlement. Was it any wonder Orbilio had attached himself like a barnacle to the hull of her business affairs? Except, just like birth, death and summer colds, one thing was certain. Claudia Seferius would not be his stepping stone to the Senate. Penniless exile was not in her plans.

'So I take it, madam, that I'm hired?' Hannibal murmured.

'You take no such thing,' she retorted, 'and, besides, what about the landlady?'

'Ah.' His mouth twisted sideways. 'I fear we are talking about the sort of woman who if a man pats her bottom will endeavour to turn it into a marriage contract, and I regret to say that orange blossom makes my nose run something wicked. You will be doing both my liberty and sinuses a favour if you tell me we have an agreement.'

'Very well.' In for a quadran, in for the whole damn money chest! 'On three conditions.'

'Name them.'

'Firstly, the pay is one sestertius per day, although I will provide bed and board.' Or rather Marcia will.

'That, if I may say so, madam, is a particularly dubious rate.'

'And you, if I may say so, sir, are a particularly dubious guide.'

He grunted. 'Your second condition?'

'You stop addressing me as though I'm running a brothel.'

'And the third?'

'You dispense with the dead canary.'

'*This?*' In a theatrical gesture of mock protection his hand covered the feathers clamped in his cloakpin. 'I'll have you know, madam, this is the same good-luck charm worn by the youngest tribune in the Roman army to lead a successful assault against Armenian rebels without a single loss to his men.'

'Really?' She peered closer. 'What happened to this illustrious hero?'

'Nothing, although he thanks you for asking.' Hannibal dipped his head politely. 'And whilst he accepts condition one regarding the abysmal pay, the dead canary stays and, since he is an officer and a gentleman, you will understand that it is beneath both of us to call you by a lesser title. *Madam.*'

Just like the traffic patrol in Rome, he was round the corner before she'd stopped laughing.

Five

Whilst Marcus Cornelius Orbilio might not necessarily have been flattered at being compared to a barnacle, it was by one of life's quirks that he just so happened to be lying beneath a boat's keel at the time. Not the most comfortable of positions, but then surveillance work rarely is, and, with his well-nourished physique and an aristocratic mien that could not easily be disguised, he was never going to blend in undercover. Besides, what did he know about caulking, riveting or any of the other processes involved in building boats? So he lay beneath the tarpaulin on the floor of the boat shed, chin in hands, watching timbers being sawn and joints being planed, with the whirr of the hand drills loud in his ears and the dust tickling the insides of his nostrils as he mused on the pageant he should be attending.

Today was the day of the Trojan Games, in which two troops comprising the cream of patrician youth paraded through the streets of Rome astride the cream of Arabian horseflesh. Fully armed and in uniform, these young men would perform complex drill movements designed not so much to entertain the crowds as impress them, and Orbilio remembered the flutter of nerves in the pit of his own stomach when he had taken the reins for his first parade. He'd just turned eighteen and was poised to take up his post in the Imperial Mint as his first step on the road to the Senate. Today it was his nephew's turn, and Marcus pictured his sisters and brothers-in-law, cousins and aunts cheering the lad on from the steps of the Capitol, totally uncomprehending of why his uncle deemed lying on his belly up to his armpits in sawdust more important than supporting his family.

But just as it was vital that the complicated drills and mock combats of the Trojan Games instilled in the people of Rome that whilst commissions might be bought leadership was nevertheless in capable hands, it was equally important that someone clamped down on the bastards who peddled young flesh to perverts who in turn insisted that tiny children actually enjoyed sex.

Orbilio consulted his mental notes as the overseer made his daily inspection. The trafficking was done from this yard, that much he knew, but unless he caught the boatbuilder in the act of passing a child to a punter, the case wouldn't stand up in court. He needed proof, and proof, as he knew from experience, came only after a great deal of stiffness and aching. Boredom went with the territory in this job, but then how does one define boredom? What about the celebratory dinner, in which some stuffy general invariably drones on about a campaign in Galatia that everyone else has forgotten, moving mushrooms round the plate as his troops, while, on the other couch, empty-headed matrons bang on about whether it's fashionable to wear three-quarter-length sleeves this season and their husbands discuss the latest cure-all for baldness? No one moots the issue of seven-year-olds being snatched for some depraved bastard's pleasure, and, assuming politeness did force the question, they wouldn't give a stuff anyway.

Marcus shuffled under the keel. Goddammit, they bloody well should! A child is abducted, subjected to terror, but because it's a guttersnipe this doesn't count, so they call for their goblets to be filled, for another hazel hen cooked in honey, and for the musicians to play something a little more lively. For a family who had devoted generations to practising the law, not enforcing it, it would always be beyond them why he'd chosen to follow a path in the Security Police, which was lowly paid and lowly thought of, when he could be making a name for himself like his father.

His father, his father, always his father. What was so great about that?

True, the old man was a brilliant orator, but it never kept him awake at nights that his clients were guilty. Yet Marcus's father was hailed as a hero. This, the man who had hurtled towards an early grave on a chariot driven by lechery, gluttony and booze! No, thank you. Orbilio had tried it his father's way. He'd completed his statutory two years in the Imperial

Commission at the Mint, followed by a further two years as a tribune, serving everywhere from Pannonia to the moon. After that, it was time to follow his conscience, and if working for the Security Police cost him the respect of his family, so be it. He had long since forsaken theirs.

Fighting cramp in his leg, he heard footsteps. Light, fast, they were the steps of the boatbuilder's daughter, a saucy young strumpet who enjoyed taking 'short cuts' through the shed, knowing the flash of shapely leg through the fringes of her short Gaulish skirt would make the workers' heads turn, as would the bounce of her nubile young breasts. Marcus took advantage of the distraction to massage his shrieking calf muscle and, as the boatbuilder's daughter passed on, feigning ignorance of the catcalls and wolf whistles, he had to admit that he couldn't find fault with her figure, either.

And suddenly Orbilio was reminded of another young woman with dark, flashing eyes and rebellious curls. Who had the same light, confident step.

Of course, that was how Claudia used to scrape a living, once upon a time, dancing in the backstreet taverns of a naval port in the north. She had never forgiven him for finding out, though, much less herself for leaving a chink in the past for someone to crawl through, though for the life of him he couldn't understand why this troubled her. We are what we make ourselves, not what we're born with – a truth he was all too familiar with – and it baffled him, too, why she didn't come right out with it and admit that she was desperate to make a success of her late husband's business for personal pride, rather than money. Despite what she made out, she could have sold up long ago. At a price below market value, admittedly, but Gaius Seferius died a very rich man; there was more than enough to go round, and even now she could liquidate his assets any time she wanted.

As the workers returned to their sawing and hammering, he couldn't help wondering what the devil she was doing in Gaul. He supposed that, in this fast-moving age of science and technology, with concrete revolutionizing building techniques and when ships could sail from Rome to Cadiz in a week, it was perfectly feasible that she'd taken herself off to a town founded less than a generation ago to check out the

41

soil with a view to growing grapes for wine production, as she'd told people.

But somehow he doubted it!

As always when he thought about Claudia, Orbilio's loins began to stir. He imagined himself unhooking the gold girdle that encircled her waist. He saw himself lifting her peach-scented gown over her impossibly long legs . . . slender hips . . . voluptuous breasts . . . tossing it down as the sheet on which he would lay her. Her lips would part and her pupils would dilate as he slowly untied her breastband. He imagined her shuddering as he slipped down the tiny thong that covered her sex, and he wondered whether she would undress him or wait while he slipped off his own clothes?

Mother of Tarquin, would there *ever* come a time when he didn't long for this woman? Half whirlwind, half wildfire, she was abrasive, manipulative, unprincipled and wilful – and the more he saw of her, the more he wanted her, but the more he wanted her, the further out of reach she became.

Propping himself up on his elbows, Marcus returned to his surveillance work and put Claudia Seferius out of his mind.

Six

Beside the spring, where sweet water bubbled up from the ground in a pool that was as blue as the ocean and where irises proliferated in early summer, a young girl laid down her bucket, kicked off her clogs and approached the shrine in her bare feet.

'Great goddess whose name means Winding River, hear me,' she whispered. 'Thou who doth nurture and protect, listen to my prayer, I beseech thee.'

She craned her ears for a sign that the goddess had heard her. Perhaps a rustle in the trees as she came on the breeze? A coo of her sacred dove? But the only sounds in the woodland were the usual chirrups and squawks accompanied by the soft, bubbling music made by the nymphs of the spring.

'Forgive me,' the girl whispered. 'I know I should not approach thy holy place for fear of offending thee with my presence.'

Only the Druids were allowed inside the shrine. Worshippers had to content themselves by making their devotions at the beech tree.

'But my prayers have not carried to thy divine ears, and unless thou canst hear me, how canst thou help?'

Many nights had passed since her sister set off to collect berries and didn't return. Her father had been furious, her mother distraught at the shame Brigetia had brought on the family by running away, but Latuna did not believe the Druids when they insisted her sister had had misgivings about her forthcoming marriage.

'She and Orix were always squabbling,' she told the goddess in a hushed undertone. 'It does not mean Brigetia did not love him.'

But the Druids were far from convinced that Brigetia had

cared so deeply for her betrothed. In a tribunal conducted a quarter moon ago, they had listened to the villagers' testimonies, including that of Brigetia's future husband and mother-in-law, and declared her to be a self-serving minx who was only marrying Orix to advance her own social standing. Latuna had jumped up in protest.

'Surely that makes it all the more logical for her to proceed with the wedding?' she'd argued.

Her own father had slapped her down. 'Hold your tongue, child! You've heard how your sister went round Santonum, telling everyone who would listen that no place was far enough away from the tannery for her taste. And you've heard how she was down by the Carent that morning, flaunting herself around the sailors and—'

'All the villagers talk to sailors when they go into town,' Latuna replied hotly. 'That's how we've come to learn about rafts made of reeds and seas made of sand, of lumpy creatures with humps on their back and horses with black and white stripes—'

'Hush, girl! There's enough dishonour heaped on our family, without you disrupting the hearing,' her mother had hissed, adding that they both knew full well Brigetia was perfectly capable of taking off with any man who promised her a better life.

'Is that true?' Latuna implored the goddess. 'Did Brigetia really run away?'

If she'd had an accident, been gored by a boar for example, there would have been blood, the Druids argued. A thorough search of the area had revealed no signs of struggle, no flattened ferns or churned earth to suggest violence of any kind, and her basket had not been found, either. The only possible conclusion from such incontrovertible evidence was that Brigetia had used berry collecting as a pretext for eloping and, in her absence, she was solemnly sentenced to shunning, should the wicked creature ever decide to creep back with her tail between her legs.

'O, great goddess whose name means Winding River, send me a sign. Give my heart peace, I beseech thee, with a sign that my sister is in good health and no harm has befallen her.'

As Latuna kneeled before the wooden shrine, her hands

44

laced so tightly that the knuckles shone white, sharp eyes watched her every movement.

They watched her lay a carved image of a fawn, the goddess's holy emblem, on the threshold of the shrine and cover it with a garland of flowers.

They watched the heave of her young breasts.

The shine of her hair.

The long, slender fingers that brushed away the tears from her eyes.

No birthmarks, no blemishes, she was straight of limb and free of fault, but, alas, she was not perfect. The Watcher stared at the tight little nipples straining against the soft fabric of her chemise. In a year, perhaps, this girl would be ripe for the plucking, but not now.

The woodland floor was still soft and springy.

The Watcher's feet made no sound as they padded away.

Seven

'Do you believe human beings can travel through time, like the gods?' a small voice piped up, as Claudia sat in the shade of a sour apple tree.

Claudia looked down at the scrap. Six years old, with a round, pink face like a cherub and eyes as big and blue as the Aegean, little hands twisted in anxiety.

'*Do* you?' the child asked again.

'I don't know,' Claudia replied tentatively. 'Why do you ask?'

'Because Mummy said if I don't tidy my room she will knock me into next week. Is that how the gods move?'

'Only if they don't tidy their bedrooms.'

The girl climbed on to the marble seat and wriggled into Claudia's lap. 'You've come all the way from Rome, haven't you?'

'I certainly have.'

'Is Rome further than Santonum?'

'A little bit.'

'Do you think I'd get there by the middle of next week?'

Claudia sucked in her cheeks. 'Only on Pegasus.'

Big blue eyes swivelled up at her. 'Who's Pegasus?'

As Claudia explained about the winged son of the sea, the stallion who could only be tamed with a bridle of gold and who lived in the stables of the gods on Olympus, she reflected on the cut of the little girl's tunic, the quality of the leather of her tiny sandals, and wondered whom she belonged to. Marcia didn't have children, but who else would dress their daughter in Roman garments and tie her hair up in Roman-style ribbons? And why, if her clothes reflected her status, was this child tidying her own room, when Marcia had slaves for every last discipline – and Claudia wasn't just talking about hairdressers and masseurs. There were slaves of the wardrobe, guardians of the jewels, furnace slaves, wine servers, ushers for when she went out, ushers for visitors who came to the villa, foot washers, perfume custodians, fan wallahs to keep her egotistical brow at its ambient temperature.

'Wherever Pegasus stamps his hoof, water gushes out of the rock, and if poets drink from this source they will always find inspiration.'

'Gosh!' Little white teeth bit into her lower lip. 'Do you know any more magic animal stories?'

'Well, there's the three-headed dog, who guards the Underworld, and the reason he has three heads, you see, is so he can watch outwards and sideways at the same time. But since no one ever leaves the Underworld, he doesn't need a fourth head to see backwards.'

'More! Tell me more!'

'All right, what about the sea witch with snakes for hair—'

'There you are, Luci!' A young woman with tired eyes came bustling down the garden path.

'She means me,' the child whispered. 'It's short for Lucina. Bet I'm in trouble again.'

'I'm sorry if my daughter's causing a nuisance.'

Despite her Roman tunic, the woman's dark, glossy hair was scrunched back Gallic-fashion in a band at the nape of the neck, and instead of being manicured her hands were red and work-roughened.

'Hardly, she's just joined me from tidying her bedroom,' Claudia assured her, shooting Luci a conspiratorial wink.

'I doubt that,' the woman sighed. 'That child never does one damn thing I tell her.'

'Told you,' Luci muttered, wriggling down off the bench.

'Put your baby brother to bed, would you, there's a good girl.' Her mother patted the little blonde curls and then gasped. 'My goodness, would you *look* at the dirt on the back of your neck!'

'Like I'm an owl,' Luci grumbled, but she scampered inside all the same, hopscotching up the flagstoned path and singing at the top of her off-key tinny voice.

'Never have children.' The woman laughed. 'But if you do,

47

never have six. You need arms like an octopus and more eyes than Argus himself.'

'I've forgotten,' Claudia said. 'Did he have a hundred eyes, or a thousand?'

'Who cares, it's never enough. I'm Stella, by the way. Marcia's cousin.'

There *was* a resemblance, now you looked closer. Same pointed features, same slender hips. Except Stella's beauty hadn't faded through hardness or been obliterated by a plastering of cosmetics. Her loveliness was still very much evident, albeit tempered by exhaustion and buried beneath a mountain of worry.

'Won't you join me?' Claudia asked.

'There's a lot I need to get on with . . .'

'Sure?' She reached beneath the marble bench and drew out a pitcher of sherbet and a plate of spiced raisin buns.

Stella wiped her hands down the sides of her tunic as though it was an old apron. 'Maybe ten minutes.' How quickly the lines disappeared when she smiled! 'Heaven knows, there'll be enough left to do in the morning.'

Made from unripe carob pods, the sherbet was thick, sugary and bursting with raspberries, and the buns melted on the tongue in an explosion of cinnamon and ginger.

'If you don't mind my asking,' Claudia said between mouthfuls, 'why are you doing the work of Marcia's slaves?'

There were traces of charcoal on Stella's gown, and laundry stains on the hem.

'I'm not,' she replied, reaching for a second bun. 'I'm doing the work of my own slaves. My husband walked out. Left me with five young kiddies and another one on the way.'

'Debts?'

'No,' she sighed, 'that . . .' She took a deep breath. 'That's what I can't get over. He left without any explanation. Just tidied his desk, folded his clothes and then *pff*! The only thing he did was leave a note saying "sorry", but sorry for what? Not bothering to let us know whether he's alive or dead? I don't mean to sound bitter,' she said, and the funny thing about it was that she didn't, 'but because *officially* he's alive, it falls on me to support the family, but how can I? The law prevents me from divorcing him in his absence, obviously I

48

can't inherit his estate and I'm not free to remarry, even if anyone wanted me.'

'How long have you lived this way?'

'Four years that feel like forty.'

When Stella pushed an overhang of hair out of her eyes, Claudia could smell her fresh, tangy scent and decided she was too young and too decent to face such an ordeal.

'Once it was seen as heroic, me struggling to raise half a dozen kids on a shoestring. Now, other people just see me as dull, and who can blame them? You know, Claudia, it's hard to meet expenses in my situation. They're everywhere I turn. I lost the estate through debts I simply couldn't manage, and whilst I'm grateful to Marcia for taking us in I don't wish to be beholden to her more than I have to.'

Stella talked of being heroic, but heroes come in all shapes and sizes, Claudia reflected, and in this instance they seemed to come with freckles on their nose, tired brown eyes and a heart overflowing with love.

'You've done a good job of raising your brood.'

'Only because I lie to them, but, you know, I'm so *tired* of lying all the time. I'm tired of waiting and,' she added softly, 'I'm tired of hoping for news of his death.'

'Oh, don't worry. If I find him, I'll kill the bastard for you.'

Stella laughed, and ten minutes turned into twenty. 'Is it true,' she asked eventually, 'that a village boy tried to kill Marcia yesterday?'

'At the time I think he was serious, yes, but Garro struck me as a hot-headed youth and I don't think he would have planned murder in the cold light of day.'

In all probability it was passion that moderated his aim.

'I'm not surprised one of them went too far,' Stella sighed, and sighing, Claudia noticed, was something this girl did a lot. 'Marcia will pick up these young men – not usually as young as Garro, thank god – and then, when she tires of them, which doesn't take long because they have no conversation or interests in common, she discards them. Who can blame the poor boys for being bitter.'

Who indeed? They'd been petted and pampered, showered with fancy clothes and had experienced luxuries they couldn't even have dreamed of, yet no sooner had they adjusted to this wonderful life, they were thrown out on their ear.

'What are you two girls gossiping about?' Marcia breezed, rounding the hedge.

Behind her, of course, the usual flurry of flunkies dressed in her distinctive green and gold livery, and, at her shoulder, the big Basc bodyguard in his leather cuirass, looking as rough-hewn as ever.

'Men,' Stella said.

'Totally intimidated by me,' Marcia breezed, squeezing between the two women. 'I'm sure you find it yourself, Claudia, but the more one achieves, the more men are put off. Strikes at the very heart of their male pride, but I say who needs them? I have my pick of virile young studs who keep me young— I say, is something the matter?'

'Sherbet,' Claudia spluttered. 'Went down the wrong way.'

'Now, as much as I would like to spend more time with you girls, it's time for my enema. You know Koros, of course?'

An elderly man of indeterminate heritage was summoned out of the liveried ranks with a snap of imperious fingers. His beard fell long and white to his chest, his face was wizened and serious, and he wore a white robe that fell to his ankles. In fact, Koros was exactly what Claudia had imagined a Druid to look like. Right down to his meaningless, all-purpose smile.

'Delighted to make your acquaintance, my lady.'

'If you'd like one of Koros's excellent purges, let me know,' Marcia said. 'He can make up practically anything.'

'I don't doubt it,' Claudia replied smoothly. The old boy had the word 'fraud' all but tattooed on his liver spots, as did Padi, the little fat Indian soothsayer.

'Right, then, Koros, enema time! Oh, Stella,' Marcia turned abruptly, 'I couldn't help noticing that Lucina is wearing one of the tunics I'd had made for her sister.'

'Poppi's outgrown it,' Stella began.

'I've had my dressmakers run up new frocks for all three girls, matching designs naturally, and of course they're in this season's shades.'

'Luci's old enough to choose her own colours.'

'Tch, what does a child know about style? Little girls only want bright pinks and blues—'

50

'Little girls don't care about fashion,' Stella sighed. 'They want rainbows to play in—'

'Yes, play. Thank you, because that's another thing, Stella. I've brought in four new tutors from the university in Burdigala, so from now on all but the littlest one can attend studies from sunrise, instead of horsing around with hoops and spinning tops, and I have to overrule you about the housework, Stella. It's not fitting that either you or your offspring are engaged in domestic activities, and, since there is an auction in Santonum tomorrow, I'll be buying slaves to take over these tasks. Koros, this new rosemary purge you've created? Is it for mornings or night?'

As the entourage swept off into the house, Stella shrugged. 'You see how it is? My own children, and I have no say in their upbringing. She means well, my cousin, and it's not that I have any great objection to her changing our names to Latin equivalents or giving my babies a good education. I don't even mind not having a life of my own. One can hardly miss what one's never known.' She stood up and smiled sadly. 'It's having my little girls paraded as miniature fashion queens that sticks in my throat.

'Thank you for the sherbet and buns,' she said. 'I expect it's taught you a valuable lesson – that no good deed goes unpunished! But now, if you'll excuse me, I intend to take a scrubbing brush to my daughter's neck while teaching her the importance of religion in her little life.'

'Religion?' Claudia echoed.

'Luci can shin up as many trees as she likes, but she'd better start praying that mud comes out of her tunic, because, hand-me-downs or not, I'm not having any daughters of mine prancing around like a set of tiered mannequins and that's final.'

Watching her bustle away up the path, Claudia's smile was tinged with sadness. Stella possessed beauty, sparkle and life, but for how much longer, that was the question. And how long before the children learned the truth about their father from someone else? Especially now they were growing up fast.

51

Eight

Fresh from the bath house, her skin softened with elder-flowers and rose oil and her hair shining from a vinegar rinse, Claudia slipped into a gown of midnight blue secured at the shoulders with brooches of gold. Though a fool and his money are easily partying, she mused, fastening the owl pendant round her neck, that wasn't an accusation one could level at Marcia. For a start, humour didn't feature in the woman's constitution, reducing the odds of her throwing herself into any festivities with abandon to that of the Trojan Horse winning the derby. And, secondly, Marcia didn't do one damn thing without good reason, and pleasure for its own sake didn't count.

Claudia screwed in her ear studs and reached for her rings. As much as the woman claimed that a succession of virile young studs kept her young, even the most cursory glance in the mirror once her make-up was removed must prove otherwise. How old was she? Forty? Possibly not even that, yet she could pass for ten years older in a bad light, and heaven knows there was enough of that here in Gaul. So if tonight's bash wasn't for pleasure, what was her motive?

'You need to meet local businessmen,' she'd told Claudia. 'Not Gauls, I'm talking about Roman entrepreneurs – men with money, vision and style – because you'll need contacts, if you're to expand your commercial empire into Aquitaine.'

Altruism wasn't in her character, either! Clipping on a spiral bracelet set with amethysts, Claudia began to smell a rat running around Marcia's villa, and it wasn't the one her blue-eyed, cross-eyed, dark Egyptian cat had just dragged in.

'Out!' she ordered. 'You get that thing out of my room right this minute!'

'Hrrrow,' Drusilla growled, biting the head off.

Ugh. Claudia dropped a shawl over the grisly remains.

'Next time I'll leave you in Rome,' she warned, but Drusilla knew better and jumped on to the couch, where she proceeded to wash her bloodied whiskers with languorous grace.

Claudia returned to her own ablutions. The trouble with telling so many lies is that one has to remember the bloody things! She applied kohl round her eyes, softening its effect with the tip of her finger. Since most vineyards in Gaul tended to restrict themselves to the southern coasts, she'd felt pretty confident at telling people that she was here to make a study of the soil types with a view to growing grapes for wine. Then Marcia goes and springs an evening like this!

'Wine merchants are popping up like horsetails in Santonum. You need to meet them, if you intend to venture into distribution yourself.' Marcia had tapped the side of her nose knowingly. 'One must always keep abreast of the opposition, it's what makes competition so good for trade.'

Hearing chariots and gigs clip-clopping into the courtyard, Claudia mused that yes, you really do need to be behind someone before you can stab them in the back.

'I'll be expected to quote chapter and verse on vineyard practices,' she moaned to Drusilla.

'Brrrp.' The cat began to wash her ears.

'My sentiments exactly.' Stick to one angle of the business and baffle the buggers with science. *'December is the most crucial month for vines, because it lays the foundation for the forthcoming vintage.'*

She rehearsed her lines aloud.

'The soil needs just the right amount of manure, the . . . the . . .'

Dammit, what else? She fished in her trunk for the scrappy piece of parchment on which she'd scribbled her notes. Here we go. Pruning. Clearing out old irrigation ditches; digging new ones. Sharpening the stakes. Mending the fences. Weaving new— Dear Diana! Claudia turned the paper over. The list went on for ever!

'Hrrrr.'

'I know, poppet.'

She'd have to memorize it better than that, if she was to impress the wealthy merchants on whom she wanted to offload

53

her future vintage. Because she might not be checking out the soil's friability or whatever the hell they called it, but she had no intention of letting a commercial opportunity like this evening go to waste!

'Right then.' She ticked them off on her fingers. 'Manuring, pruning, ditches, snaring, branding livestock, sowing—'

The assault from the past was so sudden, so strong, that the shock of it sent her reeling. Out of nowhere, time sucked her backwards and suddenly, as though it were last week, she was reaching up to kiss her father goodbye. She felt the rasp of his stubble against his cheeks, heard the rich chuckle in his throat as he laughed. Just as quickly, the image faded, and it was her mother standing in front of her. Claudia could see the wine from the jug dribbling down her chin and seeping in to her tunic . . .

'Go away!' She screwed up her eyes and covered her ears with her hands. 'Go back to the hell where you came from!'

But, oh, this was Gaul. Home of Druids and magic, human sacrifice and sorcery, where the dead could walk and evil spirits lurked in the shadows. They turned back the clock to the time when Claudia cowered under the bed as insults and crockery rained all round her. Then the spirits in the shadows shifted and time spiralled forwards. Now it was the waiting, the waiting, the endless bloody waiting. The watching, the watching, the endless bloody watching. And suddenly, with the cruellest of clarity, she realized what had triggered this nightmare.

A splintered table rose out of the darkness. There was no dinner on the table, because a loud-mouthed drunk had tipped the housekeeping money down her throat – so there were no breakfasts, no lunches and no suppers on it, either. Day by day the wine got cheaper and her mother grew dirtier, and the demons in the shadows cackled when Claudia pushed open the door of their cramped tenement and came face to face with her mother's corpse, cold and grey, beside an empty jug and a pair of slashed wrists.

At least, she thought, Stella would be able to tell her kids that the bastard was sorry.

Claudia had had nothing.

Her father simply marched out of her life, leaving her mother

54

to fill the emptiness with whatever she could until her pain reached the point where she could take no more. Neither had left so much as a note to say 'sorry', 'goodbye' or even 'I love you'.

Too numb to weep, too deadened to hate, Claudia drizzled perfume into the dips of her collarbones and set off to join the dinner guests.

If His Majesty wanted more mushrooms, then more mushrooms it was, and never mind the poor sod who had to drop what he was doing and go tramping round these woods to collect 'em. The kitchen slave despatched at such short notice jabbed two fingers in the air at Marcia's chef and, having satisfied himself that his boss couldn't see round corners, over hills, through thickets and past trees, repeated the gesture again and again.

'Ceps, I need more ceps,' His Majesty had roared. 'You know what ceps look like, don't you, boy?'

'Course I do,' the lad had wanted to snap. 'I've collected the fonking things for you often enough.'

Instead, he'd dipped his head and said yes, sir.

'Then bring more chanterelles while you're about it, and if you find a couple of jew's ears, I'll have them, too, and for heaven's sake, don't just stand there, I need them *NOW*.'

'Well, you should have bloody well planned things better,' the slave sneered. But only to the beech trees, the oaks and the birches.

As two more yellow chanterelles joined the collection in the trug, he thought that it weren't like he *minded* collecting mushrooms. Truth be told, he enjoyed being outdoors in the open, away from the steam and getting his ribs poked with a careless ladle or a strainer dropped on his toe. And it made a pleasant change from His Majesty pinching his ear all the fonking time, too.

Finding a clump of ceps hiding behind a sapling, he fell upon them and thought, that's another thing. Being able to tell his parasols from his panther caps, 'cause the one you could eat and the other could kill you, and he liked being entrusted to go out alone, 'cause not everyone were allowed to do that. Milers, the boss called 'em, meaning give 'em an inch and they'll take a mile, being gone all afternoon if they wasn't supervised proper. Well, *he* were no miler. He worked hard and weren't that the truth, and the boss valued that, that's why he gave him the responsibility of getting the mushrooms in now. Knowing he'd fill his trug and wouldn't dawdle.

It were just the way he *yelled* at him, that were all. Made him feel small in front of the kitchens. Not that most of 'em was listening, and it weren't like he never yelled at them, either. His Majesty bellowed for Gaul. But that little Spanish girl. The new one with the hair that shone like a mirror and a laugh like a springtime cascade. He didn't want her to think he was meek or stupid or nothing, but how the fonk was she going to think well of him when the boss kept talking down to him?

Gathering more velvety chanterelles that smelled of ripe apricots, he tried to think of ways to impress her. He couldn't carve, felt too embarrassed to bring her a garland of flowers, and in the kitchens she had her run of fancy foods to nibble. Yeah, but what if he wrestled a couple of the boiler room boys? He had muscles, she'd see what he were made of then, and know that he were just being polite to the boss. Respectful like. Not gutless. The boy rubbed his grubby hands on his tunic. That were it. Strength of body, strength of character. He'd fonking well gone and cracked it with that!

The sound of a twig cracking interrupted his train. From the corner of his eye, he just caught the fleeting outline of a figure before it disappeared behind a tree trunk. Immediately, it was followed by a frantic flutter of wings as birds flew out of the canopy.

Some said the Scarecrow was the presager of death.

Others believed him to be Death himself.

The boy was taking no chances. Abandoning his ceps and chanterelles, he legged it back to the villa as fast as he could.

Vines were all very well, but sooner or later someone was bound to catch on that Claudia's understanding of viticulture extended little further than twiggy bits that had to be pruned, twiddly bits that had to be tied and late summer squalls that were perfectly capable of rendering bunches of big, juicy grapes a rotting mass fit only for vinegar. Given that Marcia

intended parading her collection of artisans to the local lumi-
naries tonight, Claudia decided to play safe – and no subject
was safer than that of her hostess's tomb! Marcia could talk
for hours about Paris's exquisite marble nymphs, Hor's intense
artistry and Semir's fastidious landscaping, so Claudia decided
to explore the menagerie before the supply of superlatives ran
dry.

Following the mournful mew of a peacock, she wound her
way down the hill, past ancient walnut trees and stately oaks,
to the sheltered valley that opened out at the bottom. So this
was where the water from the diverted stream had ended up.
Expecting Roman-style fountains and Grecian grottos, her eyes
popped. It was as though a prism had exploded. Pink plumage
from the flamingoes, grey from the cranes and white sacred
ibis reflected in the pool, yellow baboons picked at their lice,
lovebirds and finches preened in the aviary.

Give the woman her due. She said she wanted to stage an
exhibition and stage an exhibition she had! Mongooses, bears
and porcupines snuffled around in their pens. White-ruffed
monkeys chattered as they swung from the bars of their cage,
their babies clinging on to their backs for dear life, gazelle
grazed serenely in the pastures across the way, while, at the
far end of the pens, a cheetah snarled.

'Good evening, Mistress Seferius,' drawled a voice from
behind. 'May I have the pleasure of escorting milady to
dinner?'

That voice – there was something familiar about its deep
baritone. Claudia spun round, but even before he'd stepped
out of the shadows, she'd picked up the smell of sandalwood.
Unmistakably, the scent of the predator. Only this one wasn't
caged in.

'*Orbilio?*' The Security Police in Santonum? This had to
be another hallucination. 'Please, Jupiter, tell me I'm
dreaming.'

'Would it help if I kissed you? It's what dashing heroes do
in folk tales, you know. Kiss the maidens to wake them up.'

'You're right. It's not a dream, it's a nightmare.'

'And it's lovely to see you again, too.'

That was the trouble. Hallucinations don't laugh, they don't
have dark eyes that twinkle, or crisp black hairs on the backs

57

of their hands that disappear up their sleeve and— 'Orbilio, what the hell are you doing here?'

'Me?' He affected a look of boyish innocence. 'Well, you know how it is. Warm summer's evening. Birds singing. Butterflies on the wing. So I thought, Marcus old chap, why not stretch your legs before dinner?'

'Aren't you worried that they're too long already?'

'Would you care to take a peek?'

'I'd sooner drink bleach while rolling naked in a hornet's nest and whipping myself with a handful of nettles.'

'I'll take that as a yes, then.' He held out his arm. 'Dinner, my lady?'

'Marcus! Darling!' Marcia scooped up the proffered arm with the kind of smile that would have given the cheetah an inferiority complex, had it been watching. 'How's your case coming along?' she purred, and it was interesting to note that she was completely alone. No big Basc bodyguard at her shoulder. No flurry of flunkies to bring up the rear.

'Handsomely, thank you.' Orbilio shot an amused glance at Claudia. 'The evidence is mounting nicely.'

'Really?' Marcia's eyes travelled over the strong lines of his face as though searching for something, but Claudia decided that this was not, repeat not, an appropriate time to be discussing Orbilio's prospects for the Senate.

Croesus, something had to have gone badly wrong if he'd trailed her right the way out here. It wasn't tax. Heaven knows, the dodging of contributions to the imperial coffers was a serious enough offence and yes, she'd built up quite a backlog one way and another. But the outstanding balance wasn't so large as to warrant such a heavy-handed approach, and, besides, he was an investigator, not a debt collector. Snooping was what he did best.

'Tell me, Marcia.' She linked her arm with her hostess's and thought it had to be that little sneak Burto. Dammit, she should have known better than to get involved with that bastard. A few probing questions and Burto squealed like the pig that he was, dropping her in it to save his own skin, and fraud *was* a serious enough offence to bring the long arm of the law here to Gaul! She looked at it, draped with Marcia's scarlet linen sleeve, and wondered how much evidence it had collected and how much was bluff. 'Are those Egyptian water lilies you're growing in the pond over there,' she gushed, 'or are they the fragrant variety? And you really *must* tell me how you get such wonderful blooms on your heliotrope. Mine produce such weedy specimens.'

Along the line, she thought she heard a deep male laugh, but she must have been mistaken, because when she glanced behind Marcia's shoulder Orbilio was coughing into his white linen handkerchief.

'And those monkeys,' she said. 'Such darling things. Are they any use as pets, do you think?'

'Hm.' Marcia rolled her tongue under her lip. 'Qeb. Qeb, are you there?'

'Ma'am?'

Wearing a pleated linen kilt like his brother, the Egyptian stepped out from behind the ostrich pen, making everyone jump. It was impossible to tell how long he'd been there, and Claudia felt the flesh creep right the way down her backbone at Qeb's downcast expression, the slouch of his shoulders, the shine on his immaculately shaven head.

'These monkeys,' Marcia said. 'Do they make good pets?'

'No.'

That was it? No explanation, such as 'they bite', 'they pine', 'they turn blue if you keep them indoors'?

'No matter, Qeb will find you something to play with, won't you, Qeb?'

'Indeed.'

Hardly the chatty type, then.

'That's settled,' Marcia declared. 'Come. I must return to the festivities or my guests will think I've deserted them.'

'I'll catch you up,' Claudia murmured. 'I just want to . . . take another look at your tomb. It's so . . . so . . .'

Sadly, the store of superlatives had run dry.

'It's so *perfect*,' Marcia finished for her, 'and that's why you should always surround yourself with purists, darling. Excellence is these men's stock in trade. Personal pride means they will settle for nothing less than perfection. It is a rule I follow myself, in everything from business transactions to my health regime to couture.' She shook her expensively cut sleeve to prove the point. 'Compromise cannot be a virtue,' she sniffed. 'Relinquishing half what one wants is weakness and I can never respect such inadequacy. Now, Marcus, about this case of yours. Is there anyone I can put you in contact with, who might be of help to your investigation?'

Claudia watched them go. Marcia was wearing scarlet tonight, and the woman was no fool. Had she chosen that robe in the belief that red was the colour of allure? Possibly, given the way she was pressing it against Orbilio's long patrician tunic, and red has the advantage of giving its wearer maximum impact, especially in a crowd like tonight. But red is the universal warning of danger and, as the spotted toadstool and humble ladybird will testify, it's a colour designed to repulse. Once again, Claudia reflected on the absence of bodyguard and slaves and mused that red also makes for a conspicuous target . . .

Why *had* Marcia invited her to stay at the villa? What was the purpose behind tonight's banquet? And, more importantly, where did the Security Police figure in Marcia's plans?

Keeping a safe distance between them, she followed Orbilio and his hostess back to the house. But instead of continuing on into the banqueting hall after them she remained in the portico, listening to the music fluting into the warm summer air, the murmur of relaxed conversation, the laughter of gentry enjoying themselves. After several minutes, Claudia picked up her skirts and quietly turned the other way.

Behind the villa, no one noticed a flock of greenfinches twitter out of the bushes. The slaves were too busy washing and perfuming the feet of their guests, fetching wine, fetching sweetmeats, topping up goblets, running errands, and, for their part, the visitors were too busy greeting friends, snubbing enemies and cutting deals to fret about a small feathered flurry. The musicians, bless them, were already lost in their instruments, clowns and buffoons far too engrossed in entertaining their audience for the outside world to impinge, and hired acrobats practised their routines in the yard with knitted-brow concentration.

So when a blackbird then came screeching out from the undergrowth, no one was even remotely concerned.

Nine

The moon was high, the stars bright, when the second round of silver platters was being cleared away. After a prelude of music and dancing to get the guests in party mood, the banquet had formally begun with a toast to the hostess, followed by a first course of fattened dormice, larks' tongues and snails accompanied by oysters from the Carent estuary served on a bed of blanched lettuce. This had been allowed to settle while a group of Kushite acrobats turned somersaults, the idea being that with white 'bones' painted on their bodies they were turned into leaping skeletons. During this interlude, Claudia had been stuck between a tin importer and Hor, and frankly she'd found little to choose between them in terms of conversation.

Of the two, the artist had the edge, because although the tin importer was widely travelled his personal interests revolved solely around the intricacies of bee-keeping and dear Diana, did that man understand the full meaning of the word drone! With an assurance that it was so fascinating she was inspired to take bee-keeping up herself, Claudia switched her attentions to Hor. Bad move. Here was a man able to quote chapter and verse on the virtues of red ochre over haematite crystals (or was it the other way round?), but knew sod all about current affairs, either amorous or political. No first course had ever lasted so long. No skeleton had ever rattled quite so monotonously.

'That's quite a cheetah your brother's got,' she cut in, as Hor drew breath about the merits of Spanish armenium.

His liquid dark eyes hardened to steel. 'Qeb?'

'Why? How many brothers did you bring with you from Egypt?' It was meant as a quip, a light-hearted throwaway, but Hor wasn't the jocular type.

'Qeb's my only family. I have to look after him, but—'

'Surely he's a decade older than you?' Maybe that was the answer? Maybe Qeb was a bit simple?

'Nearer eight years,' Hor corrected. 'But the cheetah?' He leaned towards her, his eyes narrowed. 'You saw it?'

'And heard it.' What was so odd about one snarling cat? His intensity was starting to give her the creeps. Seemed it was a family trait.

'Heard? Oh. The menagerie, you mean.'

He relaxed, picked a bit of meat out of his teeth, examined it between manicured fingernails and then ate it. Claudia clapped the retreating skeletons so hard, they thought she was demanding an encore. Bugger.

'Any time you want your walls painted – ' Hor indicated the magnificent frescoes that adorned Marcia's banqueting hall with a long artistic finger – 'be certain you look inside the artist's box before hiring him. Don't be afraid to poke into all the compartments, and satisfy yourself he's using pig's bristles for his brushwork, because nothing else is good enough, and if he says any old scoop will do for measuring out pigments, don't hire the fellow. There's no substitute for bronze. Other metals only compromise—'

'He doesn't say much, your brother.'

'Qeb?'

No, the other half-dozen! 'Yes. Qeb.' This time she wouldn't bloody well clap them and the skeletons could take as much offence as they liked.

'He prefers to talk to his animals,' Hor explained. 'Oh, and another thing. Plaster.'

'Qeb talks to . . . plaster?'

'Don't let anyone put fewer than three layers on your walls or you'll get all manner of faults cropping up. But no more than six, either, because—'

Lightning couldn't move faster. Before the skeletons had finished their last leap, Claudia was off that couch and collaring the usher before he'd even reached for the next course's seating plan.

'I'll just consult the scroll, milady.'

As the rest of the diners slowly stretched and rose from their couches for the next reshuffle, Marcia's voice could be heard explaining how Paris couldn't make it tonight, he had a nymph to see to.

'Expect he's seen to plenty of *them*,' a woman close to Claudia sniggered under her breath.

'Quite the lover, I would imagine,' her companion whispered behind her hand.

'He's from Argos, my dear, and you know what they say about *their* men! Goes right back to the time of Jason and his Argonauts, and don't tell me *those* boys didn't have stamina!'

'And his hair! The way it falls back in place when he shakes his head!'

'Never mind the head, what about the *body*?' The first woman rolled her eyes in admiration. 'And his hands! So slow, so careful! I mean, if he's that meticulous with his statues, can you *imagine* what he's like in bed?'

Her friend giggled. 'He can leave his sandals under my couch any—'

'If you would care to follow me, milady?' Trust the usher to go and spoil it. 'This is your couch, with the merchant Piso and Her Ladyship's gardener, Semir.'

Wedged between a man who'd been trading in Santonum for twenty years and the genius who recommended watering gardens with wine, Claudia couldn't have planned it better herself! Maybe Piso could fill in some gaps about what happened here fifteen years ago? Kicking off her shoes, she made herself comfortable as slaves filed in with trays of venison, duck, boar and sucking pig, but before she'd reached for the first morsel, a pudgy finger was clucking her under the chin.

'I shay, you're a pretty little wench, aren't you?' When the merchant inched closer, she was engulfed by a tidal wave of stale wine. 'My wife'sh in Rome, y'know. If you and I were to—'

'Trust me, I wouldn't, even if you were sober and went by the name of King Midas.'

'Midash? I'm Piso!'

'As a newt. Semir, would you mind changing places?'

'For you, Lady Clodia, eet iss a pleasure,' he murmured, with a bob of his immaculately black, immaculately oiled, immaculately beaded and braided curls.

In fact, there was so much oil on his body, not to mention his tongue, it was a wonder the Babylonian didn't slip off the couch. A peacock of the very first order, Semir had no intention of fading into the background. Whereas in the gardens he wore nothing but a skimpy loincloth, tonight he'd chosen a long yellow robe embroidered with griffins, and if that wasn't enough it was bordered at both hem and neck with a band of deep blue edged with silver. On his feet he wore soft fabric slippers, and round his ankles and wrists the same bangles he'd worn in the garden. Claudia noticed him swatting a hand off his thigh, where the drunken Piso had mistaken him for a girl. How wrong could he be, she mused. Semir might be an extrovert, but a ladyboy? Never!

'Tell me about Babylon,' she said, as a plate of cheese buns was laid down.

These were what the kerfuffle was about earlier, when she was approaching the banqueting hall after searching Orbilio's room to find Marcia haranguing her chef.

'How can I possibly serve cheese and cep buns if there are no ceps, you imbecile!' Marcia's eyes glittered coldly as she'd outlined the amount she would dock from his pay for this outrage.

'Don't you think a month's wages is a bit steep for what, after all, is only an oversight?' Claudia suggested.

'Don't go soft on me, girl.' Angry, her voice grew even deeper. 'These bastards will bleed me dry if I don't keep a close watch on them. I won't tolerate slackers and I won't tolerate pilfering, because in my book they're both the same, and I don't tolerate whingers, either.' She rounded on the chef. 'Tell that oaf who left the mushrooms behind in the woods that I'm selling him at the auction tomorrow.'

'He's a good worker, your ladyship—'

'Bollocks! He was tasked with one simple job and what did he do?'

'The Scarecrow panicked him, your ladyship—'

'I do not argue with minions, neither do I repeal my decisions. Consider the oaf sold, and for heaven's sake, man, try and get *something* right with the banquet!'

Claudia bit into the cheese bun. Marcia had flown into a rage because she'd wanted ceps added, but ceps were too strong for these little dainties. By accident or design, they were perfect.

'Ah, yess, Babylon,' Semir was saying. 'But iss so big, so exciting, where do I start?' He made an airy gesture with soil-stained hands that even his herbal oils couldn't disguise. 'Would you like I tell you about the spring in the mountains, where the water that burst from the rock iss so hot, no life can survive? But! As eet crashes down the hillside, so the water cools in each leetle cascade, and thus more and more creatures make their home there.'

'Sounds interesting.'

'Or shall I talk of our salt lakes and salt glaciers—'

On the adjacent couch, Orbilio was reclining next to Stella. With her glossy hair pinned up in a mountain of curls that framed and flattered her oval features, and in a gown of the finest lavender-blue cotton adorned with gems that no doubt came from her cousin's jewel box, she looked every inch the Roman matron. Smart, elegant, clever and attractive, with her freckles covered up with white chalk, the only thing missing was the essence of Stella. Marcia's grooming had completely tidied it out.

'. . . . our lush green deltas, where the mangroves grow tall and where our people build housses of reed up on stilts. Ah, but look. The ross petals!'

As a contraption from the ceiling began to shower blossoms over the diners, expert eyes scrutinized the fragrant snow.

'It iss as I commanded,' he said, picking one up, turning it over, then sniffing it carefully. 'White rosses gathered in early summer then stored in linen cloths that have been soaked in ross oil. Thiss way, the fragrance is preserved through the winter?'

'You really advocate watering the bushes with wine?'

Black eyes flashed sideways. 'Eef you grow garlick beside rosses, eet enhances their scent. The rosses, of course. Not the garlick.'

'Why white wine and not red?'

'And eef you grow mint underneath, you will not see a single greenfly all season? Ah, but look. My gracious hostess iss beckoning me.'

Strange, but Claudia hadn't seen Marcia snap her manicured

fingers. But off he oiled, Semir and his beads and his bangles, leaving her alone with Piso, who, praise be to Juno, had fallen into a snorting, open-mouthed sleep.

'My dear, you mustn't be alone at a party, I absolutely forbid it.' Stella's hand reached across the divide. 'Come and join us. There's just Marcus and I on this couch, and –' She leaned over and whispered – 'he's divorced, you know.'

Claudia smiled prettily at Orbilio. 'I'm not surprised.'

'I think you're missing the point, dear,' Stella continued under her breath. 'I mean, here's you. A widow . . . young . . . pretty. And here's Marcus!'

'I'm not his type, Stella. He likes girls with big chests and small drawers, don't you, Marcus, and, besides, we're just about to move round for the pears stewed in wine and the almond-stuffed dates that Marcia tells me comprise her dessert course.'

She fluttered her fingers, but Fortune, the bitch, had it in for her. (Dammit, that was the last time she'd leave that goddess a bracelet!)

'Glad you could join me, after all,' a rich baritone murmured, as the usher escorted her to her new seat. Orbilio's eyes danced as he raised his glass in a toast. 'Did you find what you were looking for, by the way?'

'Yes, I did, as a matter of fact.'

'I knew the lock on my satchel wouldn't deter you.'

'Lock? Satchel? Orbilio, what on earth are you wittering about?' The lock was no problem, it was his notes written in Greek that she'd had trouble with. 'I thought we were talking about seating plans? And, dear me, if that isn't the couch I was looking for. That one over there by the fountain.'

Sweeping over, she leaned down and hissed in the occupant's ear that this was her bloody seat and would he kindly sod off, she was sitting here for dessert and that was final. Too late, she realized who the occupant was. Under the floral crown that each diner wore, she hadn't noticed that the hair was long, or that it was neither red nor brown, but some point in between, like the colour of a kestrel's flight feathers.

'Well, well. Claudia Seferius,' drawled the most powerful Gaul in Aquitaine. 'If we're not back on your favourite subject of hospitality.'

66

Ten

In Rome, the lull between harvest and vintage was filled by sixteen days of Games featuring feasts and processions, horse races and athletics, theatrical productions and gladiatorial combat. Unfortunately for the Gauls, there was no such lull in their farming calendar. The instant the harvest was home, it was time to pick apples, pasture out the swine among the oakwoods and crop this year's yield of horse beans. Stone slabs from the quarries still needed to be brought in by river and piled along the quay, ditto timbers, and, since there was nothing to compare to Gaulish leather when it came to army tents, stock breeders busily prepared their hides for export as well. There was a sense of urgency about the work, too, because in less than a month the seas would be closed until spring. Shipments had to be despatched for fear of storms sweeping in from the ocean and upsetting an already precarious sailing schedule, so for the people of Santonum it was more important than ever that the Hammer God should be appeased.

A vulnerability the wily Emperor seized upon by playing up the *Vulcanalia* and declaring two days of markets and fairs followed by a public holiday funded entirely by the state!

It didn't matter that Vulcan was nothing like the Gaulish Hammer God. History proved that local customs were quickly absorbed into Roman religion, it was a simple matter of building marble temples in place of wooden shrines then endowing them with glorious statues. A generation on, who remembered that the local deity had been cast in Minerva's image? Or that their sun god bore a striking resemblance to Apollo? Gradually, the differences would blur and in Santonum Vulcan the Olympian Smith had been selected to take over.

The Emperor could easily have chosen Jupiter, who also sent thunderbolts and storms. But from the production of charcoals to the making of wheels, from the rings around barrels to the manufacture of ploughshares and from the forging of gelding knives to the forging of swords, furnaces and fire lay at the heart of Gaulish society. As did trade. Two days of profiteering would soften the buggers up, the Emperor argued. By the time the *Vulcanalia* dawned, all but the most bigoted would be receptive to compromise. The Druids were losing ground fast.

'Lord, how I loathe drinking companions who remember in the morning what happened the night before,' a rich, fruity voice groaned in Claudia's ear. Despite the bleary eyes and stubbled chin, his purple striped tunic was clean and uncreased, and the feathers in his cloakpin looked positively perky. 'Luckily, madam, your servant was spared such company, though he wishes the pounding in his head would dissipate the merest of fractions. Or I have missed two whole days and the *Vulcanalia* is starting already?'

'No, Hannibal, that's workmen you hear.'

As the Emperor's expansion plans took shape, so the whole perimeter of Santonum became one huge building site of baths, aqueducts, temples and shops. There was almost as much dust in the air here as in Rome.

'I am heartily relieved to hear you say that, madam.' Hannibal wiped his brow in mock relief. 'For years, these cunning Gauls have been advocating their barley beer as a cure for midriff expansion. But alas! The only thing I have lost in that time is a fortune – oh, and perhaps three or four days in the winter.'

Claudia glanced at his tight waistline, remembered that he'd hardly spent any time here in Gaul, and saw that the eyes were red rimmed, rather than bloodshot. 'You don't drink anywhere near as much as you make you out, you old fake.'

'Absolutely right, madam. I can go for hours without touching a drop.'

Around them, the run up to the *Vulcanalia* was being celebrated with singing and dancing along the main streets, with jugglers and acrobats capering between the stalls in the Forum. To add to the festive atmosphere, practically every threshold, hall, atrium and altar in Santonum had been decked with garlands of blue borage, as well. Since Vulcan and the Hammer God

68

were both patrons of fire, borage wasn't merely decorative, it emitted sparks and explosions when burned, and, to complete the imperial jigsaw, the Emperor had shipped in fire-eaters, fire-walkers, fire-dancers and fire-throwers. The city was hopping.

'The man whom you seek,' Hannibal murmured, drawing Claudia into the doorway of a man selling harnesses.

Her heart leaped. 'You have news?'

'None whatsoever, madam, much to my regret. However,' he lowered his voice as the harness-maker moved forward, sensing a sale, 'last night I made the acquaintance of a fellow who indicated that he *might* be prepared to talk for a small fee—'

Here we go! 'How small a fee?'

Hannibal's expression was wry as he waved the harness-maker away. 'Thirty gold pieces.'

'What did you drive him down to?'

'Drive him down?' He seemed horrified by her reaction. 'Madam, I told the scoundrel to crawl back into the wood-work where he belongs.'

Give me strength!

'Come, come, madam. Surely you would not trust the word of a man who is prepared to sell his fellow countrymen for a few coppers?'

'Hardly a few, or even coppers,' she snapped. 'Look, if this man has information—'

'They *all* have information, dear lady. They are just not imparting it. If we have any chance of finding your father—'

'I never said it was my father!'

'Perhaps not, though you have, I fear, just confirmed it, and, since you are too young to be seeking a missing swain, having been a mere child fifteen years ago, you leave precious few options available.'

Shit.

'This stays strictly between you and me, Hannibal.'

'It pains me that you might think otherwise, but,' he glanced to where Junius stood scowling under the awning of a book-binder's workshop, 'if you need the reassurance so badly, madam, then you have my word. Returning to the matter of our informant, I will pursue this line if you insist, but I do not trust the fellow. He asked for too much money too quickly.'

'I wasn't aware we had too many choices.'

'Right now options are limited, I grant you. But patience, madam, patience. These are early days. You will recall that I only commenced my enquiries yesterday.'

Claudia's wished the same could be said of Marcus Cornelius. 'Time is not on my side, Hannibal.' Nor on that little snake Burto's, once she got her hands on him! 'Haggle if you can, but whatever your informant asks tell him I'll pay.'

'Madam, I really don't think—'

'Then keep it that way.'

He was taking this cloak-and-dagger stuff far too seriously, she decided, turning down the side of the bath house. You only had to look down any street and prosperity oozed from each marble pore. Why wouldn't one of the locals get greedy? The blood of the legate and his men still stained the soil on which they fell and the hills remained scattered with the bones of brave Santon warriors. But nothing brings the dead to life or turns back the pointer on the sundial, and in the time between Rome's conquest of these wild forests and the founding of Santonum, peace had prevailed. Whatever had happened here fifteen years before had been outside any political arena, and thus if there were no records of any incident it could hardly be serious. Besides, cold hard cash breaks any conspiracy of silence and what, after all, was thirty gold pieces compared to the cost of this visit? Especially since it was thirty gold pieces that Claudia would be fiddling from her taxes, anyway.

Across from the bath house, a surveyor was hunched, hands on knees, mapping out yet another warehouse. As he lined up his plumb bobs, so his assistants adjusted their rods accordingly until the satisfied surveyor finally nodded and the post was hammered in the ground to define the warehouse's limits. Because of this surveying work, traffic had been funnelled into a narrow and often bad-tempered stream, as wheels locked in the restricted accessway or some slow-moving ox cart held up everyone and caused a trailing backlog. Luckily for pedestrians, they could skip up the steps of the adjacent Temple of Hercules and cut across.

This temple was yet another example of the Emperor's cunning. Whether Roman or Gaul, there was no denying Hercules as the ultimate model of courage and integrity, and, also, as patron of commerce (the lifeblood of Santonum), trade deals were traditionally sealed at his altar. This was the first link in the imperial trust chain. The second being that, since Hercules was also leader of the Muses, it proved that men did not have to be bullies to be heroes. The Emperor was well aware that such values struck at the very heart of Gaulish society, just as he knew that by the time it came to military processions culminating at Hercules's intrepid feet few Santons saw further than the Great Feast that followed.

Rather than Rome cocking its leg and marking its territory . . .

Claudia was halfway across the precinct when she spotted a familiar blond head scrutinizing one of the statues with an intense expression.

'Admiring the competition?' she asked.

Paris turned slowly. 'Show me just one where there is life, a living soul inside rather than marble, and I will give it my admiration, but these?' The contempt in his voice was colder than hoar frost. 'Never.'

Claudia thought of the subtle swing of the knife-edge pleats of his marble nymphs. The carelessly tied girdle on one, a ringlet escaping from its stone hairpin on another, the amused arch of an eyebrow on yet another. Taken in isolation, they were nothing, but together they pulsed out character and individuality. Just as Hor had breathed life into the inside of the tomb, Paris had giving the tomb a personality all of its own.

'Marcia said you were a purist.'

'I am from Mycenae,' he said, as though that explained everything, and, hell, maybe it did. Despite most of its original splendour having been devastated by earthquakes, the palaces, villas and tombs of Mycenae stood testament to the skill of its craftsmen so that, even four and a half centuries on, their civilization remained a byword for excellence.

'Mycenaen sculptors are the best in the world,' he added with the confidence of a young man who was bloody good at his job and knew it.

'According to half the women at last night's banquet, they also make the best lovers.'

One nostril flared dismissively. 'Those fat old trouts imagine I would dissipate my energies on pleasuring them?'

Interestingly, his blue eyes were on Marcia's litter as it

swayed back and forth above the heads of the crowd in a shimmer of green and gold drapes. He turned back to Claudia, and the expression in his eyes softened.

'You have no idea what it's like to start with a piece of stone – a virgin, if you like – and, as you slowly caress the marble with your chisels, feel the passion within her awaken.'

Gives a new dimension to the phrase 'married to the job', she supposed.

'Why aren't you at the tomb at the moment, arousing your marble nymphs?'

'I'm looking for Herakles.'

'Your dog?'

The softness vanished. 'The son of Zeus,' he snapped, 'who completed twelve impossible labours and was carried by the gods to Olympus.'

Ah. Hercules. Just like he meant Jupiter and not Zeus.

'Marcia wants the Governor to see how important she is every time he comes to dine, so she's decreed work on her tomb be deferred in favour of a statue of Herakles at the entrance of her estate. I am in Santonum for inspiration.'

'You could just copy the one inside the temple.'

'That monster?' Paris sneered. 'Its neck is too thick, its head is too small, its hands far too big and the expression on its face resembles that of a constipated griffin.'

Jupiter, Juno and Mars. How often had Claudia heard philosophers on the steps of the Rostra debating what stimulating conversation would be inspired, could the cream of intellect and ability be gathered in the same room for just one night? Now she knew. Marcia had collected the finest professionals from around the world – and they bored the spots off a leopard. Talent they might possess by the bucketload, but conversation? Personality? She'd had more fun talking to glow worms.

Santonum's Forum was packed with stalls that had spilled out of the market square and which offered everything from fruit presses to jars of honey, shaggy woollen tablecloths to salt meat. The air was heavy with the smell of ripe fruit and barley beer, of smoked hams that hung from hooks strung over makeshift rails, and the babble of trade and laughter drowned out the sound of cobblers bent over their lasts. At

72

the top end of the Forum, prisoners in leg irons were being paraded on a platform under the watchful eye of an armed guard, while at the southern end of the Forum something similar was happening, except these were not criminals.

Dark-skinned Iberians, big brawny Germans and hook-nosed Phoenicians stood, heads bowed, with cards around their neck that displayed everything from their age to their health to their various skills, but failed to mention their name or their family history. To people like Marcia, prodding the muscles of a redhead with frizzy braids, such matters were unimportant. These were not people. They were chattels. Objects, to be bought and sold at auction, like the kitchen boy scared out of his wits, whose fear of the Scarecrow provoked not protection or concern from his mistress, but anger that he'd left a few paltry mushrooms behind, and who cared that he would be torn from his friends and his family? As Marcia moved along the platform to peer inside the mouth of a Greek girl to examine her teeth, Claudia felt something slither under her ribcage. Reeling away, she slammed straight into a wall of leather. The wall smelled of dense, dark, cedary forests, his hair was cropped in a neat Caesar cut and the eyes above it, she decided, were, yes, *definitely* the colour of chestnuts.

'You have not thanked me for saving your life,' Tarbel said.

'Funny. I wasn't aware that you'd saved it.'

His rough-hewn features almost smiled. 'I didn't. But most people wet themselves in such situations and then, when the crisis is over, fall over themselves to thank me. Especially the ladies.'

If he expected her to ask how these ladies thanked him, he was in for a long wait. 'You make it sound as though such situations are commonplace.'

'I wouldn't say it's a weekly occurrence,' the Basc rumbled, his hand nevertheless covering his dagger, 'but, *sí*. The Mistress has made a lot of enemies, doing what she does.'

'Which is what, exactly?'

Marcia had never said what had earned her so much wealth. Only that there was no embarrassing way to stockpile it.

'You must ask her that,' he said, scanning the crowd. 'Gossiping about the Mistress behind her back is the surest way for a man to get himself fired.'

73

Claudia glanced round to where Marcia was busy inspecting, prodding and poking her way along the platform, surrounded by the usual bunch of quacks, charlatans and liveried slaves. He might wear a green tunic beneath his cuirass, but whatever faults he might have, she reflected, Tarbel was by no means a toady.

'Posts for mercenaries hard to come by these days?' she breezed.

'I'm a soldier,' he growled.

'You kill for a living. That's a mercenary in my book.'

'I fight,' he said. 'There's a difference.'

'Really.'

Dark chestnut eyes locked into hers and held them for a count of perhaps ten. 'Are you looking to fight me?' he asked quietly.

'Isn't it strange how you men always think in terms of waging war.'

'Maybe it's because I spent the last fifteen years serving your army in the auxiliaries.'

'Another ten and you would have received automatic citizenship.'

'Another ten and I'd have been just as broke when I quit, only with rheumatics in my bones and a bad case of haemorrhoids.'

'So you resigned and sold yourself to the highest bidder. Or have we had this conversation before?'

'Then I'm a whore,' he snapped. 'Is that worse than women who marry old men for their money?'

Claudia adjusted the strap on her shoe to cover the sudden rush of colour to her cheeks. He couldn't know. Tarbel couldn't *possibly* know . . . Then she realized that his sharp eyes were no longer scanning the crowd for danger, but were centred on his employer.

'Marcia's finished her bidding,' he said. 'I must go.'

'One question.'

An expression crossed his chiselled face, though it was far too fleeting for her to identify. '*Sì?*'

'Are you happy in your job?'

There was a momentary pause. 'If you're asking what I think you're asking, you're on the wrong track,' he said slowly. 'Not every bodyguard lusts after his mistress the way your pretty boy does, and what makes you think I wouldn't enjoy what I do? Protection work pays a hell of a lot better than your Roman army, that's for sure.'

Yes, it does. She watched as he slipped into place at Marcia's shoulder. But it was odd that he hadn't actually answered her question. (Plus any idiot with half an eye could see that Junius was the sulky type, not a yearner!) Wrestling her way through hordes of children entranced by the exploits of the Arabian fire-eater, between stalls packed with bargain hunters and past fortune-tellers bent over their charts, Claudia fought her way to the north end of the Forum. They were an ugly bunch of villains on display and no mistake. She scoured the notices that had been nailed to the platform, and saw that tonight they would be paying the price for a suitably ugly list of crimes, too.

Murderer. Double Murderer. Child killer. Rapist. The list just went on and on, though, looking at them now, naked and in chains, vilified and spat on, she wondered how much those few seconds of pleasure were worth. One or two of the cockier prisoners made an attempt at bravado, but the bluster did not extend to their eyes, and the overwhelming impression was of a group of men wracked with self-pity and not a shred of remorse for their victims.

'Will you be staying for the executions, Claudia Seferius?' a voice drawled in her ear. 'Your Emperor has sent a team of gladiators all the way from Rome to despatch them.'

'I have no great desire to watch unarmed criminals being pitched against professional killers, thank you, Vincentrix.'

'Come back in six months, when the amphitheatre's finished,' the Druid replied smoothly. 'Then you'll be able to watch them being pitched against bears and tigers instead.'

'I meant, I prefer engagements where the combatants are equal.'

'Yes, I'd noticed,' he murmured, and she smelled the peppery tang of his skin. 'Did you enjoy the dessert course last night, by the way? Personally, I found the stuffed apples a little on the cold side, but then maybe that was simply because they'd cooled by the time I'd settled into my new seat.'

'Your chivalry was much appreciated.'

Still no priestly robes, then. At the banquet he'd blended in by wearing a white belted tunic over his pantaloons, just as he had merged with the landscape on his private island. Today, wearing a pale blue-grey tunic over flint-coloured breeches tucked into high, soft, black boots, he could be any Gaul. They all wore the same amulets round their wrists for protection against evil spirits, draped the same gold torcs round their necks and restrained their long hair with the same soft kidskin headbands. Was the most powerful Gaul in Aquitania really quite without ego? she wondered. Or was he so powerful that everybody recognized him, whatever he wore? There was, of course, a third alternative . . .

She looked at the way he'd whitened his hair with lime this morning. At the reddish-brown stubble that darkened his jaw. By disguising himself as Everyman, Vincentrix became invisible among subjects who were so in awe of the Head of the Druid Guild that they would never imagine such an exalted personage would lower himself to mingle among them! She pictured him, able to quote even the tiniest detail of their life back to them. A snippet of conversation overheard in the market. The recollection of a purchase. A meeting. A sale. For a man trained to retain information in his head, it was nothing – but to his people, his reading of minds demonstrated the supernatural powers associated with Druids. Manipulation again, not magic. And this Druid had just met his match.

'Fancy your chances?' she asked, tilting her head towards the one-eyed Syrian who was challenging the crowd to Find the Pea.

'Claudia Seferius, I never play any game I can't win,' Vincentrix said solemnly. 'Find the Pea relies purely on chance.'

'Hand me your torc.'

'This?' The Druid fingered the band round his neck. 'It's solid gold!'

'I should bloody well hope so,' she said, pulling it free. 'Otherwise I wouldn't be gambling it.'

'Just a moment.' Vincentrix grabbed it back and placed his lips gently against the central boss before returning it to her outstretched hand.

'One for luck?'

'Actually, I was kissing an old friend goodbye.'

Claudia moved across to where the Syrian was playing his crowd. He made it look easy, as he placed his wizened pea beneath one of three identical walnut shells then shuffled them around. Zip, zip, zip – where's the pea? Several punters thought it was easy, as well. Strangely, they were the same punters who went away penniless.

'Bad luck, sir, oh, jolly bad luck.' The Syrian smacked his forehead with the palm of his hand. 'Anyone else fancy their chances at guessing which shell the pea's under?'

'Me,' Claudia said, and watched his single eye light up at the gold torc she dangled in front of it.

Zip, zip, zip. The walnut shells flew across the flagstone, but under which one lay the wizened legume? Claudia's finger hovered, then pointed. The surprise One-Eye feigned as she won was almost convincing. He shuffled again. Zip, zip, zip went the little dried pea. Oh, well. If wanted to play games . . . She dithered even longer before pointing this time. The Syrian was protesting. Weeping, almost. So much bad luck. Would she give him just one more chance? He was begging . . .

'Winner takes all?' she suggested.

The Syrian nodded, licking his lips as the torc see-sawed back and forth in her hands. 'Winner takes all.'

'And how much exactly would that be?'

It was all One-Eye could do not to drool. 'Today?' he said, throwing a cursory glance inside his money belt. 'Forty-three sesterces.'

'Not bad for two hours' work,' she murmured to Vincentrix. To the Syrian, Claudia simply said, 'Then let's play.'

Zip, zip, zip. You could almost hear his greed, it was that damn palpable. In fact, he reminded her of a bullfrog at dawn on the day the first mayflies hatch out.

'Which shell, lady?'

Claudia didn't give him the opportunity to pull a switch. Lithe as a lioness, her hand swept down and lifted the walnut shell before he had time to palm the pea. 'That one, I think.'

The Syrian spluttered in protest, but the crowd was behind her. Reluctantly he unhooked his money belt and tossed it across.

'Good guess.' Vincentrix laughed, re-fixing his torc.

77

Claudia smiled. 'Wasn't it, though?'

Live long enough amongst swindlers and thieves and you soon get the hang of it. Swiftness of the hand deceives the eye. The trick is to watch carefully, a task made all the easier when the dealer is left-handed, like One-Eye back there. Tossing a couple of coins to a street vendor in exchange for a bag of warm almond cakes, she said, 'Why isn't the Head of the Druid Guild married?'

Vincentrix's teeth hovered above the sweet-scented cake. 'Technically, I suppose he still is.' Piercing green eyes slanted her a wry glance. 'When my wife inherited a ring from her aunt, she decided to use it to fund her aspiration to travel.' He bit into the cake. 'She's been travelling for twenty-two years.'

'Some ring.' Claudia laughed. 'Was that what prompted you to take up the priesthood?'

They zigzagged through the streets until they arrived at the wharf, where several more cakes got themselves polished off and a shoal of small fish took the opportunity to find shelter in the shadow of their dangling feet before Vincentrix finally answered.

'It was never a proper marriage,' he said, staring across at the triple-gate bridge, where mules clip-clopped through, their saddlebags bulging, and carts laden with timber or stone lumbered over, pulled by oxen whose horns had been shorn. 'I was young, then. Seventeen. Impetuous and headstrong in a way that only seventeen-year-old youths *can* be, but I swear by the sun's holy light that she was the most beautiful creature I have ever seen. She was perfect. Tall, slender, with hair the colour of ripe wheat and skin as soft and white as a dove – and I wanted her. By the stars that turned in the heavens, I wanted that woman and I vowed to have her at any cost.'

'At any cost?' Claudia repeated slowly.

Were any three words more laden with doom?

'Oh, yes.' Vincentrix chewed his lip. 'I courted that girl for six months. Sent her gifts, sang her songs, but she was not interested in me.'

Claudia didn't dare look at him. Couldn't bear to see the pain on his face.

'"Marry me," I said, "and on our wedding day I will give

78

you anything that is within my power to give." "Anything?" my true love replied, and I swear to you, Claudia Seferius, that all these years on I can still feel her soft breath on my face when she whispered that one little word. "Anything," I vowed. "Draw up a contract. I'll sign it without even looking."'

He wouldn't have been the first hothead to have made a rash promise to a girl and lived to regret it. From time immemorial, boys have thrown their lives away on quite the wrong woman, though Claudia was curious to know what this particular paragon of perfection had wrung out of Vincentrix that remained a source of agony so many years on.

'She demanded you went to Britain for twenty years to train as a Druid?'

'Nothing so prosaic,' Vincentrix rasped, and the anger in his voice was barely disguised. 'The bitch demanded to keep her virginity.'

Claudia tossed the last cake down to the ducks on the river, then emptied the crumbs out of the bag for the sparrows.

'I'm sorry to hear that,' she said evenly. 'Now tell me why you sought me out this morning.'

The old woman lay in the bed staring up at the thatch. Time was, those would have been her creels dangling from hooks up on the rafters. Until her hands became claws, she'd been dead quick with the withies, she had. Weaving baskets for eggs, for gathering fruit, firewood, straw for the animals, storing blankets and cloths through the summer. Now she couldn't hardly hold a mug, and the creels that hung from the beams had been woven by the deft hands of her granddaughter.

The old woman's eyes misted. What an angel, that girl! Not only nimble fingered, but a keen eye as well, dying her willows blue, yellow and red to create patterns that sold for a canny price in the market. Always after market day, her angel'd bring home a gift for her old grandma. Sometimes a shawl, sometimes a brooch, sometimes a flagon of fine Roman wine. No, she'd not save her money, that girl, no matter how much she was told! And if it wasn't fine things, it'd be fancy cheeses, ripe peaches, fish that had been caught in the ocean to tempt an appetite that was as shrivelled as the poor body it inhabited, but, bless her, the lass never gave up. Only last week she'd blown her savings on nothing more than a bunch of red roses for her old gran, saying the perfume alone was worth the coin, and at nights she'd sit by the bed, weaving her baskets, while the old woman talked of the old days and told stories told to her by her mother, and her mother before her, until the girl's eyelids closed and the withies dropped from her fingers.

Aye, she were an angel, that child. With both parents dead of the plague three summers back, and her brothers and sisters buried alongside, it were just the two of them now. *You ought to be married*, the old woman would tell her. *While the bloom of your youth is still fresh, lass, and there's still a bounce in your step*, because, praise be to the Hammer God, that child was a beauty. Like the old woman in her salad days, she had a tight narrow waist with curves where you want them and not where you don't, and hair as fair and as glossy as a meadow of buttercups.

Only it were not like the lassie not to come home . . .

It could be she'd found herself a lover at last, and spent the night in his bed. Fifty years might have passed, but the old woman still remembered how it felt, having a man hold you for the very first time. Aye, the right man and it turned any girl's head. Made you forget your own name, if you was lucky!

But that were last night. What about today, the start of the Fire Festival, with two days of market ahead?

A terrible emptiness filled the old woman's chest as she stared at the pile of brightly coloured baskets piled in the corner, and fear crawled like a nest of snakes in her gut as the sun began to disappear behind the trees.

If only she could lift herself out of this damn bed, she'd get the Elders to start making a search!

If only her thin voice would carry a bit further, she'd call for help from her neighbours!

If only, if only, if only . . .

As darkness crept over the thatch, tears of frustration and terror coursed down the old woman's cheeks.

Down at the boatyard, the nightwatchman finished his rounds, jabbed his torch back in its sconce and then settled down with his back to the boat shed and closed his eyes. No point having

80

a dog if you have to bark your bloody self was his motto. Rome provided soldiers to patrol the streets, let them earn their bloody money, and, besides, if he didn't get a good kip overnight, how would he be fit enough to put in a full shift at the sawmills tomorrow? Dreaming of the luxury that his two jobs kept him in, the nightwatchman began to snore.

At the other end of the yard, behind a pile of seasoned timbers stacked next to the river, Orbilio yawned. Wedged between a splintery masthead and a lumpy anchor stone, he was acutely aware that waiting was the tedious part, and since waiting comprised most of his job his one consolation was unwinding afterwards with a workout at the gymnasium – weights usually, or a game of small ball if there were enough chaps to make up a team. This would be followed by a long, hot soak to relieve the stiffness from being stuck in the same position for hours on end, then a massage with warm, aromatic oils to rid himself of whatever smells he'd been stuck with all day, in this case hemp, pitch and sweat. Such treats, though, were impossible after a night on surveillance. Even assuming the bath houses opened that early, mornings were reserved for the gentler sex, which meant that if Marcus Cornelius wanted a bath, he'd have to go back to Marcia's villa, and, whilst he couldn't put his finger on the exact reason, he just didn't feel comfortable there.

A soft scuffling halted his train. He craned his neck, peered into the blackness, saw a rat scamper over the ramp and relaxed. Take a Spaniard, he thought, or a German, in fact any stranger to imperial ways. Put him in any house anywhere in the Empire and life invariably follows the same pattern. Visitor knocks. Guard dog barks. Janitor opens up. Porter leads guest through the vestibule to the cool airy atrium, its decor differing only in the colour of the marble, the depth of gilt on the stucco and the design on the elaborate mosaics. Visitor waits, inhaling the fragrance of the oils that burn in the braziers. Eventually, a steward leads him through the house, usually to the shade of the portico, where the lady of the house is draped on a couch under a fan. It's never the master who greets him. The men of the house are invariably out – on their estates, in the libraries, with their mistresses. It's the women who receive guests. The women who wait so patiently at home, prisoners

81

of their class, but, even more, prisoners of their own snob-
bery.

With Marcia, everything was upside down, and it wasn't
that Orbilio was a chauvinist. He saw no reason why women
should not own property in their own right or run business
empires equal to men. As far as he was concerned, it made
no sense that men could divorce their wives for infidelity yet
their wives were not free to do likewise, and in his view it
was downright unfair that women were barred from pleading
in court. One-sided justice was no justice at all, and as for
the idea that women were so weak and helpless that they
needed a man's protection from cradle to grave – absolute
bollocks. Admittedly, there were women who fell into that
category, but thank god they were few, which surely made
the argument all the more convincing that the arrangement
should be one of choice? Something agreed, like the terms of
her dowry, which was laid down in the marriage contract?
Otherwise you ended up with the sorry situation you had now.
Needy, greedy women with no conversation beyond fashion
and gossip. How could they stand their own company?

So it wasn't that he held Marcia's wealth and status against
her. Quite the reverse, truth be told. He admired strong women
who fought for their corner and succeeded against all the odds.
It was the atmosphere in Marcia's villa that sat uneasily with
him. Maybe it was because she was host and hostess rolled
into one. Or that her masculine voice combined with her crisp
manner was at odds with the fashionable gowns and dripping
jewels, the elaborate coiffure and girlie cosmetics. Then there
was the way she hectored and flirted at the same time, the
way charity came with a price (and he had yet to discover
his!), the contradiction between her hard head for business
and her predilection for fakes. In all his travels, Orbilio had
never seen so many toadies gathered together in one room!
What on earth went through Marcia's head, when she hired
the likes of Koros and that lisping Indian soothsayer?

Perhaps that was it? Perhaps that's what lay at the root of
his unease, the fact that she'd surrounded herself with so many
yes-men that she no longer saw the complete picture, only
what she wanted to see. They say power corrupts, but people
forget it's two-way traffic. Once you divorce yourself from

impartiality, objectivity evaporates and the ego magnifies out of all proportion. Ruthless in her business dealings, it was not entirely surprising that Marcia's monstrous ego needed to be satisfied at home. The trouble is, if no one stands up to you, you start to believe yourself invincible . . .

A creak of timber down by the river's edge made him sit up. He strained his ears in the blackness, but heard only the nightwatchman's snorts. Then two cats began squaring up to each other, setting off the dogs in the distance. With a grunt, the nightwatchman grabbed his torch. Orbilio hunkered down into the shadows. But the search was cursory, and having satisfied himself that the cats weren't thieves in disguise the nightwatchman scattered them with a few judiciously thrown stones then quickly fell back into sleep.

Marcus rubbed his hands over his weary eyes. At least he wasn't stuck under a tarpaulin for hours on end, he supposed, with sawdust tickling his throat and the noise of constant hammering ringing in his ears. But he'd had to do it. He'd needed to monitor the comings and goings in this boatyard during the day, because the boatbuilder's accomplices would more than likely turn out to be men whose presence would not arouse suspicion, and whilst he was by no means certain that their peddling of childflesh would take place at this yard, river access lent itself to clandestine dealings.

As an owl hooted on the opposite bank, Orbilio folded his arms and shifted his feet so they rested on a coiled hawser. Working this trip to Santonum had been easy. Given the humidity and heat that made Rome such a perfect breeding ground for the plague, it was no wonder that half the city decamped to the country during the summer (the rich half, that is), and his boss was no exception. This meant that, as senior officer in the Security Police, no one questioned Orbilio's decision to take himself off to Gaul to – what was it he'd written in his report? That's right, how it had come to his attention that there was a plot by a group of hardcore rebels to retake Aquitania by marching on Santonum and assassinating the Governor.

He ought to be another Terence or Euripides, he thought. Penning scripts for the theatre, his fiction was so bloody good. But he'd had to come up with something, because he'd finally

83

wrung out of Claudia's steward that she was headed to Gaul and it was obvious the woman was up to something. And when Claudia was up to something, it was usually illegal and highly dangerous! The age-old combination of wealth and status worked its magic in the form of a fast ship to Massilia, then he cut across land on a sleeping cart, eliminating the delays in inns and posthouses that Claudia would have had, because the only time Orbilio's drivers stopped was to change horses. This meant he'd actually arrived ahead of her, but no sooner had he reported to the barracks (with a different fiction to explain his visit!) than a note was left in his room at the tavern where he was staying.

Like most tip-offs, it was anonymous. But a few discreet enquiries among army colleagues, coupled with gossip picked up at the inn, suggested that there had indeed been instances of beggar children disappearing from the streets of Santonum, and, since the note was quite specific in naming both boatyard and owner, Orbilio's nose told him to follow it. As outlined in the note, he was careful to make no mention to anyone of what he was investigating, and although he could probably use the contacts Marcia offered to provide, far better she, and everyone else, believed he was investigating fraud than have the paedophiles inadvertently alerted to his activities.

Unfortunately, surveillance work didn't allow much free time to follow other trails and he was still none the wiser about what Claudia was up to in Santonum! According to one source, she was tracing a man who had passed through some years before, but Marcus very much doubted that. Claudia Seferius was not the type of woman to look to the past. Only the future.

He listened to the slap of the water against the bank, to bats squeaking on the wing. Clouds had moved in to cover the moon, but the night was still warm and, all around him, crickets rasped out their lonely refrain. Refolding his arms, he wriggled his back against the masthead, because there was no reason to suggest the child peddlers would act tonight. In fact, he was resigned to this being one of many long waits and, behind the clouds, the constellations of Pegasus and Hercules moved round the heavens.

Ah, but suppose she was trying to trace a lost lover? Orbilio jerked up straight. Could that be why she rejected him? Because there was someone in her past who still had her affections? *Had she set out to find the one man she'd truly loved?* The churning in his stomach subsided. Whatever had happened in Claudia's past, she hadn't just buried, she'd cremated and scattered the ashes. Quite frankly, the idea of Claudia trailing after a man who'd walked out on her was simply risible. All the same . . . A black demon stirred in the darkness, as his thoughts drifted to her bodyguard. The same bodyguard who always stuck close to his mistress. Just how close, he wondered? And what kind of mistress?

Wouldn't you like to know what goes on between those two when they're alone? the demon asked – not for the first time.

Something wrenched under Orbilio's ribcage as he thought of the blue eyes that never left Claudia, not for a minute. What had those sullen eyes seen? And what did she see when she looked back? Youth, strength, rippling muscles, lean, tanned torso – and you had to remember that she was young, too.

Too young to remain celibate, whispered the demon. *Too young to have her womanly needs go unsatisfied.*

Marcus pursed his lips until they were white. He pictured those hands, those rough, bodyguard's hands, exploring parts that he could only dream about—

The creaking of oars pulled him up short. Craning his neck, he heard the dull clunk of wood as the boat nudged the bank, followed by a muffled whimper. Picturing the child, restrained by heavy hands under a stinking blanket, Orbilio's gorge rose. Of all the dirty jobs in the Security Police, living with the knowledge that he was sacrificing this child's innocence was the worst. But the only way to break this abomination once and for all was to follow the chain, because sure he could have had legionaries stationed around the boatyard. The child would be spared, the gang would be captured, but what of the mastermind who would remain free to set up his monstrous traffic elsewhere?

The little mite began to sniffle and Orbilio's gut clenched. He forced himself to blot out the sound, because what was important was to identify the child's abductors. Peering into the blackness, he recognized the carpentry foreman and one of the riveters.

'Oi!' The nightwatchman's sleep had not been as deep as

Orbilio had thought. 'What d'you lot think yer doing? Get outta—'

The gurgling sound make Orbilio's blood run cold. He recognized it instinctively from both the battlefield and his stint with the Security Police. The all too distinctive rattle a throat makes when its windpipe's been severed. That unmistakable mix of blood, air . . . and sheer terror.

As the poor man fought frantically for a life that was already over, Orbilio thought of the wife, the children, the mother, the brothers whose lives would also be wrecked. A splash testified to the disposal of the nightwatchman's body, and a more callous act he could not imagine. To the Gauls, burial of the corpse meant eternal peace through the soul's reincarnation. Trussed inside the blanket slung over the foreman's shoulder, the child began to sob and anger boiled up inside him. Reaching for his dagger, Orbilio withdrew it silently from its scabbard and crept round the timber pile. Too late he heard a sound behind him. Saw the flash of bright steel as the moon came out behind the cloud. Caught a whiff of a woman's perfume.

Then the heavens exploded in a million white stars.

Eleven

Claudia was well aware that there were many risks a girl could take in this life, but walking round the backstreets of a strange town with a chap you didn't know and twenty-two gold pieces weighing you down was surely up there with the best of them.

'Eez not far now,' her guide muttered sullenly.

'I should bloody well hope not,' she retorted, because that was another thing. In Rome, you snap your fingers and a litter comes trotting. In this part of Santonum, litter meant discarded pies, slimy cabbage stalks, broken pots, slops, and let's not even mention the piles of steaming manure left by the hordes of draught beasts! Shuddering, she picked her way behind the young tribesman and wondered if Hannibal hadn't been right all along.

'I implore you, madam, do not go with this fellow. I distrust his motives with every fibre of my well-travelled body. The man is a scoundrel, I can smell it.'

Turning into the Gaulish quarters, Claudia was beginning to believe him. At the time, it seemed the right thing to do, leaving Hannibal and her bodyguard in the Forum and coming alone, as the young Santon insisted. Given that robbing a Roman citizen was punishable by being sold into slavery and that the taking of Roman life was discouraged by crucifixion – a deterrent, incidentally, that was fiercely effective, since a strapping, fit warrior could take two days to die on the cross, sometimes three if his torturers were proficient – it was obvious to Claudia that Hannibal's informant was after secrecy, not acting with criminal intent. I mean, what man in his right mind is going to sell out his comrades in public? she thought. But that was half an hour ago, in streets full of Romans, where people spoke a language she understood . . .

Thatched houses gave way to the wooden shacks of one of the poorer potters' quarters. Frowning earnestly over their wheels and sweating from the heat of the kilns, some applied glaze, others drew intricate patterns, while over here they painted faces on drinking mugs, over there they stacked vases for export, and everywhere young boys scurried about fetching baskets of charcoal, buckets of water, running errands left, right and centre. The guide led her on through the twisting labyrinth, turning left, cutting right, and at every corner assuring her that it wasn't far now. Claudia thought of the thin blade strapped to her calf and took a modicum of comfort from it.

'Eere.' The youth finally stopped outside a jumble of scaffolding, platforms and ramps. 'Ze man says to meet you eere.'

Bastard! He'd led her through all those stinking backstreets when he could have brought her here in a third of the time! All the same . . .

'Are you sure?'

Claudia shouted to make herself heard above the din of hammering and the cranking of the giant crane, but when she turned round, her surly guide was nowhere in sight. *Double* bastard! But before she could ask one of the carpenters sawing over their trestles which was the best way back to town, or attract the attention of one of the million bricklayers beavering away with hods and trowels as sweating apprentices mixed piles of wet concrete, a horn blew. As one, the workers dropped tools and scurried down the ladders.

'What's happening?' she asked a stonemason who'd stopped to brush the dust out of his eyebrows.

'Midday, m'lady.'

He gave his stomach a fond pat as he trotted off after the others, and she couldn't believe how, in less than a minute, the site was transformed from industrious ants' nest to deserted ghost town, where only the gentle swing of a rope and the odd settlement creak of a plank testified that a labour force had even been here. And suddenly she understood why Hannibal's informant had chosen this place for a meeting. Far enough out of the main crush to render it impressive, yet not so far that people wouldn't make the effort to come and worship, right now the Temple of Augustus was nothing more than an empty, roofless shell. Where better than a deserted building site to sell out your nearest and dearest?

'Hello?' she called out. The air was sour and dry, and near her feet a lizard scuttled under a pile of loose stones. 'Anyone there?'

'*Oh-oh-oh,*' her voice echoed back. '*Anyone there-ere-ere?*'

Choosing a stone block in the shade of the soaring temple, Claudia sat down and prepared to wait. The informant would want to give the workers ample time to get clear and, as she unhooked the heavy money belt, her pulse quickened at the thought of the information this purse was about to buy. Dear Diana, she hadn't slept a wink last night for the excitement, and as for Hannibal's concern, honestly! Did he really think she didn't know she was being ripped off? Hannibal had beat his informant down from thirty to twenty-two gold pieces, but she would have paid twice that – three times – four! – to find her father. Only how time had dragged since Hannibal first told her of the appointment. She had just returned from Santonum and was crossing the peristyle when he'd come loping over, little Luci piggyback on his shoulders.

'Down you go, young lady.'

'No, *more,*' Luci squealed, tugging on his purple striped tunic. 'More, Uncle Hanni! More, more!'

'Uncle?' Claudia laughed.

'Her mother's idea, I assure you,' Hannibal droned, as he swung the child round in an arc that billowed her little dress out like an angel's. 'My own flesh and blood can never be far enough away in distance physical, financial or emotional.' He set the laughing child down and mopped the sweat from his brow with a theatrical swipe. 'You have killed me, young lady. I lie mortally wounded, but am honoured to die in your presence.'

'You're not dead!' Luci rolled her enormous blue eyes and tutted as he dropped to his knees, clutching his chest. 'Mummy says you're as strong as the Bull God and *everyone* knows the Bull God's immortal!'

'Then I shall take comfort from that, as I writhe here in agony. Now run along and help your mother, there's a good girl, because Luci and I have an agreement, don't we, Luci?'

The little girl nodded. 'I help Mummy with the washing

89

and in return Uncle Hanni shows me how to climb trees without tearing my frock.' She pulled at Claudia's ear and whispered into it. 'The trick is to tuck your dress into your knickers, you know.'

'I'll remember that,' she said solemnly, and Luci skipped off, yodelling at the top of her off-key voice. To Hannibal, Claudia had said, 'Strong as the Bull God?'

'Not what you're thinking, madam, not what you're thinking. But it pains me to see good women beholden to bad and thus, when I am not lurking in taverns in search of information regarding certain missing persons, I see no reason why I cannot chop the lady's firewood or help haul the water.'

'Stella won't be needing your help for long,' Claudia said, musing that it was an interesting choice of words to describe Marcia. 'Her cousin bought half the slaves at the auction this morning, so Stella won't have to do those chores herself.'

'And sold them,' Hannibal murmured, darting a sharp glance towards the kitchens. 'Don't forget selling them, madam.' He swallowed what could have been a bitter taste in his mouth. 'Which reminds me. Our informant has made contact . . .'

The details of the appointment were then followed by a lengthy sermon on trust, folly and greed, but Jupiter alone knew how long that went on for, because Claudia backed away quietly and left Hannibal lecturing himself. All the same, you'd think any decent stool pigeon would arrive on time for his own bloody meeting! She pulled out her travel sundial, set it flat on a stone and flipped up the central pin. More time passed, in which the only sound was the hammering of metals far in the distance and the mewing of a buzzard high in the sky.

She thought about the temple. What it would look like once it was finished, a masterpiece of local limestone clad in Pyrenean marble, its portico lined with works of art, its precincts dotted with gaily painted statues and its carved entablature gilded and gleaming. This temple was earmarked to house a library, someone said, adding with a snigger that it wouldn't need much of a room, bloody ignorant Gauls couldn't read. Not yet, she'd thought, but give it a generation of free schooling and inequalities would soon level out – and she pictured the Druids, trapped in their secret language of runes, becoming more and more isolated from a people who no longer needed priests to do their thinking for them. *Oh, Vincentrix. What tricks will you turn to then?* Pushing the enigmatic Druid out of her mind, she imagined instead the Emperor strutting round the echoing halls of his temple, nodding his handsome head in approval at the magnificent works, while his heart mourned his best friend and Rome's finest general, the man who'd laid out the grid plan for Santonum and who'd been ferried across the River Styx long before his allotted span was up.

Hey, ho. Claudia felt an emptiness weigh down her heart as she snapped her pocket sundial shut. The informant wasn't going to show now and whatever paths might lead to her father, this one was blocked, and the only surprise was the pain that twisted inside. Ridiculous, really, to imagine that the first trail would lead her straight to him, but—

'*Lady Claudia?*'

The voice didn't belong to the surly young guide. It was deeper, had greater resonance and clearly belonged to a much older man.

'*Lady Claudia?*' it called again. '*Are you there?*'

'OVER HERE!' she yelled, grabbing the money belt as she jumped off her makeshift seat.

Bloody guide, she would skin him alive, she thought, racing into what would, in a year or so, be the sacred back room where Augustus's mighty statue would be housed. The sullen little bastard had led her to the *back* of the temple and god knows how much precious time she'd wasted while Hannibal's informant had stood pacing up and down at the front!

'Coming,' she called, 'I'm just – *youch!*'

Emerging from shadows into what would one day be a magnificent portico fronted by a flight of white marble steps, the sunlight was blinding and her shins cracked painfully against a plank. Pitching forward, from the corner of her eye she caught a flash of movement overhead. Heard a low, grating sound.

Instinctively, Claudia hurled herself against the temple wall.

Just as half a ton of masonry crashed to the ground.

It could have been an accident. A falcon she'd seen from the corner of her eye as she tripped. A dove alighting on the

91

scaffolding. And who's to say it wasn't a frayed rope or snapped swallowtail clamp that caused the block to slip from the platform? This is a building site, for goodness' sake. Accidents happen. But even before the clouds of choking white dust had settled, Claudia knew this was more than sloppiness on the part of a temple stonemason.

Unable to stem the flood of tears that were pure liquid reaction, and with limbs that were shaking like aspens in a gale, she forced herself up the ladder, one rung at a time, where the evidence was plain for all to see. A lone plank, still rocking from where it had been used as a lever. A hastily abandoned crowbar lying beside it. Leaden legs descended the steps, but wait! There was still the possibility that it was mischief, not attempted murder, because with so many workmen's tools lying about this was a thieves' paradise. Maybe one of the gang panicked, using the levered block as a distraction to divert the attention of any security guards poking around. Because all building sites have to have guards, and the Temple of Augustus was no exception.

She cursed herself for not remembering them before, and almost tripped again as she raced through the precinct towards their hut. Bursting open the door, Claudia was confronted by three burly guards, sure. Except they lay slumped over the table and she could picture the next bit. Site foreman returning from lunch. Taking one glance at the empty goblets in front of them and sacking the men on the spot. But there was another smell that lingered in the warm, midday air. Barely discernible over the wine and stale sweat, it was hard to spot unless you were trying. Cloying and not particularly pleasant, Claudia recognized it at once. Oil of narcissus. From which the word narcotic derives . . .

The shaking in her limbs was replaced by the stiffness of truth, and something primordial slithered in her stomach. The youth had not ushered her to the back entrance by mistake. There never had been an informant waiting. No misunderstanding in which the two parties waited in different parts of the building, unaware of the other's presence.

This was a carefully planned attempt at murder.

The idea was so simple, she had to admire it. Leave your victim kicking her heels in the shade, so that by the time her name was eventually called, she would be well and truly dazzled by the sunshine out front. Temporarily blinded, she would, of course, fail to spot the plank that had been so carefully laid across her path, causing her to trip in the very place where the block was designed to drop. '**X**' marks the spot, as it were.

And it had nearly – so nearly – succeeded.

Leaning over the workman's fountain to wash her face, Claudia half expected to see the Grim Reaper peering over her shoulder. But Saturn clearly had an appointment elsewhere, and the only thing that stared back was a pale creature with distended pupils and white hair cascading around her shoulders. It came as a shock to realize that the reflection was hers.

Hastily brushing the limestone dust from her hair, Claudia pinned her wayward curls into place, smoothed the pleats of her robe, pinched the colour back into her cheeks, and by the time she found her way back to the Forum she had not only removed every last trace of her close call with death, she'd also controlled the jumping at every creaking wagon that passed, the flinching at each brush of a hand.

Squeezing past pack mules and porters, there was no outward suggestion that many nights would pass in which she would be kept awake by a continuous replay of half a ton of limestone smashing to the ground within inches of her.

But at least Claudia Seferius would have the satisfaction of knowing that the bastard who planned this wouldn't sleep, either.

Twelve

Orbilio opened one eye, felt a stab of white pain bounce off the back of his skull and quickly closed it again. So, then. Not dead. As far as he knew there was no sunshine in Hades – and he didn't imagine it was filled with pretty girls with apple cheeks and liquid black eyes pressing their young, firm breasts against his arm as they mopped his brow, either!

'Where am I?'

The first time he awoke, he truly believed himself to be in the Halls of the Dead. Through misty vision and great waves of nausea, monsters and giants closed in on him. Dwarves and serpents gurned in the flickering torchlight. The second time he awoke, he realized they were painted plaques. Grotesque, but harmless, in fact the very opposite of harmless, but it hadn't been the most auspicious moment to be introduced to the Gaulish custom of sticking gargoyles on the wall to scare off any evil spirits who tried to enter the house.

'Sssh,' his ministering angel cooed. 'Lie still and rest, my lord. You're all right now.'

She could have fooled him. His head pounded, his brain was on fire and every tooth in his jawbone was screaming. 'Someone hit me,' he said.

'Yes, me.'

She laid a cold compress over his forehead, drenched with healing comfrey and witch hazel, and at the same time contrived to press another warm breast against his shoulder. The feeling was not altogether unpleasant, even allowing for the pain in his head.

'Would it be too much of an imposition to ask why?'

Vaguely he remembered the stakeout in the boatyard. Witnessing the senseless murder of the nightwatchman and a

94

child being smuggled ashore. After that, though, things started to get a bit hazy.

'Well, if I hadn't clobbered you with that lump of wood, my lord,' she said matter-of-factly, 'they'd have killed you like they did Rintox.'

'Rintox being the nightwatchman?'

Even the simplest deduction sent daggers into his brain, slicing it into a thousand pieces.

'He was a lazy git and no mistake,' the girl said, wringing out the cloth for another compress that she placed behind his ear. 'That's why my stepfather hired him, and it's why he wouldn't have no dog in the yard, neither. Said if you had the right guard dog, you could never turn your back on the bugger, and if you had one you could turn your back on, then it weren't worth the trouble of keeping. But no one deserves to die like Rintox did, do they? Can you try to sit up, my lord? I've got a potion here what'll put paid to the queasiness.'

As she plumped the cushions behind his back, he smelled the same scent he'd smelled last night in the boatyard, and now he remembered where he'd inhaled it before.

'You're the boatbuilder's daughter.'

Like everyone else in the yard, he'd been too distracted by bouncing breasts, swaying hips and the flash of her shapely calves to notice the girl's face, and he felt his cheeks burn with the shame.

'Stepdaughter, my lord.' She held the mug to his lips. 'You won't get me calling that bastard Dad – now look, this stuff ain't nice, but do drink it all if you can.'

The shattered mush that was his brain slowly reassembled itself. 'The anonymous note in my room? That was you?'

'Certainly was. Come on, you can do better than that, my lord. That's the ticket.'

'Mother of Tarquin!' His eyes were streaming from the vile brew. 'What *is* this stuff?'

'Told you it weren't very nice, and frankly you don't wanna know what it is. Now then,' She sat on the bed and leaned earnestly towards him, 'what are we going to do about them child-peddling bastards, my lord?'

'*We*,' he groaned, 'aren't going to do anything.'

He stared at the grimacing monsters covering the walls, felt

95

the bitter aftertaste of her concoction strip the taste buds from his tongue and gingerly explored the swelling behind his left ear. Right now, he wasn't sure Rintox hadn't got off rather lightly and was immediately ashamed of his thoughts. Rintox's death was no joking matter. He might have been lazy, as Black Eyes here said, but sloth is no motive for murder. Rintox didn't deserve to die in terror and pain, any more than his family deserved to have their lives ruined, either.

'*You* are going stay here and carry on as usual,' he told her firmly. '*I* am going to take this up with the authorities.'

'Oh, no.'

Black Eyes folded militant arms over her breasts.

'Oh, no, you bloody don't, my lord. For one thing, I ain't staying a minute longer under the same roof as that flesh-peddling creep, and while me Mam won't hear a word said against the dirty bugger she'll find out soon enough what he's like, so I won't lose no sleep over that. And for a second '

She paused only to plunge the cloth into a bowl of cold water redolent with hyssop and comfrey and wring it out as though it were a chicken's neck.

'For a second,' she said, slapping it on to his forehead, 'I'd be very careful who I told about this, if I was you. I mean, it ain't poor folk who can afford tender young flesh, if you gets my drift, and I'm pretty sure, from the odd bits I've over-heard, that there's some powerful people involved here.'

'Like who?'

'Well, if I knew that, I'd have told you in me note, wouldn't I!'

Orbilio was plunged back to his childhood, to the times when he'd been stuck in bed with mumps or the itching pox. The family nurse hadn't had much use for meekness, either.

'I suppose the only thing in our favour,' she said, 'is that the bastards don't know we're on to them—'

'I do wish you'd stop saying "we".'

'Why?' Her liquid black eyes widened in incomprehension that it could possibly be any other way. 'We're a team, ain't we?'

'No,' he sighed wearily, 'we are not a team.'

Or at least that's what he would have said, had his face not been muffled by two soft, warm bosoms.

'Glad we got that settled, then,' Black Eyes announced cheerfully. 'Now upsy-dupsy, my lord. Let's get your old head bandaged up, cos we can't have you here when me Mam gets home, can we? That's the ticket.'

With a brisk flick of the wrist, she tipped the water from the bowl out of the window.

'Which is the quickest way to your place, d'you reckon?'

For the female pheasant strutting proudly across the woodland clearing with a string of chicks in tow, the appearance of yet another predator to deplete her brood was met with a series of almighty squawks followed by a good few indignant clucks as it became obvious that the predator in question was not stalking her. Further on, a robin fluttered from the forest floor into the safety of the branches overhead and the rapid whirr of wingbeats into a bramble thicket testified to the nervousness of a pair of dunnocks.

But the Scarecrow had grown used to this and didn't notice the slithering of an adder from the stone on which it had been basking, or the chatter of a squirrel as it dropped the acorn it had been nibbling between its paws to scamper up the oak tree in a blur of rusty red. The Scarecrow was watching out for other things.

By crouching down and pulling back an overhang of dog rose, one was afforded an excellent view up the gently rolling hill to the meadow where the horses pastured. Their sweat carried on the summer breeze, rich but not unpleasant, as did their snickering and snorts, the swishing of their tails and the crunch of grass being pulled up in clumps by soft, prehensile lips. They were fine horses, some of the best, but the Scarecrow had not risked everything in creeping this close to the villa in order to sit and watch a herd of grazing animals.

The overhang of dog rose gently fell back into place and the Scarecrow moved on, to a view through a patch of gorse to the adjacent meadow. Here, the grass was still long and lush, and this was where the horses would be moved to next, once the paddock they were feeding in had been cropped back. Right now, though, it was full of squealing children, five of them to be precise, twin boys aged eight, a girl perhaps one year older and another girl a few years younger, plus a tot as naked as the day that he was born and browner than a stack of berries. From the noise they were making, you could be forgiven for thinking there were twenty-five rolling down the bank, not just five, and the reason they were shrieking was the antics of a middle-aged man in a purple-striped tunic with a clump of feathers pinned to his breast.

The Scarecrow watched as the man, lean and tanned and fit and strong, played Wolf with them, his patience never straining at the constant repetition or the increasing number of grass stains that were accumulating on his tunic, or the fact that the littlest one found that the surest way to attract the man's attention was to pull his hair. It was a fine head of hair, the Scarecrow thought. White at the temples, admittedly, but no signs of thinning, and his energies didn't diminish as he strode round the meadow, growling and snarling and gobbling the children up, or jumping out from behind trees and scaring them witless. The Scarecrow noted how easily he incorporated the noises floating up from the menagerie into the game. The reverberating snarl of the cheetah; the mewing of peacocks; the gibbering of monkeys and parrots.

Then suddenly a small child with hair of gold and eyes as big and blue as a full summer moon came running into the meadow, her little Roman robe billowing out like a pink cloud as she hurtled down the hill.

'Uncle Hanni!'

When she threw her little arms round the man's neck and smacked her rosebud lips against his weathered cheek the Scarecrow felt something churn inside.

'Uncle Hanni, you're home!'

'Am I?' The man spun round, looking over this shoulder, then beyond that, until he finally spotted his own shadow. 'So I am, little Luci,' he declared. 'So I am!'

'I've seen Qeb's cheetah. It's really scary, but ever so, *ever* so pretty. It's got emeralds for eyes and it's all enamelled, and it's got a blue collar round its neck of shiny lapsed lizards.'

'I think you might mean lapis lazuli, and I think you might also have been poking this ' he gave the child's nose a gentle tweak – 'in places where it doesn't belong. Did Qeb say you could go sneaking around in his quarters?'

98

'You won't tell Mummy, will you, Uncle Hanni? Only last time I got caught playing in somebody's room she made me scrub the latrines, clean out the pig-pen and I had to shuck peas for a whole week.'

'I hope you washed your hands before shelling those peas.'

'*Promise* you won't tell?'

'Very well, young Luci,' the man said, laying a hand over the feathers pinned to his chest. 'I swear I won't breathe a word of your indiscretions to your mother.'

'Thank you, Uncle Hanni, oh, thank you, thank you!' A shower of wet kisses descended upon him. 'Now can we play pirates? Please can we?'

'We'll have to put it to the vote.' He turned to the other five, knowing their eager eyes had already lit up. 'What d'ye say, me hearties? Do we let this 'orrible wretch join our rebel gang, or shall we make 'er walk the plank?'

Filled with shame and an uncontrollable sense of self-loathing, the Scarecrow turned back into the woods.

Whilst fighting off a gang of slave traders with one hand and stamping out fires on the oar deck with the other, Hannibal noticed a flock of doves take off from the woods down in the valley. At the same time, half a dozen rooks rose from the tree-tops, then circled noisily.

'Break out the mainsail, men! Stay the foremast, set the sprit, put the cat out!'

The rooks settled. The pigeons were nowhere in sight. The horses in the next meadow grazed contentedly.

'Why, shiver me timbers, if that isn't the Minotaur!' he yelled, drawing an imaginary sword as one of the estate dogs wandered into the paddock and cocked his leg against a poplar. 'After him, men! Don't let the brute get away!'

With a series of bloodcurdling shrieks, Hannibal's pirate gang tumbled up the hillside behind him.

In her bed, the old woman clutched at her heart. The pain was horrendous, but the old woman didn't mind. However long she had to endure it, this was nothing compared to the agony of knowing that her granddaughter would never set foot inside this house again, or the terrible imaginings that tortured her when she thought about what her darling must have endured during her final moments on earth.

'I'm coming,' she cried. 'I am coming to join you, my angel.'

She wanted to curse the fiend that had snatched this beautiful child from a golden future and denied her the happiness she so richly deserved – a loving husband, a house filled with the laughter of children, the right to grow up and grow old with loved ones and friends – oh, how she wanted to curse this vile monster, but her ancient body was failing her. There was no breath left in her to call on the gods, but surely the Shining One, who saw everything, would take pity on her? Surely the Hammer God would strike out for vengeance?

'May your evil bones never be buried,' was all she could rasp, as the pain clawed ever deeper into her heart. 'May your black soul never rest!'

In the final throes of her spasm, the very last gift that her granddaughter had given her fell from the bed on to the floor. Typically thoughtful, it was a carving made from ivory of a wolfhound, just like the hound the old woman used to keep when she and her man were first married. The old woman had wanted to die clutching this gift as something she could show the God of the Underworld, that he might see how beautiful her angel was on the inside, as well as the outside. Now she would just have to tell him, but the Horned One was patient, as well as a good listener. Through pains that rent and twisted her frail, shrivelled body, the old woman was content that her angel would be reborn in goodness and light. Mustering one final breath, she called one name.

'*Esus!*'

Esus, the Blood God, because those who he slayed or were slain in his name were condemned to eternal torment.

In the corner, layers of dust faded the bright colours of the baskets woven by her granddaughter and made grey the pillow where she'd laid her lovely head.

Thirteen

Shadows were lengthening and the setting sun had cloaked the landscape in a dusky heather pink as Claudia followed the path beside the stream, but work on Marcia's tomb continued unabated. She could hear the chip-chip-chip of chisels and the clip-clip-clip of shears as she approached, along with the unmistakable thwack that an axe makes when it's engaged in felling trees.

'I thought you were supposed to be working on Hercules,' she said to Paris, kneeling on the scaffolding where fifteen marble columns were slowly being sculpted into nymphs.

One tanned and muscled shoulder shrugged, but his concentration didn't waver.

'Marcia wants me back on the caryatids,' he said, blowing away the marble dust that had accumulated in the nymph's left ear. 'She insists the tomb take priority again, so I've delegated the statuary to her hired workforce, given them sketches, dimensions and so on, and then it's just a question of adding the personal touches myself. Some of them,' he added grudgingly, 'aren't too bad.'

Praise indeed from a man who could turn a lump of stone into the youthful personification of spring.

'That doesn't bother you?' she asked. 'Delegating to a team you didn't pick?'

Right from the outset, it struck her as odd that men such as Paris, Hor and Semir were working alone. Most experts, especially those in the artistic field, were accompanied by a whole squad of apprentices and labourers. Men who understood every inch of the business their maestro was engaged in, down to the last nuance and wrinkle, and who were thus easily entrusted with the more mundane tasks and repetitive jobs. When Claudia raised the subject with Marcia, though, the woman had been adamant.

101

'My dear girl, I provide the staff,' she'd sniffed, 'not the hired help!'

This way, she insisted, she always knew exactly where each stage was at, whilst at the same time ensuring there could not possibly be any pilfering going on under her roof, much less any lingering about on time that she was bloody well paying for.

'In other words, if bread's the staff of life, this way you're sure the life of your staff isn't one long loaf?'

'Hm.' Marcia had looked at her in much the same way Claudia imagined she might inspect a cockroach in her bed, before turning on her fashionable heel to harangue the fan wallah for not flapping hard enough, while clipping her maid-servant round the ear for eavesdropping.

And whilst Claudia could see exactly why Marcia, who needed to be in control of every waking moment, would ship in scores of slaves to work on her precious project, she couldn't understand why the likes of Paris, Hor and Semir would agree to such terms. Surely artists of that calibre also had a need to be in control of their work? If only out of personal pride, rather than ego?

'What *bothers* me,' Paris snorted, polishing the nymph's earlobe with a soft cloth, 'is being made to employ imbeciles who can't tell the difference between a right foot and a left.'

He cast a scornful eye over the statues that were scattered round the precinct in varying stages of completion. For all her talk about purists, it would appear that Marcia was more than happy to compromise on quality in favour of early comple-tion of her undertaking. This was nothing short of a produc-tion line.

'Thanks to one incompetent fool, I'm faced with the choice of mounting a discus thrower with two left feet on the podium,' the Greek snapped, 'or I end up with a satyr surplus to require-ments, because I've had to shear his feet into hooves.' His voice softened. 'Isn't she beautiful?'

'Marcia? Um, yes. Absolutely.'

'No, no, the caryatid.' He ran a lover's hand over her stone shoulders. 'Do you know what the word means?'

'A clothed female figure used in place of a column.'

'Caryatid means "woman of Caryae",' he corrected.

'A Spartan?' Claudia had had no idea.

'Spartan women were reputed to be the most beautiful in the whole of the Greek world.'

'As well as the most intelligent, the most spirited and the most independent.'

'Exactly, and can't you see the way this one is thrusting herself out of the marble? The more I work on this woman of Caryae, the more aware I become of her turning into flesh and blood. I feel her character form in my hands and then I start to sense the pride she feels, holding up this roof not just for a few years, but for centuries.' He leaned back on his knees and admired his handiwork. 'Centuries,' he whispered. 'Can you imagine that?'

And suddenly there was the clicking of internal cogs as it became clear why Paris had agreed to waive his usual practices. Marcia needed a tomb to outshine all other civil monuments in Aquitania not simply to impress people during her own lifetime, but to secure for herself the nearest thing to immortality.

Paris, too, was looking far beyond the immediate future.

Paris was looking towards a time when people would be able to look back and marvel on his works, in much the same way they used to marvel at the achievements of his Mycenean ancestors. Except that whilst Greek statues in those days were finely executed, they were also stiff and unyielding. Paris had contrived to combine his stoneworking skills with modern art that embraced the human psyche every bit as much as it revered the human body. His statues reflected real people doing real things, rather than elevated ideals. In capturing the soul, Paris had also ensured his own immortality!

Locked in his obsession with his marble, he didn't even notice her slip away. But the concept of immortality lingered, as Claudia reflected that Hor was Egyptian ... and a race more obsessed with the afterlife she had yet to meet.

She wasn't sure whether he'd even noticed her, absorbed as he was with his brushwork. But he had.

'Good evening, my lady.'

He flashed her his wholesome smile before returning to his work, and Claudia thought Hor would be much better looking if he only went outside once in a while. His skin was so pale it was unhealthy, his hair was flecked with dandruff from too much time spent indoors, and it couldn't possibly be good for his eyes, working by lamplight from morning till night.

Picking up one of the hand-lamps, she toured the tomb, again dumbstruck by how expertly Hor had managed to cram everything in. The banquets, the trade deals, the villa, the boat, and more scribes, accountants and secretaries than Augustus employed to run the whole Empire. Of course, on the walls all these people were perfect. No warts, no squints, no birth-marks, no ugliness was permitted inside or out of this tomb. In each scene, a timeless Marcia was surrounded by beautiful girls, although, so as not to distract from the point of the exer-cise, they were either shorter or depicted seated so that each had to look up to her, physically, not just figuratively, and in every setting she was adored by bronzed, handsome hunks. No detail had been spared. Hor had painted the rich harvests from the fields and the abundant game from the forests with draughtsman-sharp accuracy, and if he couldn't reproduce the animals intended for the menagerie with anatomical precision he left a space and rough outline for later completion.

'The artwork is exquisite,' Claudia told him truthfully.

'Thank you.' He responded with all the grace of a man used to receiving compliments, but for whom they had little meaning.

'I recognize that outfit,' she said, peering over his shoulder to the scene he was painting. 'Marcia wore that robe to the banquet.'

'Did she?' He continued to define the features of the face. 'I don't remember.'

Not just the scarlet gown, either. He'd captured every detail from the silver tiara to her cerise slippers, even down to the engravings and whorls on her bracelets. It was just unfortu-nate that the face, though undoubtedly well executed and undeniably stunning, happened to be two decades younger than the woman who'd worn that eye-catching outfit. What was wrong with growing old?

'I lose track of time,' Hor added wistfully.

And he wasn't the only one, she thought, leaving him to it. Without doubt, Marcia would accept that lovely unlined face as hers. In fact, Claudia saw a time – not far off, either – when mirrors would be phased out of Marcia's life. Once she was no longer capable of luring young men (like the unfortunate Garro) into her bed and was forced to hire gigolos, she would have no need of mirrors. Instead, she would surround herself with people offering constant reassurance of her loveliness, and just a short stroll round this tomb would corroborate their lies.

Here, Marcia never grew old.

Here, she remained young and beautiful, for ever rich, for ever cherished, and only those around her would know differently.

But! Claudia set off in the direction of the menagerie. She'd come down here to find Hannibal, and Hannibal wasn't here. Frankly, she hadn't been a bit surprised when she had returned to the Forum shortly after midday and found Junius waiting alone outside the basilica.

'Hannibal's gone back to the villa,' he'd said.

'Now why doesn't that surprise me,' she'd muttered under her breath.

But how strange. Having searched high and low, he was nowhere to be found. Dammit, Hannibal, you're here somewhere, I bloody know it! Across the far side of the pond, now every bit as pink as the flamingoes that were giving their wing feathers a last fluff before bed, gazelles flicked off flies with their stunted, wagging tails as they grazed with quiet elegance, blissfully unaware of the cheetah's ever vigilant gaze. But still no Hannibal.

'There, there, my pretty-pretty,' a monotone cooed behind one of the walls. 'There, there, my pretty girl.'

Claudia peered over, expecting to see Qeb with something small and furry in his hands, and recoiled instantly.

'It's a king cobra,' he said.

Sitting cross-legged on the floor of the enclosure, the setting sun reflecting cherry-red off his gleaming, shaven skull, he held the snake behind its head with one hand and stroked the loose skin that flared into a hood when threatened with the other. Interestingly, he didn't lift his eyes to meet hers once, although, to be fair, that might have had something to do with the creature in his hands.

'Venomous, although primarily it eats other snakes.'

105

'How reassuring.'

The damned thing had to be at least twice as long as Qeb was high, and he wasn't a small man. Six foot if he was an inch!

'Cobra venom paralyses the nerve centres that control the heart and lungs, did you know that?'

Claudia looked into the cold, bronze eyes of the cobra and thought, hell, the bloody thing wouldn't even need to bite.

'The spitting cobra is even more fascinating.' Qeb continued to stroke the snake's hood as though it was a kitten he held in his hands. 'That's capable of spraying venom from a distance of up to eight feet –'

Claudia took a step backwards.

'– and aims for the eyes, causing immense pain and temporary blindness.'

Lovely. Paris makes love to his statues, Qeb makes love to his snakes. Who said this wasn't a progressive society? Claudia wound her way up the path back to the villa. She knew who had made the attempt on her life this morning, and she knew why, but more importantly she was well aware that the killer wouldn't give up just because she'd had a lucky escape. What had gone through that murderous mind, she wondered, when it was obvious the plan had failed? Killers can't afford to hang around, for fear of being identified, because no matter who or what your status Rome doesn't take very kindly to its citizens being picked off in broad daylight. The killer would have bolted like the rat that they were, but she had no doubts her would-be executioner would try again. Only this time she would be waiting. Waiting, and ready to turn the tables on this person who valued human life so very lightly . . .

'Ah, there you are, Hannibal.'

To his credit, he actually jumped.

'Madam!' By the light of the torch flickering in the sconce on the wall, she could see the colour that flushed his cheeks darken to the hue of cut peat then spread all the way down to his neck. 'I – I didn't expect to see you there.'

No, I'll bet you bloody didn't.

'Sorry to startle you,' she said sweetly.

Although quite how else he could have been expected to react, she couldn't imagine, since she'd been standing behind

106

that laurel for half an hour, until he eventually emerged from a certain door at the far end of the east wing.

'Only I have a favour to ask.'

Hannibal smoothed back his hair with his hand and adjusted his buckle. 'Ask away, madam, ask away. I am yours to command,' he added, with a theatrical bow. 'Even at one lonely sestertius a day.'

Claudia drew a deep breath and forced herself to respond to his clowning with a smile. Since it made her cheeks ache, she stopped. 'I want you to forget about finding my father—'

Frown lines furrowed Hannibal's weathered brow. 'Don't tell me that scoundrel had reliable information after all?'

'Oh, my, you'll never *believe* what happened there!' Claudia rolled her eyes and wondered whether any of her ancestors had been actors. 'For a start, that idiot guide led me to the opposite end of the temple from where your informant was waiting, but the worst part, Hannibal, this HUUUGE lump of masonry fell off the platform, and, of course, this brought people running –' he'd never know that was a lie – 'which scared your informant away. Anyway, the thing is . . . Hannibal, are you listening to me?'

'What? Oh, yes. Yes, of course, dear lady, of course. You want me to forget about tracing your father.'

'I do. You see, Vincentrix went to a lot of trouble to seek me out in Santonum yesterday morning.' She paused, picturing Everyman with his lime-whitened hair and pantaloons tucked into his boots, confiding the heartache of his tragic marriage as they munched sweetmeats by the river. 'He wanted to know what I could tell him about the Scarecrow, but all I could pass on was what Marcia told me. Namely, that this character lives in the forest and, whilst creepy, seems perfectly harmless.'

'Though not without cunning,' Hannibal muttered. 'Stella informs me that her elegant cousin regularly despatches trackers to hunt down this fellow and drive him out of her woods, but as fast as the dogs pick up his spoor they lose it again. There is only one possible conclusion to be drawn. Our friend the Scarecrow employs a substance to put the hounds off the scent. But I am curious, madam. Why should the Collegiate of Druids be interested in the wild man of the woods?'

The very question Claudia had put to Vincentrix, because

clearly the Scarecrow wasn't Santon or the locals would know all about him – and if the locals knew, so, of course, would the Druids – and it was unlikely the most powerful Gaul in Aquitania had nothing better to do than satisfy an idle curiosity about a person who didn't remotely concern him.

'It would appear that a number of young women have gone missing lately,' she told Hannibal. 'Late last spring, the sister of a man who makes millstones disappeared, but it seems she'd always had a wanderlust and everyone assumed she'd just taken the first boat out of here, and, who knows, maybe they were right. Then the wife of a root-cutter left without a word, but, again, she was a flighty piece, often running off with different men, so no one gave her leaving a second thought.'

Except the root-cutter, presumably.

'There was a girl who churned cheeses.' Claudia ticked the victims off on her fingers. 'Then Brigetia, the tanner's daughter, and now a young basket-weaver has failed to come home.'

'To wit, Vincentrix believes our friend, the Scarecrow, is responsible for their mysterious disappearances?' Hannibal stroked his jaw thoughtfully. 'I will certainly ask around. See what the slaves here have to say, what the local people think. But meanwhile, madam, I urge you to have caution when dealing with the Druids. They are not what they appear.'

'Who is?' she replied, locking her gaze firmly with his.

He held her gaze, but only just. 'They pass themselves off as preachers and philosophers, wise men who have learned their wisdom from the ancients, and when they make worship they speak in riddles to confuse their subjects, because the more secret their knowledge, the greater their power. But what you have to remember here, madam, is that the Druids practise human sacrifice.'

'Used to,' she corrected. 'Rome has put paid to all that.'

'So the Druids would have us believe, dear lady, so the Druids would have us believe.'

There was no joking in his manner now. The low tone was deadly serious.

'But there are places in this forest a full day's march from here where the soil is black from scorching and where the stains against the oak are suspiciously sticky. The wicker man

108

is not dead, madam, that I assure you. The Collegiate has not forsaken its ways.'

With a mighty groan, Esus the Blood God woke from his long sleep. Through the blackness, he had heard his name being invoked. An old woman calling for vengeance.

Half man, half bull, Esus lumbered to his feet, shook the dust off his stout horns and bellowed.

The death rictus on the old woman's face slowly relaxed into a smile.

Fourteen

The minute Orbilio booked Black Eyes into an apartment overlooking the basilica, he realized his mistake.

'Ooh, my lord.' The girl's dark, liquid eyes widened in delight as she fingered the soft damask furnishings and ran her hand over the smooth planes of the maplewood and oak. 'You *are* a dark horse!'

Elbowing their way through the crush of the market, and with his head throbbing like Vulcan's celestial smithy, it had seemed the logical thing to do, renting a furnished apartment for the girl. Well, he could hardly turn up with her at Marcia's villa then pack her off to the slave quarters, could he? The girl was freeborn, for heaven's sake! On the other hand, Marcia was never going to welcome what she'd consider the peasantry under her roof, no matter whose protection the girl was under. A furnished apartment off the Forum was the answer, and personal pride would not permit him to hire anything cheap. Except that the instant Black Eyes set foot inside, he knew she'd misunderstood his motives.

'Not that I'm saying I don't want to, my lord.' She plumped herself down on the soft, swansdown mattress, so her bouncing gaze travelled up and down his body with what could only be described as approval. 'Only – well, it's come as a bit of a surprise, that's all.'

He forced himself to tear his eyes away from the playful puppies that were threatening to burst out of her straining bodice and tried to explain his reasoning, a technique that sadly only served to make matters ten times worse.

'Stands to reason you won't want your wife to know,' she said sympathetically, wriggling further back on to the pillows and releasing the band restraining her long hair.

'I'm not married,' he explained patiently.

110

'Course not, my lord.' She tapped her nose knowingly. 'I understand. Your Zina's the very soul of discretion.'

Zina. The strumpet's name was Zina. And she *wasn't*, dammit, his!

Not that he wasn't tempted. Single man, single woman, no strings on either side, where's the harm? He didn't have to think back very far to Zina cutting through her stepfather's boatyard, teasing all the workers with her swaying hips and shimmering breasts, and pretending not to notice their ogling and catcalls. Looking at her now, pouting provocatively as she arched her neck, it wasn't as though she wasn't willing, and, judging by the unexpected jolt in his loins, it wasn't as if he wasn't able, either. (Despite the lump behind his bloody ear!) How easy it would have been to succumb. To have reached out and buried his face in the thick, dark curls which tumbled over her shoulders. How easy to imagine Zina as someone else. Someone, for instance, whose curls were streaked with the colours of the sunset, and, as his hands explored Zina's voluptuous curves, to imagine it was another woman's naked body writhing beneath him. Another woman moaning with pleasure as his lips brushed against her skin, crying out when he entered her.

So what held him back? Mother of Tarquin, it wasn't as though he was in love with Claudia! There was no pain to love. He didn't love her, or his heart wouldn't thrash in agony whenever he was with her, any more than his liver would feel as though it had been ripped apart by wild beasts when she left. No, no, no. Whatever it was, it wasn't love, so why not follow his natural instincts? Quite why he found himself making excuses about raging headaches, previous appointments and official business to attend to, he had no idea.

'Very well, off you pop, my lord, if you've got stuff to do.' His nubile misunderstanding stretched luxuriously over the scented damask counterpane. 'And while you're sorting that out, I'll see if I can't find out where that flesh-peddling creep took that little kid last night. Bastard couldn't have gone far with her, there weren't no cart waiting in the lane, so I'll have a snoop around.'

'You will do no such thing!' He'd been horrified. 'Zina,

111

these men are dangerous and I absolutely forbid you to go poking around, endangering yourself!'

She shot up straight, her black eyes flashing like twin fire-balls. 'Here, I might be your bloody mistress, but you don't tell me what I can and can't do, now!'

'For gods' sake, Zina—'

'You Romans can put all the fetters you like on your bloody wives, but I'm a Gaul. No one orders me about, not even you, my lord! Now give us a kiss before you go. Come on, a proper one. That's the ticket!'

Orbilio groaned as he now pushed his way through the crowds celebrating the *Vulcanalia*. Until now, if he'd given a thought to his own courage, which of course he hadn't, he would have put himself at about eight on a scale of one to ten. Never mind his two years in the army, working for the Security Police had left him facing some pretty hostile situations, yet he'd never hesitated. Fist fights, knife fights, sword fights, it was fairly bloody stuff, and over the years he'd gone charging into burning buildings to rescue the inhabitants, been beaten up and tortured. Dammit, it was fast approaching the point where he could not see skin for scars. But, frankly, he'd rather face a dozen axe-wielding maniacs any day than a seventeen-year-old buxom minx . . .

He postponed his return to the wretched apartment as long as he could, spending the night, talking, watching, listening in search of information, and, as a patrician, he had an obligation to attend the morning's sacrifice to Vulcan, hadn't he? But all the time the bull was being led around the altar, Marcus's mind was in another place. A dark and lonely place, where a small child whimpered pitifully, slave to a pervert's pleasure . . .

When the bull was finally brought before Vulcan's holy priest, its horns gilded and beribboned, Orbilio noticed that the acolyte's hands were shaking when he purified the creature first with salt and then with holy water, but then whose wouldn't? That was one massive lump of cattle snorting its hot breath into his face. Orbilio waited while the prayers were sung, but when the priest cried *Strike!* – the cue for his attendant to stun the sacrificial bull before its throat was cut – he turned away. The memories of what had befallen Rintox in the boat yard the night before were far too raw, and, in any case, he was worried what Zina would do next.

Throw her arms around his neck was what she did.

'You don't understand,' he said, disentangling himself.

'Course I do and it's bound to tickle, a big bump like that. But better I whacked you one than have the gang see you, cos I know what that ugly bastard's like. Dunno what me mam sees in him, I really don't. He'd have slit your throat, my lord, as soon as say hello—'

'Marcus. Call me Marcus, *please*.'

'Then Marcus it shall be, my lord, but I've had a good old poke around the boat yard, and wherever he's keeping that poor little mite, it ain't in there. Any luck your end?'

'Not a bloody thing,' he admitted ruefully.

Taking Black Eyes' advice, he'd made no mention to anyone in authority that he was investigating the abduction of small children, instead letting it be known around the bath houses in Santonum that if anyone knew where he could find young flesh, and the younger the better, wink wink, he would appreciate it. But the only thing he'd been met with was revulsion, and who could blame them?

'There's more bad news,' he told Zina. 'Despite reporting the fact that I'd seen a body in the river as I was taking a midnight stroll along the bank, Rintox hasn't washed up.' He wasn't sure how to phrase the next bit. 'The thing is—'

'It takes three days for the gases to build inside as the body rots,' she said bluntly.

He had forgotten that she'd lived beside the Carent all her life.

'I'm just hoping that when he bloats up, we'll be able to fish him out and bury him, poor bugger. Cos if we don't, he'll not find reincarnation. He was a lazy git, Rintox, like I said, but he don't deserve not to find eternal peace.'

Orbilio had never been convinced of the logic behind this reincarnation lark. Peace, Zina called it, but as far as he could see life was one long, lonely, uphill struggle – which the Gauls seemed to want to keep repeating. Stepping out on to the balcony, he saw that she'd already installed a pot brimming with marigolds and asters. They really needed to have a talk, Black Eyes and him!

'It's such fun, this Fire Festival,' she said, stepping out to join him.

Beyond the basilica, smoke rose from the Great Inferno in the Forum, which would burn until daybreak tomorrow. This was the time of year when people began to work by candle-light and these roaring, spitting flames were lit as an auspicious start to the closing of the summer.

'All our shrines are stuck out in the middle of the forest,' Zina said. 'Takes all bloody day to hoof out there, and ain't as though you can understand a word the Druids say.' The fringe of her short skirt vibrated distractingly as she jumped up and down. 'I *much* prefer the idea of celebrating Hammer God Day with races and dancing!'

Young and vibrant, she would, of course, and in another twenty years, the whole of Aquitania would be scornful of the old ways, of furtive practices carried out in secrecy and silence by a priesthood that hardly anyone remembered. Already, for a nation new to public spectacles, the concept of Games was opening up a whole world of fresh horizons.

'Chariot races, horse races, foot races, I can't wait for this afternoon,' she said, clapping her hands in delight. 'Oh, Marcus, my lord.' She slipped her arms round his waist and nuzzled her head against his shoulders. 'Isn't this just *wonderful*?'

'Yes, Marcus, my lord, *isn't* this just wonderful?' a voice cooed from below.

'Claudia!' He took the stairs three at a time. 'Claudia, it's not what you think.'

'And what do I think, Marcus, my lord, when I see you standing on a bedroom balcony draped around a pretty girl whose hair is as loose as her morals? By the way, I do hope it's a quality place that you've rented.'

He made a sweeping gesture with his hand. 'A man of my stature settles for nothing less than the best.'

'Best, as in more fleas per square inch?'

'Keeps a chap warm in the winter.'

'Yes, and talking of fires –' She indicated the massive bonfire burning in the Forum – 'did you know that in the olden days people didn't just throw fish into the flames like we do today, they used to toss small animals in, as well? I'm thinking of rats, in particular.'

'That's not fair!' He spiked his hands through his hair, and wished now he'd taken that bloody girl after all. 'There's a lot more to Zina than meets the eye.'

'Really? Looks to me like you can see most of it through that flimsy handkerchief that passes as a frock.'

'You know full well that all Gaulish women wear their skirts short, and, dammit, you've no right to question my private life. Not when your relationship with that – that –' he jerked his thumb at the sandy-haired Gaul scowling at him from lowered brows – '*boy* is the talk of the whole bloody town.'

Claudia seemed intent on examining a piece of jewellery around her wrist, a silver band which wrapped round twice, rather like a snake, and which was etched with whorls and inset with red enamel.

'Did you know the Gauls believe dwarves have healing powers?' she asked sweetly. 'I must remember that, next time I see one clowning in the theatre. See how healthy the rest of the troupe is and make comparisons.'

There was an ugliness surfacing in Orbilio that he was not proud of, but the mental images that confronted him – the two of them entwined, bedsheets askew, as the candle flame burned ever lower – were too powerful to ignore.

'Well?' he persisted. 'You could at least deny the rumour.'

'Orbilio, I have no intention whatsoever of discussing the relationship between my bodyguard and myself,' she said cheerfully. 'And certainly not in the sense you're suggesting.'

Contrition overwhelmed him. For Croesus sake, what got *into* him – and what the hell was he thinking of, prying into her sex life? What she did in the privacy of her own bedroom wasn't any of his bloody business!

'I am so sorry,' he said, and he meant it. 'When I used the word relationship, I wasn't talking any "sense" in particular—'

'Do you ever?'

Her eyes defied him to follow her as she disappeared into the celebrating crowd.

For the children, especially, the idea of spending weeks making their own offerings to throw into the fire had been particularly successful. Some of the older boys had carved elaborate wooden fish or animals to burn, while the girls had sewn or knitted theirs (with the aid of patient mothers), though the youngest simply tossed in whatever they'd been given. For most Santon children, this was their first experience of a party held right there in the middle of the street, to which everybody was invited, young or old, rich or poor, sick or ailing. There was music, made by all kinds of instruments. Trumpets, horns, pan-pipes, cymbals; there were harpists on the steps of this temple, lyre players on the steps of that; dancers everywhere. Some were costumed, some were masked, some mimed stories as they leaped, others performed breathtaking balletic feats and everywhere, but everywhere, there was food. Hot sausages, chilled wine, crumbly pies and crusty bread, sweet cakes made with almonds, honey, wine or dates, savouries filled with cheese or nuts or olives.

Through the giant flames, Claudia could see Stella's brood tossing their offerings into the fire, their eyes wide and shining as Hannibal guided their childish throws so they would hit the target. Balanced on the crow's nest of his shoulders, the littlest one clung on with fists clenched white, chortling merrily as his fish-shaped pastry landed in the middle and exploded with a whoosh that suggested Hannibal had filled the little chap's offering with oil. By his side, Stella clapped and laughed. She was dressed in Roman garb again, her dark, glossy hair pinned up in tight, obedient curls secured with pins of the finest ivory, and her tunic had been girdled in the latest fashion with the exact number of pleats that this year's style dictated, with the embroidery just so and a gold border round the hem and neck, and, just like at the banquet, she looked the prosperous, neat, attractive cousin she was meant to be. But again, just like at the banquet, it was as though the essence of the girl had been ironed out of her. How much longer, Claudia wondered, before Marcia sucked the whole lot out?

Moving on to where fire walkers drew both gasps and silver from their flabbergasted audience, she was distracted by a soft tug on her sleeve. Turning round, fully expecting a beggar child or perhaps a vendor at her elbow, the last thing she expected to see grinning back was the unctuous smile of Marcia's short, fat Indian soothsayer.

116

'If you're going to tell me I'm about to meet a tall, dark, handsome stranger,' she told Padi, 'I've already bumped into him this morning. He was tall, he was dark, he was handsome, and he was stranger than you'll ever know.'

'That is not what the rods spoke of,' he replied in his soft, sibilant voice, and again Claudia was reminded of a snake slithering through the long grass. 'The Great Mistress asked me to cast them for you, and to consult the Stones-That-Talk, that I might be able to divine your future.'

'Is it good?'

'Indeed, Mistress Claudia.'

'Am I blessed?'

'Exceedingly.'

'Are there any nasty surprises in store?'

'Oh, no, no, no.' Padi placed his plump pink palms together and bowed. 'The rods speak of long life and perfect health. The Stones-That-Talk cannot lie and they tell of riches and happiness, a husband who adores you, children who will live to their full span. Come, I will show you how they fell, and in any case the Great Mistress wishes to speak with you. She is curious to know how your soil tests are coming along.'

So *that*'s why Claudia was invited up to the villa. The devious bitch wanted to plant her own vines over these Santonian hills! Until Claudia's arrival, no one had even considered planting grapes here, but, shrewd businesswoman that she was, Marcia had sniffed a new market, and rather than waste her own money on analysing conditions why not let an expert do the job for her and then bleed her dry?

'The soil tests aren't looking good,' Claudia said solemnly. 'Perhaps you can cast your rods for me, Padi? See what the future holds for my vines, only the experiments we've conducted so far are depressing in the extreme.'

Blatant little fraud that he was, he was hardly likely to go against a specialist's assessment, now was he? And I ask you, what sweeter way for Marcia to discover that her potential new money-spinner was a non-starter? Which, now Claudia came to think about it, and bearing in mind what little she knew about vines, might not actually be the case. The conditions, she suspected, were absolutely perfect for growing the

117

little beggars and the knowledge surprised her. She'd obviously picked up more about viticulture than she'd supposed . . . and something fluttered under her ribcage.

'Come,' Marcia said, when she joined her. 'I want to introduce you to some of my suppliers.'

'Exactly what business *are* you in?' Claudia asked.

'Anything, everything. I told you before, there's no embarrassing way to get rich, and there's money to be made in times of conflict.' When she leaned close, Claudia could smell the balm of Gilead she rubbed into her skin, so rare, so expensive it had been the Queen of Sheba's gift to Solomon. 'An awful lot of money,' she confided. 'But I wasn't talking about business. I want you to meet the merchants who supply me with textiles. You see, I have what I *believe* to be the finest cottons shipped in from the Indus Valley and the highest quality of linens that come out of Egypt, but we are somewhat out on a limb in Aquitania.'

'And you'd like confirmation –' not as an introduction to good fabric merchants or a second opinion on girlie issues, but as someone who lived in Rome and who'd know about these things – 'that you're not getting fobbed off with second-grade rubbish?'

'Exactly.'

Well, Marcia didn't sell charm as one of her character traits, so she could hardly be accused of double standards . . .

'Meat pie, anyone?' Claudia breezed, as a hot-food seller approached wheeling his barrow. 'Marcia? Padi? Tarbel?'

'Tarbel doesn't eat between meals, the Indian takes his meat raw—'

'Really?' Claudia turned to the soothsayer, who nodded in smarmy confirmation.

'. . . and I need to watch my figure. I say, you! Yes, you over there!' Her masculine voice stopped half the traffic and one of the fire eaters nearly did himself a mischief. 'That vellum you sent round.'

The merchant in question flushed crimson as people turned to stare.

'I specifically asked for kidskin and, mother of Heaven, that stuff you sold me was mutton on its last legs. It's too late to return, I've already used it, but if you think I'm paying full price for that inferior junk you're mistaken. Five per cent is the most I will go and that's final.'

The merchant was torn. His reputation publicly shredded, was it better to fight and risk further humiliation, or accept her unreasonable terms and melt quietly away? He opted for the latter, and Claudia wondered if that hadn't been Marcia's plan all along. She had no doubts whatsoever that the merchant's vellum was top grade. He just happened along in the wrong place at the wrong time, because Marcia was forty years old, her beauty was hanging by the most slender of threads, but, most of all, she was alone. Despite her outward denials, these things mattered very much to her and the void they left had to be filled somehow, regardless of who got trampled along the way. This incident showed the whole town that she was as rich and powerful as ever, and, since this was also the capital of Aquitania, she'd ensured the whole of western Gaul knew who they were dealing with.

'Tell me about your husband,' Claudia said, as a rope walker balanced his pole above the Great Fire. 'Do you miss him?'

Marcia's sneer could have extinguished the flames. 'Let me tell you how we met,' she said, 'then you decide. I was twelve years old when one of your soldiers snatched me as I was walking home one cold December afternoon. The next thing I knew, I was being sold to a dealer.'

Claudia's maths weren't the fastest, but even she knew that if you subtract twelve from forty, then you're left with twenty-eight. And twenty-eight years ago, Rome was no longer making examples of rebellious Gauls by enslaving them as prisoners of war.

'Rome and the Santons had a peace treaty going by then,' she pointed out.

'My dear girl, a legate and his entire army were slaughtered! Regardless of pieces of paper, there was – and remains to this day, I might add – hostility on both sides, leading to all manner of atrocities, and, let me stress again, by *both* parties. Invariably, it is the innocents who are caught up in the backlash.'

'Of which you were one?'

'Not for long!' Her hard eyes glittered. 'Do you have any

idea what it's like, being thrown into a Massilian brothel at that age? No, of course you don't, nobody does until it happens to them, but you could say I was lucky. Shortly after I joined, a man comes along. He takes a shine to the little girl with blonde hair and no breasts and decides to keep her as his personal pet. This man is rich, he's Roman, and, though the girl's lost her innocence, there are times when knowing the tricks of the trade comes in handy. One night, when she's brought this pig to the brink of ecstasy, he agrees to marry her.'

No. Claudia didn't suppose you would miss a husband like that. 'How did he die?' she asked.

'Slowly. During which time I learned a lot about the money that can be made from the black market.'

Bitter, lonely – but, Janus, was this girl a survivor! As the fire walker was applauded, there was one thing Claudia did not understand.

'Why come back?'

'Why not?' Marcia shrugged. 'It's my home.'

'But you've distanced yourself from your people in favour of the very people who sold you out?'

'I would trade with Hades if it turned me a profit. Besides, you only have to look around to see that this offers a far better life and, moreover, it's the way of the future. Ah. I've just seen someone I need to talk to. We'll do the textile people tomorrow, and don't forget I have a front box at the races this afternoon. Do be there.'

High in the hills, inside the cave from which the Spring of Prophecy bubbled from the rocks, the Arch Druid Vincentrix sat cross-legged on the floor, only this time it was the sun's progress that he followed as it traversed the heavens, not the moon's.

From here, he could not see the rooftops of Santonum shimmering in the heat of the afternoon, nor the smoke rising from the thatches of his people's homes. All he could see were the first hints of the autumn across the canopy of trees, and a pair of buzzards rising on the thermals, mewing to one another as they spiralled ever higher.

Vincentrix tossed another handful of magic herbs on to the

fire, pressed his eyes into the palms of his hands and blotted out everything but the blackness inside his head. Leaning over the smoke, he inhaled deeply, rhythmically, and waited.

How many hours had passed he did not know, but finally he became aware that he was no longer alone inside the cave. Removing his hands from his eyes, he saw the Horned One, born of the winter solstice and Master of the Underworld, seated on his left, and on his right sat the Piercer of Shields, father of twin sons, Terror and Panic, who led his people into battle and then directed them onwards to victory.

Our influence is waning, Druid. You have seen for yourself how it is, for it is not the Thunderer our people propitiate today. It is the foreign smith they worship.

'Those are only silly cakes they toss into the flames,' Vincentrix replied in the same secret tongue. 'Is it not good that they are happy?'

The soul cannot perish, because it passes from one body to another after death, but only you are the conduit to this new life, Druid.

'I am aware of this, my lieges. It is why the Collegiate elected me.'

You are the only one with the powers to make this happen. But think! Think what will befall our people, should they choose to enter foreign Halls of the Dead. Neither we nor you can reach them there – and if we cannot reach them, Druid, their eternal souls will perish.

'And they will be no more than dust, blowing on the wind.' Vincentrix finished the ancient text for them. 'But I have kissed the Stone of Honour,' he reminded them, 'and wear the Ring of Pledge on my right hand that, though I might grow weary, I will never cease to serve the gods as they command.'

He closed his eyes, and when he opened them he expected to find himself alone again.

It is not enough that you serve us, loyal Druid. Our hearts have lightened at the safeguards you have put in place against such terrible contingencies, but our influence is waning, because we ourselves are growing weak.

This time, the Thunderer stood before him, hammer in his hand, his skin as black as the dark clouds that he rumbled.

You know what we need to make us strong again?

121

'I do,' he said heavily.

Then do it, another voice said. The voice was gentle, coaxing, full of warmth and love. Mother, lover, sister, friend and wife rolled into one. *Do it for us, Vincentrix. Do it for our people, I beseech you.*

He searched the Healer's sweet, smiling, innocent face and found comfort through the pain.

'Of course,' he said at last, kissing the ring on his right hand. 'Of course you will receive what is owed you, and your people will receive what they deserve, too. Peace through eternal life.'

He prayed with all his might that his next life might bring the same kind of succour to him.

Fifteen

'Correct me if I'm wrong,' Claudia said, 'but isn't today Saturday?'

She and Stella were sitting on their favourite seat in the garden, munching on chunks of warm chestnut bread, spiced liver sausages, smoked ham and other delicacies, all washed down with a large jug of chilled white wine. The chief attraction of this seat was the rippling fountain alongside, which was ringed with hibiscus and fragrant oleander. A soft breeze wafted scents of heliotrope, roses and summer narcissi over the topiaried box trees.

Stella squinted across to the calendar nailed to one of the portico pillars. 'Yes, today's Saturday. Why do you ask?'

'No reason,' Claudia replied, 'no reason at all.' Yet her eyes continued to follow Semir, stripped as usual to the tightest of loincloths, as he planted out Trojan irises to flower the following spring, pausing occasionally to gnaw on chicken legs and bite-sized sesame buns as he worked through his lunch break. 'Just that I've lost track of time lately,' she lied.

'Me, too.' Stella sighed, pushing a lock of dark hair out of her eyes with the back of her hand. 'Now Marcia's brought in a welter of servants, I've nothing to do and it's driving me crazy. Every day is the same as its predecessor.'

Nearly a week had passed since the *Vulcanalia*. A week in which the first turnips began to be pulled, red deer started to rut and neither hide nor hair of Hannibal or Orbilio had been seen.

'It's not as though I could pass some of the hours sewing clothes for the children, Marcia's taken care of all that. She's brought in tutors from the university in Burdigala to (quote) relieve me of my obligation to teach them their letters (unquote), and our quarters are so organized that I barely recognize them. Thanks to her, my laundry's taken care of, likewise the meals, and I can't even grow my own vegetables and herbs, because Marcia won't have me what she calls "labouring like a common peasant in the fields". If you have any ideas, I'm open to suggestions.'

Claudia leaned back on the marble seat, reached for another delicious oyster from the Carent estuary and turned her face towards the sun. It was said that winter in these parts didn't start before December and lasted only until the end of February. That left nine glorious months in which the summers were not too hot, the springs and autumns not too wet, and two thousand hours of sunshine to spread between them. That was a lot of time to be doing nothing, she reflected, even assuming Stella was the tapestry type.

'Marcia's threatening to swamp me with wardrobe and cosmetics slaves,' Stella added drolly. 'So far, I've managed to fend off that particular invasion.'

Claudia studied the simple belted tunic in the palest mint green linen that showed off Stella's long, glossy hair to perfection. She'd stopped short of restraining it Gaulish-style in a ribbon at the nape, but her uncomplicated bun told its own story, and no doubt Marcia was having kittens at the freckles on show and the distinct absence of kohl around her eyes. But the truth was, Stella looked stunning. If only the worry lines would disappear . . .

'You need a man,' Claudia pronounced.

This wasn't something she advised many women – in fact, now she came to think about it, it was a first – but Stella badly needed a companion. A soulmate to grow old and wrinkly with. A man to laugh with in her bed, and out. A man to take her sons fishing and glower at her daughters' suitors. A man to share the burdens of her life, then take them off her shoulders and carry them on his. *Don't we all*, a little voice whispered.

'I hope you're not trying to palm me off with Semir.' Stella chuckled, following the direction of Claudia's gaze. 'He has more braids in his hair than my girls put together and more jewellery than my dear cousin.'

'His baubles are only glass.'

124

'True, but there's so much oil on that man's body, it would be like making love to an eel.'

'I was speaking generally.' Liar.

'Good, because I've had a husband, thank you very much, and the desire to repeat the experience is not at the top of my shopping list.'

'So planting vervain round the peristyle isn't your idea?' Vervain was supposed to bring errant husbands home.

'*That* old wives' tale?' Stella giggled. 'No, no, that's Marcia's doing. If Jupiter himself will have no other herb to sweep his table, why should she settle for anything less?' The vitality suddenly popped like a bubble. '*Why?*' she asked wearily. 'Why did he just walk out without a bloody word?'

The lump in Claudia's throat tightened like a knot.

'Another woman?' Stella sighed. 'Was he in some kind of trouble? Why couldn't he have just left an explanation?'

Why, indeed, she thought, and the knot just got tighter.

'Doesn't he care at all, that the older ones still cry themselves to sleep at night? That he's consigned my girls to wearing clothes they hate, living rigid lives with frigid masters that they might grow up with all the privileges money can buy, but no spirit?' The freckles stood stark on Stella's face. 'Did he hate us? Hate *me* and wanted to punish me? I don't understand. We were fine. Nothing magical, I grant you, and something must have been building up that I didn't see, but until you have five kids running amok and a sixth kicking your belly-button inside out, you can't know what it's like, and it's not as though it was me who kept pushing for the large family.'

Trapped. Trapped and caged like the lovebirds in Marcia's aviary, pretty and spirited, but doomed all the same, and yes, what kind of bastard does that? Until now, Claudia had envied Stella, believing that a note saying "sorry" was better than no note at all. She was wrong. Her father (assuming he *had* walked out) had entrusted his daughter to her mother's care, and at least her mother had waited until Claudia was old enough to take care of herself before slitting her wrists. A butterfly fluttered off from the heliotrope, taking every ounce of Claudia's self-pity with it. Orphaned, she was at least free to make her own decisions. Decide who she married, what she did with

125

her future, how she earned her living. Stella's husband had left her high and dry. Unable to divorce him. Unable to remarry. Unprepared and ill-equipped for taking over his business, until the family became a victim of Marcia's charity, the coldest charity of all.

'I don't know whether this is some kind of sick control he's exercising,' Stella added wearily, 'but what he can possibly gain by making his children suffer, I have no idea.'

Claudia rubbed weary eyes. 'You're going to have to stop lying to them, you know that? You're going to have to tell them the truth about their father's absence, because four years is a long time to be stringing them along and children aren't stupid.'

'You're right.' Stella sighed. 'Hannibal said the very same thing, said if I didn't do it quickly, the danger was they'd turn against me for betraying them.'

Hannibal wasn't wrong. 'Have you seen him recently?'

'Uh-uh.' A soft smile played at the corner of Stella's lips. 'In fact, I wouldn't be surprised if he hasn't gone roving again. Have you ever known a man with such itchy feet?'

'Probably not, dear lady,' a familiar voice boomed, 'probably not, but restless though my poor body is, I am not a pack mule. Even I cannot remain on the move all the time.' He turned the corner into view, balancing the littlest one on his shoulders. 'Think of the strain on my poor weary legs, not to mention my wallet.' he cast an oblique glance at Claudia. 'And, in any case, Stella my star, Hannibal *never* leaves without saying goodbye.'

Fond farewells were the least of Stella's concern. 'What happened to my son?' she squealed, jumping to her feet.

'Small boys, I fear, are like pigs, in that they are addicted to rolling in mud.' Hannibal tickled a little fat midriff and was rewarded with a loud chuckle in his left ear.

'I'm a pig, I'm a pig.' To the chuckles were added a series of snorts. 'Oink, oink, oink, Mummy. Oink, oink.'

'I'll turn you both into bacon,' Stella exploded, as he was heaved down. 'Marcia will be needing that tomb tomorrow, if she catches you in this state,' she scolded her son, 'and as for you!' She rolled her eyes at Hannibal. 'That tunic is filthy! Give it here before Marcia sees it or you'll be banned from the house. You know how she baulks at the slightest imperfection.'

'Now, Stella my star? Here? And in *public*?'

'Yes, of course, now, here and in public.' Stella unbuckled his belt as though he was just another one of her brood she was undressing. 'It's a lovely warm day, you'll have it on your back within a couple of hours.'

She didn't even blink at the lean, tanned torso that was revealed, or the strong sinewy arms that had been previously hidden by baggy sleeves.

'Now, what's this little piggy been up to, eh?' She tucked the three-year-old under her arm like a bedroll and carried him back to the house. 'Oink, oink, little piggy-wig.'

'Oink, oink,' the bedroll echoed back. 'Oink, oink, oink.'

Once they'd rounded the corner, Hannibal flopped on to the bench beside Claudia. 'You have no idea how exhausting that tribe can be, madam, no idea at all. Tell me,' he leaned sideways and lowered his voice to a whisper, 'are there really only six of them, or does the witch keep another set indoors as a spare?'

Oh, Hannibal, Hannibal, what sorrow you sow . . .

'Like the horses of the Gaulish sun god, they feed in special pastures overnight to replenish their energy,' she quipped. 'What did you find out about the Scarecrow?'

'Well, for a start, it would seem your Druid friend's tally is correct.' He reached for a spiced sausage. 'First, the sister of a man who made millstones went missing. Number two was the root-cutter's wife. Three was a young woman who used to churn cheeses. Number four was the tanner's daughter, Brigetia, who was due to be married to a local boy called Orix. And, finally, the fifth victim is the granddaughter of an old woman who'd passed her basket weaving skills down through the family. Sadly, the old dame died of a broken heart,' Hannibal added, munching his way through a plate of rissoles, 'and I understand the root-cutter has not been the same since his wife disappeared, either, despite her reputation for lifting her skirts at the blink of an eye.'

The tavern-keeper's words replayed in Claudia's memory. *It's never just one man*, she had said. *It's always somebody's father and somebody's son, a brother, a lover, a friend. Let it go*. Wise words, because it was never simply an isolated incident. Whole families are destroyed in the process, and if Claudia was unable to let go of the past, how on earth could these families hope to move on?

'I'm told the Druids conducted a thorough investigation after each girl's disappearance, but no traces of violence were found. No blood, no trampled undergrowth or broken branches to suggest these women had fought for their lives, and, since there were no signs of struggle in their homes, it was accepted they'd plotted in advance to elope.'

'Bollocks. Even the most hot-headed lovers will take some cherished possession with them.'

'Ah, but there speaks the voice of wisdom and experience,' Hannibal intoned, reaching for a plum. 'These villagers have not travelled further than Santonum. They do not understand the significance, not so much of these girls' disappearances, but the *manner* of them.'

Something uncoiled in her stomach. 'You mean . . .?'

Perhaps the plum was bitter, because he tossed it into a bush. 'They were stalked, madam. Like hinds at a drinking pool, someone watched them, followed them, knew their every move.'

'Knew when and where to strike.'

'Precisely so, dear lady, precisely so.' He drew a deep and thoughtful breath. 'And there is a common denominator among these missing creatures. The ladies in question were not necessarily beautiful, but each was without blemish and in the richness of youth. In short, madam –' He filled his glass – 'they were plucked in full bloom.'

Silence descended, in which the only sounds were bees buzzing from plant to plant heavy with pollen, and the distant low of cattle in the water meadows.

'Tell me,' Claudia said eventually, 'if you were a tribune in the army, how come you wear a tunic with narrow purple stripes?'

'This?' Hannibal looked down, then gasped. 'Good heavens, I've been robbed!'

She smiled dutifully at the clowning, whilst remembering how he'd slipped away from the Forum while she'd gone to meet his informant.

'The stripes.' She was damned if she'd let him change the subject. 'I'm curious.'

The rules of class were simple. You're an aristocrat? Then you sew wide purple stripes on your tunic that can be seen a mile off, and, just in case the viewer's sight is fading, you wear a long tunic and red boots so there's no mistaking you for any old oik. But aristocrats were a minority. Most citizens were simply freeborn, but in between there existed a sizeable class of merchants, bankers, landowners and senior civil servants known as equestrians. Claudia's husband had been an equestrian and he, too, had been entitled to wear narrow purple stripes on his tunic. Most inherited their rank, but some – again, like Claudia's husband – could be promoted to the order provided they were of free birth for two generations and had assets totalling half a million in sesterces. Hannibal was struggling to hang on to half a sestertius, never mind half a million, and whilst being born into the order explained his education and manners, it didn't explain the tribune bit, when only patricians qualified for the role.

'Curiosity does terrible things to cats,' he rumbled, reaching for a chunk of smoked ham, 'but if you must know, I am the son of a senator. Not necessarily the legitimate heir, but flesh and blood all the same.'

'Were you close to your father?'

'Let me see. Are you meaning close as in the number of times my mother and I stood outside the Senate House hoping for a quick glimpse – her, not me? Or are you referring to the number of visits he made to the house and dandled me upon his knee? Because if it is the latter, madam, you can count those on the fingers of a man with no hands.'

'Yet he bought you a commission in the army?'

'He also paid that I might have a good education. Athens University, no less. Ah, dear Papa! Taught me so many things.'

'Like how steadfast men can be?'

'You, young lady, will cut yourself with your own tongue one of these days.'

Never mind that. 'Did you just say *Athens*?' All this time she'd been working out ways to translate Orbilio's case notes from Greek, and now the gods had thrown her a man who had been to university in Athens!

Hannibal reached for the chicken and nodded. 'Wonderful city, magnificent architecture, shame about the drains. In fact, it was while I was studying there – could you pass the bread, please? – that I discovered my true vocation in life. Frankly, I am not sure what my father would have made of my purveying pitch at the shipyards, because I never had contact with the dear fellow, but since my mother was already in her grave—'

'She died young, then?'

'I'd call thirty-six young, wouldn't you?' He demolished the rest of the oysters. 'Tumour,' he explained. 'And do you know, that woman died with his name on her lips. Can you believe that?' He wiped his mouth with the back of his hand. 'Hadn't seen the man for twenty years yet loved him to the end. Now, I ask you.' He tossed back the last of his wine in one swallow. 'How bloody stupid is that?'

Dawn cast her soft pink veil across the landscape of rolling hills and gentle woodlands, bringing verdant fields to life with birdsong and the scent of wild herbs and giving warmth to the early autumn air. Along the water meadows, dragonflies dried their wings. Horses, cows and sheep lumbered to their feet, stretched the stiffness from their limbs and began to graze on grass made moist and succulent with the dew.

Inside the villa, the slaves' quarters were already bustling, as furnaces were stoked to heat the Mistress's water, wood chopped, bread baked, floors swept, chairs polished.

In a den of leaves lined with soft moss deep in the forest, the Watcher gazed upon unqualified perfection. With streaming hair and streamlined hips, and without mark or blemish to stain her flawless skin, she waited for the sun to rise over her loveliness.

In breathless wonder, the Watcher stared, mesmerized by the spectacle of so much youth, vibrancy and beauty. Dare one? Dare one touch such embodiment of purity without polluting its very innocence in the process? Tentatively, one hand reached down towards her perfect cheek. Her eyes did not flicker when the shaking finger stroked her skin, nor did she flinch as trembling lips were laid on hers.

Her lips were cold. Icy cold.

The Watched waited for the sun to rise and warm them.

Sixteen

Claudia was dreaming. In her dreams, the fertile fields that swept down to the Carent were being ploughed by oxen lowing softly in the endless sunshine. Behind them, lines of singing workers planted vines, and among the bent-backed labourers was a woman with dyed blonde hair and pointed, painted features, whose beauty had long faded.

I wish I'd thought of vineyards, Marcia sang. *We wish, we wish, we wish*, the chorus followed. *It's such a respectable way to grow rich. Grow rich, grow rich, grow rich*, the chorus added.

The stems in their hands were thick and black with age, the leaves free of mildew, and, as Marcia tipped amphorae of vintage Falernian red over the vines, bunches of dark, purple grapes brushed the ground, the yield was so heavy. Claudia ticked the hours of endless sunshine off on her tally-stones, and with each click of the stones gold coins showered from the heavens. Then she lost track of the count, because hounds baying in the distance distracted her tally. Louder and louder it grew, as the dogs came closer and closer, until she realized she was no longer dreaming.

'Hrrrowwl.'

On the counterpane beside her, Drusilla was standing with her back arched and ears flat, her hackles so sharp they could cut stone.

'Hrrrrrowwwww.'

Leaning out of the window, Claudia counted a dozen dogs in the courtyard straining on the leashes of their handlers. Turning circles on their leads, squirming, jostling, twitchy and tense, the dogs were eager to go, and Claudia pulled the wooden shutters closed, which blotted out much of the sound, although that wasn't her motive.

'You can't take them all on,' she told Drusilla. 'You're staying in until I get back.'

Vicious hooks clawed at the shutters, but they were no match for a strong metal bar.

'Mrrrrp?'

'Cute won't work, either,' she told Drusilla, who'd taken to posing prettily on the pillow. 'You're grounded.'

'Frrr?'

'Yes, I'm afraid I will be gone some time. I need to go into Santonum.'

'Hrroww.'

'Sorry, poppet, Hannibal left me no choice.'

She remembered how he'd stood up, his shadow consigning the delphiniums to deep shade, when she'd told him she had a favour to ask.

'Is it about your father?'

She'd felt a mule kick inside when her gaze locked with his. 'No.'

'What a strange species you fair sex are,' he had drawled. 'You hire me at a measly one sestertius a day to find the man who abandoned you, yet you are prepared to pay thirty gold pieces to a rogue for information, but before you even meet with the scoundrel, you order me to drop my enquiries and follow up on the Scarecrow instead!' His eyes narrowed. 'Is there something you are not telling me, you saucebox?'

I could ask you the same question, she thought. Instead she asked him if he would translate a set of documents written in Greek, because although Orbilio had gone nearly a week, who knew when he might return?

'Rrrrr.'

'Exactly,' she told Drusilla. 'How was I to know he had an aversion to the Security Police?'

No matter that she was the one who'd be breaking and entering, she was the one who'd be stealing them.

'At the risk of repeating myself,' he'd said firmly, 'penal servitude is not on your faithful servant's agenda.'

Dammit, she needed to know what Orbilio had on her, because it wasn't just blocks of falling masonry that had kept Claudia awake this past week. Heaven knows what that little snake Burto had confessed to, but she had a horrid feeling that he'd blabbed everything about their lucractive venture then embellished it tenfold in order to cut a deal and save his skinny hide at the expense of her, and she knew it was fraud he was investigating, because Marcia had said so.

'He doesn't confide the full details,' she'd said, tapping the side of her long pointed nose. 'Discretion personified, that man, but yes. Quite a high-profile case from the sounds of it.'

'What do you think, poppet? Would you consider the fraudulent activities of the only female wine merchant in Rome to be high profile?'

Particularly when one has evidence that said female wine merchant had inveigled herself into marriage with a man above her station who'd died a violent death and is therefore living off a will which is illegal? There was only one course of action left open. Throw herself at his mercy and hope for the best! Shutting the door on Drusilla, Claudia was surprised to find herself colliding with Tarbel on the gallery. What on earth was he doing in the upper-class quarters?

'So sorry, I didn't recognize you without your armour,' she breezed.

Chestnut eyes stared down at her for a beat of perhaps three. 'But you recognize the Mistress's livery?'

Ah. Wearing Marcia's colours made his skin itch, after all. So what made him stay on, she wondered? Was the motive purely financial, as he claimed? Purely, therefore, *mercenary*? Or was there another – more personal – reason?

'Why is every dog in Gaul camped in the courtyard?' she asked him.

Tarbel shrugged. 'The Mistress has it in her head that if she can track down the Scarecrow, it will bestow even more kudos on her.' He paused. Shifted position. Folded his arms over his massive chest. 'It seems another local woman has gone missing. No trace of the girl, no signs of a struggle and the villagers are starting to fear that Death himself stalks these woods.'

'Maybe he does.'

'Anything is possible, *sí*,' the Basc said. 'But I am a soldier. I do not hold with shapeshifters and superstition. That scarer of birds is flesh and blood, nothing more, and it is flesh and blood that I fight.'

'Or rather don't,' she said sweetly. 'As we've already established, you're unarmed and unarmoured.'

Something rumbled deep in his throat, and it didn't sound like a laugh. 'The Mistress has ordered me to stay at her side.'

'And you're a soldier, as you said, so you obey orders.'

'*Sí*,' he snapped. 'I obey orders.' Turning on his booted heel, he strode down the corridor, leaving a smell of dense, cedary forests in his wake.

'It's fascinating what one stirs up when one mixes a brew,' a voice cackled from the shadows.

'How much of that did you hear, Koros?'

He stepped out from behind one of the tapestries that hung on the walls, stroking his long white beard. 'My lady, a man can hear everything around here,' he said, with a shrug of his bony shoulders. 'Provided he knows where to stand.'

Claudia tried to count the wall hangings and gave up. 'Then maybe you can tell me who told Marcia about the connection between the missing girls and the Scarecrow?'

Koros's wizened face creased into a grin that was, for once, neither all-purpose nor meaningless. 'I may have overheard a conversation between the Mistress and the Arch Druid to that effect.'

'*Vincentrix?*' The impression Vincentrix gave Claudia was that he very much wanted their disappearances to be played down.

'Those two are closer than you might think, my lady.'

Was that a hint of malice that sparkled in his rheumy eyes? 'You're a wicked old man,' Claudia told him.

'It's why you like me.'

'Doesn't it trouble your conscience, prescribing Marcia daily enemas?'

'Why should it?' The twinkle in his eye clicked up a notch. 'Or do you take issue with my diagnosis that the Mistress's bile duct is blocked?'

Claudia tried to imagine what might happen if Marcia's bile built up any more and decided old Prune Face had a point. All the same. 'Forgive me for being blunt, but I'm detecting a certain deficiency in the loyalty department.'

In a blink, the humour was wiped from his face, instantly replaced by a sober expression and neat, empty smile. 'My loyalty to the Mistress is undying,' he insisted, bowing so deeply that his long white robes swept the floor. 'What she asks for, I give. I am hers to command.' When he straightened up, the piety had gone again, to be substituted by a sly and slanting smile. 'You see?' He spread his bony hands and laughed. 'I am what she wants me to be.' Koros paused, sombre once more. 'We all are.'

'Actors,' she asked, 'or magicians?'

'Both,' he said woodenly, making a farewell gesture with his hand that Claudia recognized as Eastern, but beyond that couldn't place. Hell, though. Maybe that was phony, too. Everything else was around here.

Cocking an ear in the direction of the baying of the hounds, the Scarecrow detected an increase in their numbers from packs in previous hunts and this was coupled with a sense of urgency that had also been missing in the past.

A chill rippled up the Scarecrow's spine. It was the chill of a net that was closing in. There was no time to waste.

Wrapping a few precious belongings in his ragged cloak, he kicked over the traces of his camp fire, collapsed his makeshift tent of yew branches and hides, and buried it beneath a mound of leaf litter.

Grimacing at the painfully low level of liquid in his little blue phial, the Scarecrow headed down towards the river at a run.

'I thank you most humbly for permitting me to ride with you into Santonum,' Padi murmured in his ingratiating lisp. 'The Great Mistress does not permit us to travel free on personal business.'

As the gig clip-clopped along the forest track, Claudia thought how typical of Marcia to make a few extra coppers by charging her own people for transport into town! But then the traumas of her past would be a driving factor in her obsession to amass wealth, because, in her book, money equalled stability.

'You're from the Indus Valley?'

'In a manner of speaking.' His rosebud lips pursed. 'We *Padaei* are a nomadic people, which makes our children easy pickings for fast horseback raiders.'

135

A scene flashed before Claudia's eyes. A serene and tranquil place, where men water humped cattle in the river as the women pound clothes on the rocks and children splash each other in play. Suddenly there is a thunder of hooves, and before the *Padaei* have time to wonder what's happening, a group of riders charge down, their curved swords flashing in the sunlight, and while the tribespeople run for their lives, the children are snatched at the gallop. *Far away before their mothers know they are missing . . .*

And what did that say about Marcia? she wondered. It was like Claudia being sold into slavery and being called Roma. Degrading wasn't the word.

'Tell me, Padi, do your rods see Marcia's beauty lasting? Will she find love?'

'Undoubtedly,' he assured her in his soft, sibilant undertone. 'The Stones-That-Talk speak of a long and happy life for the Great Mistress, and a tomb that will ensure she is venerated for immortality.'

'Really?'

'Indeed, Mistress Claudia. They foresee excellent health enjoyed in the company of a strong man, who is prepared to lay down his life for her, such is the depth of his affection. My stones speak clearly of such things.'

Looking down at the soothsayer's little plump face, his eyes wide with sincerity, she thought his lies were so transparent, she wondered why he bothered.

'How . . .' Padi wriggled on the uncomfortable seat. 'How are your soil tests coming along?'

So *that* was what this morning was about! The lying little toad didn't have personal business in town. Marcia had sent him to bleed Claudia dry, because she knew that if a wine merchant had found the soil unsuitable for vines, as Claudia had claimed, she wouldn't be wasting time in Aquitania, but would be on her way back to Rome to oversee this season's vintage.

'It's more than simply identifying the right soil which retains water without turning to clay,' she said earnestly. 'One needs to monitor rainfall versus sunlight then factor in summer temperatures and compare them to frost cycles, then decide how best to shade the roots, whether this type of soil can cope with layering for the propagation of the vines, establish which cultivars are suitable for this climate, how one prevents the young leaves from being eaten by deer, and . . .'

Claudia leaned towards him and lowered her voice to a conspiratorial whisper.

'Purely between ourselves, Padi, these things are not looking good. Of course, I need to wait for the results of the salt tests to be sure.'

'Salt tests?'

'Too much salt in the air can kill the delicate vines,' she confided. 'And remember, we *are* less than twenty miles from the ocean.'

'Aah.' The sound was like the sighing of the breeze through a grove of poplars. 'Salt.'

And hogwash, she added silently. Don't forget the hogwash, Padi. 'If you could consult your rods for me,' she said with a radiant smile, 'I would be eternally grateful.'

On cue, the little pink palms plumped together and his little head bowed. 'My stones do not lie, Mistress Claudia,' he lisped. 'I will cast them this very evening.'

Excellent. Because if Marcia wanted to grow vines on these slopes, she could bloody well pay for her own research.

As the gig pulled to a halt in the Forum, Claudia's mind turned back to the reason she'd come to Santonum this morning. Given that she was unlikely to outwit the Security Police on this occasion, considering Orbilio had travelled halfway across the Empire specifically to nail her, there was only one solution. Dredge up the helpless-little-woman routine, then pray to every god up on Olympus that Orbilio fell for it the same way every other man had in the past. (Burto included, may his black soul rot in Hades!) And since our fine upstanding investigator preferred the well-upholstered charms of local girls to the gold and marbled luxury of Marcia's villa, Claudia had little choice but to go to him.

And, besides, what manner of floozies he associated with was entirely his affair. She didn't give a damn what he got up to when he wasn't clapping criminals in irons, and the thought of his bronzed torso rolling naked round the bedsheets didn't even cross her mind . . .

137

'Wait for me here,' she told her bodyguard, as they reached the apartment block. 'This won't take long.'

Oh, no. This won't take long at all.

Orbilio slumped down in the chair and combed his fingers through his hair in desperation. It had been a whole week now, and still this bloody case was going nowhere. Face it, the trail was colder than a witch's arse.

He rubbed the stubble on his jaw. Dammit, every waking hour had been spent on surveillance work and following up what he'd hoped were leads, and what time he hadn't spent doubled up under hot, stinking tarpaulins he'd passed in taverns, bath houses and brothels, spreading the word that he wouldn't be averse to reading bedtime stories to little children, boys or girls, it really didn't matter. And what had he achieved during that week? He'd had nothing but the honour of being branded a pervert of the very first order, and hopes of flushing out the child-abductors by offering himself as a punter were fading fast. It suggested they already had their market sewn up. But where? Who, for heaven's sake?

Zina remained convinced that her stepfather's accomplice must be local, poised out back to whisk the child away, because, as she'd pointed out, if there'd been a cart, they'd have heard it – and he agreed. Santonum wasn't Rome. Night-time traffic was unheard of here. Maybe an occasional despatch rider passing through the town, or a young blade's chariot arriving home late from a party. But neither he nor Zina had heard hooves or wheels, and for that reason she'd been pursuing the local angle, in spite of his misgivings. Fat lot of good that had done him, too!

She was well aware of the risks, thank you very much – in his mind's eye, he could still see her planting her hands on her hips, black eyes blazing, bosom heaving – *but that bastard's married to my mam, and I'll not have it bandied around that my mam's part of this, and, in any case, it might sound strange but he loves her, that he does, and if anything happened to me it'd be the death of her, and that's me safety net, my lord.*

Had he not been utterly exhausted, he might have smiled. He wasn't sure how she came about her reasonings half the time, but more often than not Zina hit her nails squarely on the head. It didn't mean the boatbuilder would have qualms about eliminating her, necessarily. It just meant he'd need to be ultra careful how he set about it.

As Zina laid a jug of wine on the table and hauled a tray of steaming, spicy rissoles off the gridiron above the hearth, Marcus scratched his neck in irritation. Half the problem was that he was working this case without access to the massive resources that he usually relied on from the army, but if 'Persons In High Places' were indeed involved in this repulsive trade, as Zina very much suspected, they would undoubtedly have soldiers in their pay. If word filtered back that Orbilio was investigating child sexual abuse, the operation would simply be closed down here and opened up elsewhere. He wouldn't risk it.

And of the two men he'd recognized in the yard the other night, the carpentry foreman and one of the riveters, all he'd been able to establish during this past week was that the former lived a lifestyle far beyond his means, with a smart town house near the Forum, his wife draped in fine clothes and his children schooled by private tutors, while the latter lived alone in a cramped apartment close to the boatyard, spending all his spare time and money on getting drunk and gambling on cockfights, often simultaneously.

'Croesus,' he groaned, 'how many more children are going to be subjected to a miserable existence because of my stupidity?'

Throwing herself at the feet of the Security Police and begging for mercy wasn't a procedure Claudia was overly familiar with. The technicalities of such a move were fraught with difficulties, not least because he sheathed his menace in a scabbard of urbanity. She'd had to think.

In terms of appearance, it wasn't difficult. Once inside the apartment block, a quick wipe over her face with a damp cloth removed the artfully applied cosmetics that concealed the black hollows round her eyes caused by too many sleepless nights and filled in the worry lines that had furrowed her forehead. Add a tweak of a seam here, the pull on a pleat there to create a hint of dishevelment, together with a slight readjustment of her girdle and mismatched alignment of her ivory hairpins and trained investigators would soon pick up the signals. There was no need to overdo the female-in-distress thing. Less was definitely more. All the same, worms slithered inside on an industrial scale as Claudia mounted the stairs. For years she'd worked to rid herself of the stink of the slums, and now her future hung in the balance once again, only this time it was a hundred times worse. She had eaten of the lotus and found its taste very much to her liking. Whatever it took, she thought, whatever it bloody well took . . .

'Croesus,' she heard a familiar baritone groan, 'how many more children are going to be subjected to a miserable existence because of my stupidity?'

The front door was ajar. Through the gap, she could see him slumped in a high-backed chair, head in hands, while a girl wearing a skirt that was little more than an oversized belt with a fringe round the bottom kneaded the tension out of his shoulders.

'It's not your fault, Marcus, my lord,' she told him gently. 'We're in this together, remember.'

And how, Claudia thought, looking at the cosy little domestic scene through the open crack. Table set with home-cooked food. Jugs of wine. Fresh bread. The bitch could cook, as well, it seemed. That was mustard Claudia could smell, with coriander, garlic, veal and olives, and her mouth might well be watering had it not been for the rumpled, unmade bed in the corner of the room and the obvious stubble on the Security Policeman's chin. Oh, well. Maybe this was a good time, after all. He'd be relaxed, after a lengthy bout of couch athletics . . .

What had they said?

She ran it back through her mind. Orbilio bemoaning the miserable fate awaiting kids due to his stupidity, and Curvy Thighs telling him that it took two. The worms in her stomach were replaced by something else.

'I can't stop thinking about how we could have prevented this poor child—'

'Too late to worry about that now, Marcus, my lord,' Curvy Thighs replied briskly. 'We'll just have to make sure there won't be no more.'

Claudia's fists clenched white.

140

'I wish you'd be more careful, Zina.'

Claudia watched as he turned round in the chair to look up at the girl with big black eyes and even bigger bosoms.

'You've really got to take precautions.'

'Well, you're a fine one to lecture people!' The black eyes rolled. 'I don't recall you thinking much about precautions the other night! Oh, no, not you! You just went at it like nothing else mattered in the world, and I'm all for passion, Marcus, my lord, but when there's consequences like this kid—'

Claudia couldn't stomach any more.

Throw herself at the feet of this arrogant patrician, who goes round getting local girls pregnant then puts the onus of responsibility on them? The sun could freeze over and Hades ring with laughter before that day came to pass! She stomped down the stairs, straightening her girdle and pinching her pleats black into place. Orbilio could whistle for his bloody fraud. Just let him damn well try and nail her for it. Just let the bastard try!

Orbilio heard the clump of footsteps on the stairs and shot out of his chair. Shit. He hadn't shut the door properly after Zina had let him in, and he knew he was dog tired and probably overreacting, but suppose the boatbuilder or one of his accomplices had grown suspicious of him and/or Zina and had followed one or other of them here, overheard them talking, then gone back to report?

In the corridor, he caught the whiff of a distinctive spicy Judaen perfume and, leaning his head over the balustrade, was just in time to see a familiar coil of ringlets flouncing out the door. What was eating her? She knew about this apartment and since she'd already misread the situation (a common practice among women entering this establishment, it appeared!) Claudia was hardly likely to conceive a sudden disapproval of what she'd perceived as his amorous activities. Jealousy, unfortunately, was out of the question, so what on earth made her come here in the first place, then storm off in a huff?

From the balcony, he watched her elbow her way through the crowded street and thought, hell, you could chargrill cutlets on Claudia Seferius at the moment. He shook his head, and wondered if he'd ever crack the mystery that was Women.

141

After all, it wasn't as though she was involved in the paedophile gang; her exploits in the world of forgery and fraud were solely confined to what she considered 'victimless' crimes, and it wasn't as though he and Zina had been engaged in anything untoward. Mother of Tarquin, they'd only been discussing . . .

Oh, shit. He slumped against the door jamb. Holy, bloody *shit*.

'Whatever's the matter, Marcus, my lord? Are you ill?'

'Zina,' he said, 'if I die, promise me you'll burn my bones. I know how much reincarnation means to you Gauls, but please, please, *please* don't let me come round again.'

The thought of enduring this hell for eternity was simply too dire to contemplate.

Seventeen

Semir was bending earnestly over what appeared to be an empty flower bed as Claudia rounded the corner of the peristyle.

'If it's your modesty you're looking for, you left it in the atrium,' she said. 'And your mother should have warned you that wearing loincloths that tight plays hell with the circulation.'

'Thank you, Mistress Clodia.' The Babylonian grinned. 'I shall bear eet in mind.'

'As long as that's all you bare.' Those seams were stretched to breaking point.

'Eet iss my crocus I want people to gasp at,' he laughed, 'but I am hopeful.' He probed the soil with a gentle finger. 'They will flower next month, during first rains of autumn, very pretty, and over time will colonize thiss whole bed, eef eet is kept properly watered.'

'With wine?'

Semir wiped an errant braid out of his eye. 'And thees,' he said, pointing to the massed ranks of blue vervain, 'Hor say thees flowers spring from tears of his Egyptian Isis. I think maybe goddess was unhappy, yess?'

What about Hor? she wondered, sweeping on. Was he unhappy, yess, or did the artist famed throughout the whole of Alexandria find fulfilment working like a mole, with skivvies rather than trained artisans for his assistants? The closer she drew to the stream, the louder the chip-chip-chip of chisels as Paris supervised his equally unskilled labour force – but wait. It was unfair to write off Marcia's enslaved workforce as amateurs. Many were just labourers, true, but that tomb was more precious to her than anything else and she was never going to compromise immortality for the sake

143

of workers lacking in qualifications and experience. Marcia might want the project finished quickly, but she was shrewd enough to grasp that there was nothing wrong with a well-supervised production, provided the end product was of sufficient quality. So what if Hor painted what he was told to paint and Paris shipped in mass-produced torsos and simply stuck a head on to personalize the statuary? This was what Greek sculptors had been doing from the dawn of time, and if the artwork on this tomb propelled them up the social ladder then good luck to both of them.

Near the pool, where flamingoes dabbled and sacred ibis stood in all their stately ugliness, a small girl with golden hair and big blue eyes was playing with a kitten.

'Qeb says I can keep her when she's old enough to leave her mother,' Luci said, as the kitten chased the ribbon that should have been tying the girl's hair back but was now torn to shreds. 'I shall have to smuggle her into my bedroom, though, cos Mummy says there are already too many mouths to feed as it is, and I heard her tell Uncle Hanni that half the time she's not sure she isn't raising a clutch of cuckoos, we're growing so fast.' She scooped the kitten into her arms and it started to rattle. 'I like Qeb,' she announced, 'don't you? He strokes my hair—'

'Oh, does he.'

'Yes, and it feels really nice, too, but can you keep a secret?' She put the kitten down and cupped her hand to Claudia's ear. 'He keeps a cheetah in his bedroom. I've seen it. It's lovely and smooth and has blue lizards round its neck, but Mummy says I'm not allowed in there, so you won't tell her, will you?'

Claudia tickled the kitten's little grey ears and thought about a grown man stroking a small child's hair and what exactly made Mummy ban her daughter from his quarters . . .

'No, I won't tell her,' she promised.

'And you're not to tell her that Qeb lets me feed live mice to his snakes, either,' Luci said. 'Shall I show you how it's done? It's ever so easy, you just hold them by the tail and drop them in the cage, then the snake eats them and you can see a big bulge where the mouse is in its tummy.'

In her arms, the kitten squirmed and Claudia didn't blame it at all.

144

'Maybe you can show me later,' she said. 'There's something really urgent I have to do and I'm afraid it can't wait any longer.'

A week had passed since the attempt on her life in the Temple of Augustus. A week in which her would-be executioner believed she thought she'd had a lucky escape from a freak accident, because, hey, that's building sites for you, these things happen. The hell they did. But revenge, as women everywhere will tell you, is a dish that's best served cold, and what better time to start dishing up than when the target is off guard? Waiting was the hard part. When someone tries to kill you and you not only know who, but also why, there's a great temptation to rush in and start tearing livers and lungs out with your bare hands. It had taken every ounce of Claudia's self-control to let the killer think they'd got away with it, but the time had finally come to turn the tables. However, before those tables could start moving, there were three things she had to lay her hands on first.

'What are they?' Luci asked.

Claudia told her.

Luci laughed.

Having finished work for the afternoon, half a dozen slave girls tumbled out of the back door of the villa and ran arm in arm towards the stream, giggling and gossiping as they did every day. Since one peeled vegetables in the kitchens, another cleaned the bath house, a third aired the Mistress's linens and so on, this was the first time today that they'd met up, and with so many people coming in and out, as well as the extra workers employed on the tomb, the girls were never short of who-did-whats, you'll-never-guesses and you-won't-*believe*-what-old-so-and-so-said-when-he-thought-my-back-was-turneds.

Down the hill they ran, exchanging tittle-tattle, embellishing rumours, until they reached the river bank. Throwing off their soft cotton tunics, they let out their customary squeals as they jumped into waters that had been heated by the sun. Soon, they were joined by other slave girls from the villa and, in no time, everyone was horsing about in the reeds.

They had no idea that sharp eyes followed every movement.

145

The swinging of wet hair. The way they tipped their heads back when they laughed. They way they shrieked when dainty toes collided with sharp rocks.

The Watcher sighed. Having scoured the local villages and picked out the very best, it was depressing to see how many young women were left whose bodies were already ravaged by poverty, childbirth and diet. At least these girls would still have their teeth by the time they were thirty. Nourishment was never an issue at the villa. In fact, looking at them splashing about in the river, many were already overweight. The Watcher's lips turned down as ripples of fat bounced about in the water. They were almost as bad as the skinny ones, whose hipbones stuck out through their skin. That one has a squint. That one has warts. The redhead has a nose you could launch ships from, and will you look at the breasts on the blonde one! The Watcher shuddered. It was grotesque, breasts that big, absolutely revolting. On a par with the one who keeps pulling her hair out, strand by irritating strand. Yes, we all know it's caused by anxiety, but a woman of twenty going bald? Disgusting.

But for all that, there were many bathers whose beauty *was* ripe, unblemished by physical disfigurement and not despoiled by the march of time. Unfortunately, it was just not possible to take girls this close to the villa. The Watcher frowned. With the villa out of bounds and the villages depleted, where else could be found the perfection that was so crucial to the cause?

Walking up the hill from the menagerie and leaving Luci with her kitten, Claudia listened to the squeals and splashes of a group of young women making the most of the late-afternoon sunshine.

Passing a stand of stately silver birches, she felt a cold chill ripple down her spine.

Someone's watching me.

She turned, but none of the undergrowth moved. Ridiculous! If it was the Scarecrow she'd have heard a churr from a magpie, a squawk from a pheasant, a grouse from a grouse. It was nothing. Just Claudia's imagination working overtime, because Marcia's huntsmen had returned empty-handed, the dogs having lost his spoor again. The Scarecrow was unlikely to strike again so quickly after such a narrow escape. He'd feel threatened by the hunt, not emboldened. She was simply over-reacting.

The Watcher's eyes followed the familiar bounce of Claudia's ringlets as she resumed her march back up the hill, the luscious curve of her breasts, the unlined skin around her neck, the moist red lips and finely arching brows.

Now that – the Watcher's pulse quickened – now *that*, my friend, is perfection . . .

Eighteen

Set like crystals in a cupola of jet, a million stars twinkled in a cloudless sky, cradling the new moon like a baby. Outlined against them, wooded hillsides smudged the night's horizons, giving shelter to bright-eyed stoats and curious fox cubs, while badgers tumbled in the clearings and bush crickets rasped continuously in the brambles and nettle beds.

Inside the room, Claudia waited.

Through the open window, she smelled honeysuckle and wild basil carried on the breeze . . . but not the scent of the person she was waiting for.

She could see ghost moths swaying backwards and forwards over spikes of yellow mullein, whose white woolly leaves shimmered in the dark . . . but of her would-be killer there was no sign.

She heard rodents rustling about in the undergrowth . . . but not the rat she was waiting to trap.

Time strode seamlessly forward and, with each star that moved round the heavens, Claudia considered the cold-blooded tactics of the assassin, the icy planning and callous disregard of human emotions, and felt no discomfort as she crouched in the corner. Only a sense of purpose and satisfaction. She did not bother to keep track of the hours. Time didn't matter. She had a job to do, and she was going to do it. Possibly even enjoy it.

At last, footsteps approached. Door hinges creaked. She had measured the distance earlier between door and oil lamp. Counted the seconds before it would be lit, and her training as a dancer held her in good stead. The timing for the next bit was crucial.

Sssss. As the tinder was struck, she untied a small bag. The wick ignited and, as the first flame flickered to light up the room, she tossed the contents in the killer's direction.

148

'Ribbit, ribbit,' the outraged frog croaked, as it landed unceremoniously at a pair of feet.

The feet jumped.

'Don't you recognize me?' Claudia whispered.

'Ribbit, ribbit, ribbit,' said the frog, thoughtfully keeping pace with the sidestepping feet.

By now, Claudia had opened her second sack. Naturally, the owl panicked.

'Do you recognize me now?' she called softly, as it flew at the walls and banged into doors.

With flailing arms, Claudia's attacker ducked to avoid the flapping wings – the very moment she'd been waiting for! Grabbing the contents of her third bag, Claudia lunged, only this time there was no incensed amphibian, no terrified bird. Just cold, hard steel in the form of a pair of leg irons, on loan from the prison guards.

'What the bloody fuck—?'

'Tut, tut, such language.' She jerked him backwards by his hair into a chair. 'And from a priest, as well.'

She'd propped the broom handle by the door in readiness and now she shoved it between his outstretched elbows across the back of the seat. Like a winkle on a pin, she thought happily. Like a winkle on a bloody pin. She let him kick and thrash while she opened the front door. The owl flew out straight away, but she had to nudge Froggie with her foot. Claudia closed the door and calmly lit another lamp.

'Good heavens, Vincentrix, I'd credited you with better manners than swearing in front of a lady.'

'What the bloody hell do you think you're playing at?'

'Playing, Vincentrix? Now tell me, honestly, does this knife look like a game? Ooh, did that hurt? And it was just a teensy little nick on the side of your throat, too.'

He stopped thrashing. Blades that close to jugulars weren't worth the gamble.

'What do you want?'

'I thought you and I could have a cosy little chat, one shapeshifter to another and all that.'

'Those creatures weren't you in disguise. You don't have the magic.'

'If you say so.' She tested the broom handle wedged so

149

firmly between his elbows. 'But look around your lovely house, Vincentrix. Do you see any frogs hopping around this exquisite tiled flooring? Any owls battering against your magnificent frescoes?'

The only way to turn the tables on a Druid was to use his own beliefs against him, and he'd been so busy fighting leg irons and imprisoned arms that he hadn't noticed the door open and close. Surprise was the key. Surprise, and the play of light-and-dark. She looked at his bloodless face, the dilated pupils, and knew she'd judged him correctly. Ordinary people wouldn't dare play mind games with this elevated caste, least of all tangle with the most powerful Gaul in Aquitania! For a man who accepts shapeshifting as a truth, what other explanation was there?

'But now, Vincentrix, it's time for us to trade.'

'Trade what exactly?'

That was the down side of priests who swallow all that paranormal hocus-pocus. They bounce back straight away.

'Isn't it obvious? I don't stick this serrated blade into your neck, and in return you tell me what happened in Santonum fifteen years ago.'

'I would tell you, if I knew.' His green eyes shone with honesty. 'But I wasn't here. I was in Britain back then. Ask anyone.'

'I have. You were. But you know anyway.'

'I serve the gods on an astral plane; it is not in my remit to become involved in local affairs. Claudia Seferius, I swear on my life that I have no idea what may or may not have taken place fifteen years ago.'

'I hope you're ready for the Horned One, because if you think I won't slit your lying throat you can think again.'

'You won't kill me.'

'Spoken with confidence, but why? Because you think I like you? Because you think I feel sorry for you, after hearing your hard-luck virgin-wife story? How much of that was true, by the way?'

'All of it, as it happens, and, yes, I do think you like me. But the reason you won't use that knife is because it's impossible to kill someone face to face, especially once you've shared food and secrets with them.'

150

'Really? Then how come you're so adept at it?' Old trick. Win a person's trust and confidence while you probe their Achilles heel. Vincentrix was a past master at it.

He exhaled slowly, and in the lamplight his kestrel hair shone like polished chestnuts. 'Claudia Seferius, I have no idea what tonight's nonsense is about, but you are mistaken. Whoever, whatever, you think I am, you are wrong.'

'I may have my faults, but being wrong isn't one of them. Suppose we say a count of three?'

'Very well.'

Oh, dear. He still thought that business with the torc and Find the Pea had been a lucky guess. Claudia stepped back and examined the bloodied point of the blade. 'Vincentrix, you have no idea what I'm capable of. You kill people in cold blood and I am quite prepared to kill you in the cold light of reason, but the thing you need to remember is that your death won't just be the end of you. It puts paid to all hope of leading your people through the Halls of Change into the Light. That's count number one, incidentally.'

He wriggled in the chair to turn his piercing green eyes up at her.

'Do you think I have not trained up my acolytes? That other Druids have not been taught the Chant of Incarnation?'

'Undoubtedly, but it's you they look to, Vince. It's you the people trust, and this is count number two, by the way. If you're dead and they see your corpse left unburied—'

'You're planning to toss my body into the river?' Scorn rose in his voice. 'It's not far to the water, admittedly, but cadavers are heavy and you're not strong enough to haul mine on your own, and that Gaulish bodyguard won't lift a finger against a Druid, dead *or* alive.'

'I have no desire to contaminate the river with your poison. My intention is for the authorities to throw your corpse on the middens for the murderous scumbag that you are and now, sadly for you, your time's up.'

She yanked his head back by the hair.

'All right, all right.'

She held on to the hank, but relaxed the tension.

'All right,' Vincentrix repeated slowly, 'we'll trade, but not because I'm afraid of dying.'

151

Claudia nodded. Whatever else he might be, the Druid was no coward.

'The gods have visited me,' he said quietly. 'They have tasked me with a mission and it is for this reason, and this reason alone, that I agree to your terms.'

Sheathing the knife, Claudia felt a cold shiver run down her spine. She could not explain the feeling, but at the back of her mind was a horrible suspicion that, in doing so, she was making one of the biggest mistakes of her life.

There was still an hour or more before dawn would start to break over the forests of south-western Gaul and yet, on the Druid's island where three arms of the stream converged, the sense of a new beginning was already strong.

It did not come in the form of the sultry night air, nor the rasp of cicadas or the churr of a nightjar. There was no crack of light in the east, no change in the breeze, no leap of the first feeding fish. But it was there. Pulsing, throbbing, pushing through the soil and surging through the currents, to create a newness that only comes with rebirth, and for a split second Claudia understood what Vincentrix experienced when he began the Chant of Incarnation to guide the dead on their voyage through the Halls of Change until they finally emerged in their new bodies.

Then the moment was gone.

The island was simply an outcrop of land where three branches of the river met. Where bats swooped low over the slow-flowing waters. Where reeds whispered to one another on the wind. More than that, it was a solid physical island rooted in a solid physical world where people were people, not butterflies hatching out from some bloody chrysalis!

But that didn't diminish the sense of new beginnings that stirred in Claudia's blood. What she was experiencing had nothing to do with Druid magic or the Gauls' belief in reincarnation, not even any eerie prequel to dawn. It was the knowledge that a gateway had opened and she was taking the first real steps toward tracing her father, and the knowledge was as exhilarating as it was scary.

Listening to her little rowing boat clunk softly against the river bank, and with the light from Vincentrix's house shimmering like a glow worm behind her, she mulled over the Druid's story.

'First of all,' he'd said, 'you need to put this into context.'

Remember the history of this region, he reminded her. Remember how Julius Caesar sent an army to conquer these lands, and what happened to the legate and his men. Remember how Rome despatched more soldiers to avenge the dead legions, and how easily the Santons had them routed, too. Finally, he'd added, remember that although on the surface relations between the two parties were running smoothly fifteen years ago, with Augustus having proclaimed Santonum the capital of Aquitania and the tribes prospering on the back of the increase in trade, rancour and mistrust still tarnished the alliance.

Immediately, an image was conjured up of a twelve-year-old girl being kidnapped and sold into prostitution for no other reason than that she was Santon. *Atrocities were committed by both parties*, Marcia said, hinting of blood feuds and vendettas that lingered to the present day. What turmoil must have existed fifteen years ago when a Santon village was suddenly attacked by a band of renegades?

'An entire village was razed to the ground,' Vincentrix explained. 'The women were raped, the men killed so their heads could be taken for trophies, livestock were slaughtered, shrines desecrated. Even the smallest children were tortured, and it is said the smoke hung in the air for six days.'

It made no difference that this was an isolated village on the edge of the Empire. An entire community had been destroyed, butchered on an unimaginable scale, and feelings among the tribespeople ran high. Rome was supposed to protect them, they screamed. You siphon off our harvests, you force us to pay taxes, you yoke us to your imperial plough and subject us to your laws, yet, instead of defending us, villages are being wiped out!

'Amid the sense of outrage on the one hand and betrayal on the other, who can blame the Santons for ignoring Rome's pleas to let their cohorts hunt down the renegades? Mustering a group of vigilantes, and bearing in mind our Gallic fondness for horseflesh –' it was the closest the Druid came to a smile – 'it didn't take the warriors long to track down thirty or so Parisii sitting round a camp fire, laughing and drinking so hard that the first they knew of any assault was when the warriors fell upon them.'

Fine so far. Claudia could easily see why Rome wanted the matter hushed up. The Governor had failed to take adequate precautions for the safety of those in his care, and if a whole village being wiped out didn't destroy his career then a full-scale rebellion by the Santon people certainly would. No wonder so many natural disasters befell the official records! Mice, mould, floods? The Governor probably imported rodents for the very purpose! What she didn't understand was why the locals wanted it swept under the rug.

'Ah, you Romans. Always so impatient,' Vincentrix said, and, now she thought about it, she realized he hadn't struggled against his bonds since the beginning. 'But, as it happens, this brings us to the next page in our storybook.'

As the victorious vigilantes danced in triumph round the corpses in the Forum, hacking off the heads of their enemies so that their souls would be denied rebirth, the army returned with prisoners in tow.

'It would appear our glorious warriors made a mistake,' Vincentrix said grimly.

While the hotheads went charging off on the finest horse-flesh in Gaul, the legionaries employed two centuries of tracking skills to run down the real culprits – and how did they know it was them?

'Because they produced the trophies the real bandits had been parading,' he said. 'Namely, the villagers' heads impaled on poles.'

Going through the satchels of the slaughtered Parisii, it quickly became clear that the Santons had succeeded in butchering a trade delegation on its way to Burdigala on the Jirond.

'So a deal was struck?'

'And why not?' the Druid countered. 'It was hardly in Rome's interest to incense allies who had trekked hundreds of miles to talk peace, while, far from being the heroic avengers they believed themselves to be, the Santons find they are killers of innocent men.'

Nothing like embarrassment, contrition and shame to unite

opposing factions, she reflected, pulling a stem of long grass from the river bank and chewing on the juicy end. Everyone was agreed: the delegation never arrived. No one saw them. No one heard them. The Parisii simply vanished into thin air somewhere along their arduous route . . .

The landlady's words echoed back to her. *You won't find anyone around these parts willing to talk about what happened back then, not a soul,* she had said, adding that some things were best left in the past and how it was a waste of time trying to dig deeper. She was wrong. Trying was never a waste of time. Unless you try you cannot succeed, and while Claudia was no closer to finding her father, she had at least broken through the barrier of silence. Even though it nearly cost her her life.

'You didn't have to kill me, you bastard.'

'Not a decision I took lightly.' And she wasn't sure whether the pain in Vincentrix's eyes was because he was truly contrite or whether his arms were starting to strain in their sockets. 'But you have to remember, Claudia Seferius, that if word got out about that tragic day, the Santons involved would be rounded up and made examples of.' He drew a deep, shuddering breath. 'One life sacrificed to save twenty, not to mention the families whose lives would be ruined by the disclosure? It had to be right.'

'Didn't it occur to you that Rome doesn't want this business aired, either?'

'Of course.' His kestrel head nodded. 'But once it is, there is no going back, and when you bear in mind that most, if not all, of the legionaries involved back then have retired, the consequences for Rome are negligible. For the Santons, however . . .' He let his voice trail off. 'I am sorry,' he added.

'That you missed me?'

'I didn't miss, I miscalculated, there's a difference, and what I miscalculated wasn't the drop of the block or the accuracy of my mathematical computations, Claudia Seferius, it was you. You were too fast for me.'

Always, Vincentrix. Always . . .

'What made you suspect me?' he asked.

Oh, come on! Who else could have blended in so seamlessly into a bustling building site than the Arch Shapeshifter himself?

155

'You gave the game away, Vincentrix, when you were telling me about your tragic marriage. *At any cost*, you said. You said you wanted that woman to be your wife *at any cost*, and you actually admitted that you couldn't see what was in front of you because of your obsession. The very same quality you recognized in me and played on,' she told him. 'A desperate need to find my father.'

'Your father, was it?'

'Does it matter?' She wondered whether the prison guard would have to replace the leg irons out of his own personal funds. 'Right from the outset, when I first started making enquiries about events that took place fifteen years ago, you realized it had to be something of vital personal importance that dragged me all the way out to Santonum, and you just couldn't resist showing off when you realized that I couldn't sleep from the anxiety. You played on my insecurities, Vincentrix. Exploitation of the mind is your job and I have to hand it to you, you're pretty damn good at it.'

Anger surged through his captive body. 'I serve my people through communion with the gods. That cannot be construed as exploitation.'

'Manipulation? Magic? Your argument, then, is what does it matter so long as they believe?'

'Yes,' he hissed. 'So long as they believe, their souls are safe. *That*, Claudia Seferius, is my job and *that* is what I am good at. My people entrust me not with their lives, but with eternity. I. Will. Not. Let. Them. Down.'

A fanatic with conviction in his beliefs? Or a man addicted to power and authority? Claudia did not know the answer. Leaving Vincentrix pinned to his own high-backed chair, she untied the rowing boat and silently made her way back to the shore.

From the long grass, the tabby cat watched her depart.

Nineteen

'Uncle Hanni, what does stamina mean?'
'Great Jupiter, young Luci, that's a very long word for a very short child. Let me think.' He cupped his jaw and frowned. 'What would that information be worth, do you suppose? Two copper quadrans?'

Blue eyes bulged in horror. 'Two *quadrans*?'

'Very well, two copper quadrans it is.' He fished around in the bronze purse that hung from his belt and passed them across.

'Gosh.' Luci squirrelled the coins away in the depths of her robe. 'I thought you meant *I* had to pay!'

A smile was quickly suppressed. 'Stamina, I believe you were enquiring about?'

'Yes, because Mummy told me I'd soon learn it, if I didn't eat my leeks, beans and onions.'

'How does that work?' he asked, in his rich, fruity tones.

'She said she'd make me sit at the table until they were gone and that would teach me about stamina. Only I thought if I asked you first then I'd *know* what stamina was, and then I wouldn't need to eat those horrid vegetables.'

'Those horrid vegetables are good for you.'

'Those horrid vegetables were *cold*.'

'Only because you didn't eat them.'

Crouched under the dogwood, the Scarecrow followed the interchange with an ache in his heart. He watched a tiny pink hand slip into a leathery brown one. Felt a wrench in his gut when the man kneeled down, looked deep into the child's enormous eyes and said, 'Suppose you and I play a game on your mother? Suppose tomorrow you gobble up all your leeks, beans and onions as soon as she puts them in front of you? What do you think she'll say to that?'

Luci giggled. 'She won't believe what she's seeing.'

'Precisely.' He ruffled her blonde curls. 'Then afterwards you and I shall sneak off and stuff ourselves with sweetmeats and sherbets until honey drips out of our ears.'

'Sweetmeats *and* sherbets?'

'Every day, if you play the same game on your mother.'

'I like that game, but if it makes me burp I'll tell Mummy that it's your fault.'

'My shoulders are broad, young lady, my shoulders are broad.'

The Scarecrow watched as the man hefted her on to them to prove his point, felt a stab under his ribcage as she squealed in delight. Of all the children, this little cherub whose innocence burst out of every hop, skip and jump – this one, oh, this one was special. They called her Luci, he'd noticed, and a lump formed in his throat. He had another name for the child. Belisana. After the goddess whose name meant 'the Bright One', for Belisana equated with sunshine and happiness, gentleness and warmth, qualities this child possessed in abundance.

'Belisana,' he whispered. 'Dear, sweet Belisana . . .'

His reverie was interrupted by the arrival of the girl's mother, wiping her work-reddened hands on her gown and shrieking in mock horror. 'Gracious me, what terrible visitation have the gods inflicted on me? This morning I had three boys and three girls, now I have four boys! Oh, it's you, Luci! What on earth are you doing up there, with your dress tucked into your knicker cloth?'

'Riding Pegasus!'

Her mount duly whinnied and neighed.

'Well, you can jolly well drop down from the saddle and give the floors a good sweeping. I've left the broom by the door.'

'But Auntie Marcia bought us slaves to do those jobs.'

'Indeed she did, but you'll never know the value of hard work if you don't experience it, so off you go, you idle monster. And no sweeping the dust under the rugs, either!'

'What of Pegasus, Stella, my star?' the man intoned, lowering himself to his knees. 'Do you have any tasks this fine stallion can put his hoof to?'

158

'Didn't they teach you anything in the army, Hannibal?' Stella laughed. 'Such as never, ever volunteer?'

'*I* never volunteer,' Luci confided in a loud whisper as she clambered down off his back, 'but look at the chores *I* get lumbered with!'

One day, her hair would darken to the deep, glossy brown of her mother's, the Scarecrow realized. The plumpness would fade from her cheeks and her figure would achieve the same stunning curves as the woman who was pretending to throw her arms up in despair. When that day dawned, this rosy-cheeked child would metamorphose into a beautiful, beautiful woman – but right now, the only thing the Scarecrow knew was that when Belisana coiled her little arms round the man's neck and smacked a wet kiss against his leathery cheek the pain inside was too hard to bear. With tears coursing down his face, the Scarecrow stumbled back into the woods.

'Marcus!'

Among the thick, swirling steam and rich, scented oils that clouded the air of the villa's bath house, her deep, almost masculine voice made him jump.

'How lovely to have you return to the fold!' Marcia settled herself on the bench beside the hot tub and crossed her legs. Behind her, billowing in and out of the mist, painted horses galloped over the walls as the Amazons charged down in their war chariots. It came as no surprise to Orbilio that, at the head of the column, Marcia was holding a whip in her left hand, or that her wheels were crushing the life out of a luckless Athenian.

'We've missed you,' she said.

'Nnnnnn.'

He bared his teeth in what he hoped was a smile. Mother of Tarquin, it wasn't enough that he was lying naked in the bath in front of his hostess. The wretched woman had only brought her whole bloody entourage into the room, and he regretted, now, the diet of stodge he'd been living on this past week while he kept up surveillance. Every fat-sodden sausage and honey-drenched cake seemed to be on public display round his midriff, and it was no consolation that Marcia's gaze wasn't actually on his waistline. None at all. Not when it had drifted a lot further south!

159

'Don't get out on my account, Marcus. You enjoy a long wallow while I give Tarbel his orders, then I'll let you into the secret about what my little soothsayer's been up to.'

Listening to her organize another manhunt – 'This time there will be no slipping through nets. Tarbel, you will take personal charge and bring this bastard back dead or alive, understood?' – Orbilio was conscious of the big Basc's silent scrutiny. He might be nodding at what his mistress was saying, taking everything in, but his dark eyes were fixed on the man in the tub. Interesting. Because someone had made a thorough search of his room (someone other than Claudia, that is) and it occurred to him that the most likely candidate was Tarbel. But why? And had he been acting on his own initiative or on his mistress's orders? More than ever, Orbilio was glad he'd taken a leaf out of Julius Caesar's book and written up his dispatches in Greek. The Gaulish language, when written, was not so dissimilar to Latin. Greek rendered everything in code.

'. . . I want this set in motion first thing in the morning,' Marcia was saying. 'Got that? Good. Padi!' At the snap of her fingers, the crowd parted and the Indian oozed his way to the front. 'Padi, tell Senator Orbilio what your runes read. Or –' she grinned wickedly – 'have I just given the game away?'

'Indeed so, Mistress.' He placed his pink palms together and made his customary obsequious bow. 'But I do not think the young gentleman will be too distressed at the disclosure.'

This time he bowed in Orbilio's direction.

'The Stones-That-Talk cannot lie,' he explained in his soft, sibilant voice. 'They spelled out quite clearly the letters SPQR and heralds calling you to your seat, O Great Master, and the rods spoke of you taking that seat in noble ceremony below the presidential podium.'

Orbilio wondered if he would also meet a tall, dark stranger and go on to marry a man in uniform, but decided this was probably a combination of embarrassment, scented oils and the jug of red wine he'd thrown down his throat making him light-headed.

'That is marvellous news, Padi,' he replied solemnly. And resisted the urge to fart in the water.

160

'My soothsayer also predicts a swift and successful conclusion to your current case, Marcus,' Marcia said. 'Isn't that so, Padi?'

'Unambiguously, Mistress,' the Indian lisped, 'and Aquitania will hail you as a hero for your actions.'

It crossed Orbilio's mind to ask this little fat fraud whether he saw the Governor himself kneeling at his feet. Instead, he scrubbed his chest with a sponge as the steam billowed up to the high, vaulted ceiling, playing round the gilded cherubs and swirling through the chain of stylized lotus flowers so that they almost appeared to be swaying in the breeze.

'Good heavens, Marcus, we have slaves to do that!' Marcia was horrified. 'You! Yes, you over there! Get in and scrub Master Orbilio's back!'

'Actually, I'd prefer to scrub my own—'

'Nonsense! It's what these people are trained for, and if you let them get away with it once, they'll walk all over you, darling. That girl knows I'll be docking her wages for slacking. Now then.' She stopped glowering at the slave girl and her voice softened. 'I'll have Koros fix you up with a tonic, Marcus, because you're looking a bit peaky, if you don't mind my saying so. Koros!'

The old man materialized at her elbow, and Orbilio realized how perfectly he'd been camouflaged in this hazy white atmosphere.

'Which would you recommend?' Marcia asked. 'Borage and chamomile wine or rosemary and wild celery seeds in a marjoram tea?' When she leaned forward to whisper in Orbilio's ear, he could see the cracks that had formed in her heavy make-up because of the steam. 'They work absolute miracles, trust me.'

'For the Lord Orbilio,' Koros said, stroking his long, straggly beard as rheumy eyes evaluated the patient, 'I would recommend a herbal concoction, my lady. Coriander seed, parsley, horseradish and caraway, with perhaps a slight hint of basil.'

There was no point in arguing. Falling back on his aristocratic heritage, and trying to ignore the fact that, out of the whole crowd, only Marcia's feet were protected against the scorching heat of the floor tiles by thick-soled wooden sandals, Marcus duly enthused over the tonic, complimented his hostess

161

on her generous hospitality, shot a glowing smile of thanks at the soothsayer, allowed the bath house attendant to wash every inch of his already over-exposed body and experienced more than a small glow of satisfaction that the big Basc body-guard's skin was running with sweat beneath the weight of his leather armour . . . and all this while sucking his stomach muscles in tight.

Who said men can't multi-task?

Twenty

Claudia was in the garden, peering at one of the statues (a wood nymph, to be precise) and calculating exactly how dangerous an enemy she'd made of Vincentrix, when she felt the first tingle at the base of her scalp.

Someone was watching her.

She looked round, but it was just another day up at the villa, with slaves rushing about like wasps with their stingers on fire, rolling barrels, fetching sacks, rumbling amphorae across the courtyard, while others brought in baskets of charcoal and bundles of hay or carried armfuls of linen down to the river. Surely it wasn't possible for a peeping tom to be snooping in broad daylight with so much activity going on?

She glanced through the arch of the rose arbour to where Semir, dressed, if you could call it that, in his customary loincloth, was stroking the velvety leaves of a senecio to check how it had transplanted. Further down, his shaven head gleaming every bit as brightly as Semir's olive skin, Qeb was struggling along the path with a huge crate in his outstretched hands. Whatever new addition he was fetching to the menagerie, judging by the thrashing inside, the creature wasn't going gracefully, but, although the big Egyptian was too far away for her to catch his words, Claudia could hear him crooning to the animal as though it were a baby. Immediately, she was reminded of the king cobra she'd caught him caressing. And how Qeb liked to stroke little girls' hair . . .

Moving on to inspect another of Semir's masterpieces, a box tree topiaried in the shape of a cockerel, she decided that whatever faults he might have you couldn't criticize the Babylonian's artistry or his gardening expertise, and it didn't seem to bother him, either, that he had to rely on slave labour when it came to pruning, planting and clipping. Of course, the daily drudgery of watering and manuring would be done by slaves, anyway. All the same, it was unusual for a man of Semir's standing to hand over control of his landscaping project to a higher authority, especially a woman and an amateur at that. As Claudia continued to admire the cockerel's proud crest and applaud his strutting pose, the prickles returned and she shivered. Dammit, she *was* being watched!

Adopting an air of unconcern, she moved to the cockerel's southern side. Hor, she could see now, was in conversation with his brother. Could it have been him? Their voices weren't raised, but they seemed to be arguing and, from the increase in hand gestures, Hor was becoming more and more exasperated with his older brother. Glancing over her shoulder, there was nothing to suggest that Paris had been remotely interested in her, either. Down on his haunches, he was examining the gilding on the sandals of a statue of Minerva. But the sensation persisted . . .

In two leaps, Claudia was across the lawn and diving into the laurel.

'Got you, you pervert!'

Credit where it was due, at least the pervert was freshly laundered and smelled of rich, musky oils with just a hint of . . . just a hint of . . . oh, shit. Just a hint of sandalwood.

'Orbilio, what are you doing in the bushes?'

'Right now, I appear to be flat on my stomach chewing a mouthful of bay leaves with a harpy glued to my back,' he wheezed. 'What is even more bizarre is that I don't actually find this situation objectionable.'

'You must have been in the laurels for a reason.'

'Hope springs eternal and this is proof that patience eventually pays off. Have you been putting on weight?'

'Why do you ask?'

'Because that question usually makes women jump a mile.'

'Well, you ought to know, you lecherous bastard. What are you planning to do, anyway? Inseminate the whole of Santonum while you're here?'

'Only the women,' he rasped, 'but if you don't move soon, my broken spine is going to leave an awful lot of ladies disappointed and you wouldn't want that on your conscience, now would you?'

Dear Diana, what was she *thinking* of, flattening the Security

Police then straddling them like a bloody donkey? (And why didn't she find the experience objectionable, either?) 'What's a conscience?' she asked, scrambling off.

They were solid muscles she'd been astride, too. No wonder Curvy Thighs dropped her guard (and everything else).

'Why were you watching me?'

'Don't assume everyone else has eyes in the back of their head just because you have,' he puffed, straightening the crick in his neck.

Fair point. She couldn't have pinned him face down, if he'd been looking her way. All the same, the sensation of being observed had been strong . . .

'If you must know what I was doing, I spotted this.'

'It's a doll.'

'Ten out of ten, Mistress Seferius.'

'Don't tell me, you haven't been able to get to sleep at night without Dolly and that's the only reason you came back to the villa. To collect her.'

'Actually, you're thinking of Teddy and I was careful to take him with me. What do you notice about this doll?'

'Other than the fact that she's extremely ugly and has only one arm?'

'You don't think this little cutie might be a treasured possession, then?'

'Might *have been*,' she corrected. 'Past tense.'

Carved out of oakwood and jointed, it would have been a little girl's dream when it was new. Right now, though, the doll's long black hair was caked with dust, what was left of her miniature tunic was in holes and the reason she was ugly was because her head had either been trampled or had fallen under a wheel. Which was probably how she had come to lose her arm, too.

'Uh-uh,' he said. 'Is. Present tense. Look.'

The hair was human and, like most dolls' hair, it was stitched on to linen then glued into place. When Orbilio shook off the dust, the hair shone.

'It's been washed,' he said. 'Recently. And the clothes might be ragged, but see how clean they are. In fact,' he added, turning the doll over, 'I'd say this little poppet couldn't have been lying here for much more than a week.'

165

'How fascinating, but if you'll excuse me I'll leave you honing your investigative skills in the bushes—'

'I'm not analysing dolls to keep my hand in,' he said evenly, and the amusement in his eye snuffed like a candle. 'I think this might be connected to the case I'm involved in.'

Something skittered in Claudia's heart and that something was happy. Whatever dirty pies she might have her fingers in, dolls, broken or otherwise, didn't figure! 'That's the case that brought you to Gaul, right?'

He bent down to adjust his bootlace. 'Actually, that wasn't the reason I came to Santonum, no.'

The skittering clattered to a halt and solidified. 'No?'

'No,' he confirmed. 'But shortly after I arrived, I received an anonymous tip-off about a paedophile ring from someone personally affected by the gang's activities, who felt unable to report it to the authorities for fear of involvement at a high level.'

'Anonymous?' she repeated for want of nothing better to say, because suddenly the lump in her stomach was turning to ice.

'My informant hoped the newly arrived representative from Rome would be objective,' he explained, 'but left the note unsigned just in case.'

'High places?' she echoed dully. Anything to keep his mind off her fraud. 'You think the traffic might be going through Marcia's villa?'

'It crossed my mind.'

'Then it was a very short journey,' she said. 'You know Marcia's history, Orbilio. After what happened to her, she's hardly likely to inflict the same hell on others, is she?'

'You've obviously never heard of victims repeating their own abuse?'

There's no embarrassing way to get rich, Marcia had said. And what he said was true. Victims of cruelty, whether physical, emotional or sexual, often visited the same torture on others, although for what reason Claudia could not say. Comfort in a pattern repeated? Justification on the grounds that it had done them no harm?

'It would go some way towards explaining her interest in my case load,' he added, 'not to mention her ordering Tarbel to go through my papers.'

166

At last it became clear what the big Basc had been doing on the landing yesterday morning, watched by wily old Koros behind the tapestry. Why he wasn't in armour. Why he'd felt distaste at what he was doing. For a man used to combat, snooping was not a fair fight.

'A little over a week ago, around the time this doll got dropped, I happened to witness a child's abduction,' Marcus said. 'And incidentally did nothing to save her.'

No, no, no. This wasn't right. Not the man who'd dedicated his whole life to weighing in with the warships, careering down with the cavalry and loosing off with the legionaries.

'Marcus Cornelius, there is no way you'd stand idly by and watch a child become meat for a bunch of perverts.'

'It wasn't for the want of trying,' he said thickly, and suddenly she understood the deep lines round his mouth, the frown lines on his forehead, the purple hollows beneath his eyes. 'But whichever way you look at it, Claudia, the bastards got clean away. They killed the nightwatchman, threw his body in the river where it still hasn't been found, but, yes, it was my fault they slipped through.'

She stared at the doll in his hands, soiled and despoiled like the child he had failed, and felt sick. The hands that held it were shaking, she noticed. Shaking from rage and impotence, worry and shame, but, Croesus, couldn't he see that none of this was his fault? One day, she supposed dully, he would realize that these bastards held no respect for human life. That they'd have slit his throat without hesitation and that dead he'd be no help to that child either. At least he could prevent others from falling into the same filthy hands! But events were too fresh, the guilt far too raw, for him to see the full picture . . .

'Have you—' She cleared her throat and started again. 'Have you seen Hercules?' she asked brightly. The less he dwelled on what he believed to be his own inadequacies, the quicker his objectivity would return. 'Or rather Herakles, if you happen to speak "Paris".'

Orbilio seemed to wake from a very deep sleep. 'H-Herakles?'

'Last week, I came across our drop-dead-handsome sculptor scouring for a role model for his hero. At first, when he told

me he was looking for Herakles, I assumed he was referring
to a dog, although, funnily enough, it appears I am right.'

The doll had disappeared into the folds of his long patrician tunic, she noticed, as they cut across the lawn. The man
was nothing if not professional.

'See?'

Herakles stood straight backed and square shouldered on
his podium, lion pelt slung nonchalantly over his shoulders,
olive-wood club in one hand, the golden girdle of the Amazon
queen (Labour No. 9) in the other, as he stared across to the
villa. A wayward marble fringe was poised for eternity about
to flop over his forehead, and, although his strong jaw was
set in determination, there was a twinkle behind his dark
painted eyes.

'But . . . that's *me*,' Orbilio gasped.

'Woof woof.' Although wolf might be a more appropriate
description. 'You're mass produced, of course. At least your
body is, but that's all right, considering you're already mass
producing yourself all over Santonum—'

'Does it ever occur to you that you might be wrong occasionally?'

'Never. Now take a look at Medusa.'

'One look from Medusa and men turned to stone.' Orbilio
let out a loud sigh. 'I suppose it's too much to hope Paris
fashioned her in your image?'

'Be careful what you wish for,' Claudia said. 'But luckily
for you, that's me over there.'

She pointed to Venus, and since the statue was too far away
for him to recognize Stella rising from the foam surrounded
by cherubs Claudia swept on towards the monster with the
face of a beautiful woman but whose hair was a writhing mass
of serpents. Orbilio sucked in his cheeks.

'Does Marcia know?'

Her trademark expression had been captured in stony perfection.

'The lady's objections, I believe, have been voiced.
Especially in connection with the statue's location.'

He looked up at the tree that was shading Medusa and could
no longer keep his face straight. 'A medlar. Ouch! And
Marcia's objections, presumably, were along the lines that the

168

snakes are painted purple and green, rather than the blonde tones she likes to pass off as natural?'

'It wasn't the colours she took exception to,' Claudia quipped back. 'More that they don't *hissssss* like the real oncs.' She turned and lifted her eyes to his, and the laughter died on her tongue. 'Orbilio, I want to do a deal with the Security Police.'

'Interesting,' he murmured, brushing a few specks of soil from the sleeve of his tunic. 'Go on.'

'It's about the Scarecrow and these missing girls. I presume you've heard about them?'

'I'd show you my file notes,' he said, and she detected an irritating twinkle at the back of his eye, 'only I've written them up in Greek. Five young women in the prime of their life have gone missing, yes. What about them?'

'The deal,' she said firmly. 'I mean, we are talking murder here?'

'It's beginning to look that way.'

Goddammit, the bastard was hedging. She ploughed on. 'And murder beats fraud on the Naughty Scale?'

'Usually . . .'

Don't commit yourself. 'So, if I was to help you catch a mass murderer and save lots of young women's lives, that would surely count in my favour?'

He folded his arms over his chest. 'Keep going . . .'

Janus, Croesus, the snake was making her grovel! 'I propose an exchange,' she said crisply. 'I help you track down their killer—'

'This isn't my case,' he cut in. 'I'm not involved at any level.'

'No, but solving the murder of five innocent women wouldn't exactly be a black mark on your record?'

'True.' He stroked his jaw thoughtfully. 'So let me get this straight. You make Padi's prediction come true by turning me into a local hero and . . . and I do what, exactly, in return?'

She took a deep breath and held it for a count of three. 'You drop your investigation into my business affairs.'

'Very well.'

'I beg your pardon?'

'I said, yes. Agreed.' He held out his hand. 'It's a deal.'

169

'Are you serious?'

'Would I lie to you?'

'Marcus Cornelius, you could talk the Ferryman into rowing you to Atlantis instead of Hades and still not pay the damn fare.'

'I take that as a compliment,' he said, with a firm shake of her hand.

Yes, it was a deal, Claudia thought, turning away to follow the marble path as it twisted its way through beds of mallow and hibiscus. Unless one happens to be a member of the Security Police . . .

That handshake. Far too slick. No negotiation, no questions, no verbal arm-twisting? He'd given in too quickly, which meant either he was slipping in his old age or he was turning even wilier. The answer, she concluded, as he caught up with her by the statue of Saturn, was that wolves had nothing on Marcus Cornelius.

'There seems something vaguely familiar about the tilt of the head,' he murmured, running his hand over Saturn's sickle and reaping hook. 'That stocky body and bull neck . . .'

'The head groom,' Claudia said. Very well. Let's play it your way, wolf-man. She sat down on a wooden bench over which chamomile had been planted to make a fragrant seat. 'I suppose you know that Marcia is organizing another manhunt in the morning and that she means to trap the Scarecrow one way or another?'

'She's put Tarbel in charge this time,' Marcus said, settling on the grass at her feet. 'And something tells me he's not the type to accept defeat.'

'That's why you have to stop it from going ahead.'

He plucked a blade and began to chew. 'I would only intervene,' he said slowly, 'provided I had bloody good reason.'

Claudia selected a ripe, velvety peach from an overhanging branch and tossed it to him, then plucked another one for herself. 'The problem as I see it,' she said, 'is that these girls were abducted without any sign of a struggle, which made me wonder whether this was actually true. Had the search party been looking in the right places, I asked myself, and would they recognize signs of violence if they saw them? The Santons are untravelled—'

'Untravelled doesn't mean stupid. These people understand

the land better than anyone else, and if there had been a struggle, believe me, they'd know it,' Marcus said, wiping the juice off his chin. 'They're expert huntsmen who read the forest like you read the daily gossip sheet—'

'One should always keep abreast of current affairs.'

Orbilio leaned back, absorbing his weight on his elbows. 'Most people take that to mean politics, not who's cheating on whom.'

She tossed the peach stone over the hedge. 'A lot of hard work goes into the production and distribution of those sheets. I feel it only fair that their efforts are supported.'

'And I always thought philanthropy began with an "f",' he murmured, stretching out on the grass and folding his hands behind his head.

'That aside,' she sniffed, 'and as much as it grieves me to admit it, I actually arrived at the same conclusion. No violence took place.'

'That isn't necessarily the case,' Marcus said, closing his eyes against the harsh glare of the sun. 'I can think of several methods just off the top of my head, but go on.'

'Well, it occurs to me that everyone for miles around has heard of the Scarecrow. In fact, I would go so far as to say his reputation is notorious.'

'It's human nature for people to be frightened of things they don't understand.'

'Precisely. So how come these girls didn't scream or run off at the first flutter of wingbeats in the trees? Even if they believed the local superstition that he was Death himself, they wouldn't just walk calmly up to him. But! Assuming all five *were* stupid enough to do just that, once they got close, they'd quickly tell the difference between the Guardian of their Souls and a smelly individual who lives rough in the woods. I mean, imagine his teeth.'

One lazy eye opened. 'I'd rather not.'

'Which brings me back to my original point: why no blood? *Why* no signs of a struggle?'

Marcus sat up and hugged his knees. 'There are only two possible reasons,' he said. 'One, the killer is a professional, a man who has been trained to move quietly and kill cleanly, and the second—'

171

'It's someone the women trusted. Exactly.' Claudia paused. 'Which means whoever is abducting these girls, it isn't the Scarecrow.' And if Orbilio didn't stop tomorrow's manhunt, another victim would be added to the mounting list of innocents . . . 'We need to find the Scarecrow before Tarbel,' she said.

He flopped back on to the grass with a groan. 'I do not believe it,' he told the sky. 'Marcia's people have spent months trying to flush this elusive creature out of the woods, yet milady here thinks she can do it in . . . yes, just how long *do* you think it will take you?'

'A day.'

'Are you sure you don't mean half a day? An hour? Twenty-five minutes?'

'Sarcasm is beneath you and so, incidentally, is a long, black, wriggly thing that seems intent on crawling inside your tunic.'

Orbilio jumped up and brushed the earwig away. 'Tomorrow is the Emperor's birthday. I might be able to persuade Marcia to show a bit of respect on that score, but she won't hold back for long. That woman eats, drinks and breathes glory and I'll bet Hor is already pencilling out the victorious scene on the east wall of her tomb.'

'Then he'd better wheel out the whitewash,' Claudia said. 'But in order to beat Tarbel to the Scarecrow, there's something I need you to do.'

'I had a feeling there would be.'

'Nonsense. Everyone knows the Security Police don't have feelings! Now, pay attention, Marcus. Your job is to put that manly baritone of yours to good use, shouting out orders as loud as you can and repeating them endlessly, to make sure the Scarecrow gets to hear about the impending manhunt.'

'I'm so glad my military training has some purpose.'

Claudia snorted his cynicism aside. 'It's absolutely crucial that our woodsman understands the strength of the contingent set to track him down and the fact that, this time, Rome is behind the manhunt.'

'You don't think he might become a teeny bit suspicious about the lack of legionaries clumping about?'

'Frightened men don't think logically,' she said. 'Just make sure you bark out your orders round the perimeter, so there's no chance of the Scarecrow not hearing.'

'Yes, ma'am.' He saluted. 'Anything else, ma'am?'

Her retort was cut short by the arrival of a hired courier, jogging down the path at a professional trot. 'Message for Master Marcus Cornelius Orbilio.' He handed over the letter. 'Will there be a reply?'

Claudia recognized the seal as he broke it. It was his own.

'Yes,' he said, tipping the runner with a coin from the bronze purse round his wrist. 'Tell her I'm coming at once.' Orbilio turned to Claudia. 'I've got to go,' he said.

'Zina?'

'The Scarecrow will have to wait,' he said, nodding. 'This can't.'

'It's about the child, I suppose?'

'Yep.'

She watched him race back to the villa. Dammit, the lecherous bastard could at least have lied.

'Zina's found her,' he shouted.

A lot of things reassembled themselves in Claudia's innards.

'Wait!' she yelled, although for some reason she was quite out of breath. 'Marcus, wait! I need to borrow that doll!'

Among the items that had rearranged themselves was another piece of the puzzle. With icy clarity, she knew exactly why the Scarecrow was hanging around in these woods . . .

As it happened, the Scarecrow wasn't in the woods.

For some reason, the middle-aged man in the purple-striped tunic had stopped bringing the children down to the meadow next to the paddock. Presumably he felt the grass was too long for racing about in, so he'd taken to playing with them at a spot by a bend in the river. One of the many branches that separated from, and then rejoined, the Carent, this stretch was known locally as the Solora, after the water spirit who inhabited it. Often, the lean, leathery man would bring them here to skinny dip first thing in the morning, or for a picnic of cheeses and chestnuts with hot damson pastries before they were packed off to bed.

It hadn't been easy to get close to the wide, open bank where they played, but the Scarecrow had found that by arriving early then concealing himself under an elderberry bush and waiting, often for hours, his patience was rewarded. From time to time, the man would scan the woods behind with narrowed, soldier's eyes, as though expecting to see someone, or something. But once he had satisfied himself that they were alone, he would throw himself wholeheartedly into whatever activity the children were engaged in, be it watching fish, stamping the ground to drive tiny frogs into the reeds, feeding the ducks or gasping at snakes underwater.

As sunlight glistened off the Solora and grasses nodded their feathery heads in the breeze, the children dabbled their nets in the river for tiddlers that they never caught or played Mermaids and Sea Monsters, and no one told them off for eating while their hands were still covered in mud. Most amazing of all, considering there were six siblings ranging in age from three to nearly ten, the Scarecrow could hardly believe they were so well-behaved. An occasional squabble might erupt, but when the man with the feathers pinned to his chest started clowning the quarrel was quickly forgotten.

Hidden by the elder, the Scarecrow's eyes followed the children. Twin boys, alike as two peas in a pod. The oldest girl, with dark glossy hair like her mother's, and the youngest, who still had a slight lisp. He watched the toddler, chortling with glee as his little fat legs slurped in the river mud, but especially, yes especially, the Scarecrow watched Belisana. Belisana, with hair the colour of ripe corn and eyes as big and blue as the Aegean . . .

'So that's where you're hiding!' Their mother hove into the clearing like a warship in sail, hands on hips, head tipped to one side, but the children weren't fooled for a minute.

'We've been playing statues with Uncle Hanni,' the oldest girl said.

'I was Alexander!'

'I was the Hammer God!'

'I'm Cupid,' the littlest one said, standing on one leg and toppling over.

'No, darling, you're just cute,' she crooned, hoisting him out of the mud. 'But I'd like to know what *you* are,' she said to the man.

'Extremely sorry?' he suggested.

174

'Hannibal, you know full well that Marcia insists the children stay in the classroom until the sun sinks over the stables. Right then, you lot.' She clapped her hands for attention. 'You know what this means. It means I'm going to have to teach you monsters a lesson myself, and the subject today is . . .' She tipped back her head and adopted the traditional pose of Juno, Queen of Olympus. 'Well, come on!' she squealed. 'Who am I?'

'Minerva?'

'Aunt Marcia?'

'The Emperor's wife?'

'No, she's *Mummy*!' the little one shrieked, and the statue dissolved.

'Yes, I am, darling, I'm Mummy, and Mummy supposes we'd all best get back to the villa.'

'Into line, chaps!' The middle-aged man formed his troops into a column. 'A-n-d march! Left, right, left, right.'

With a knot round his windpipe, the Scarecrow watched as the littlest one, struggling to keep up, was scooped under the arm of the slender young woman with dark, glossy hair and bounced along in formation. As the army marched off through the trees, Belisana broke away, racing back to collect the rag doll she'd left propped up against a fallen tree trunk. Watching the bounce of her curls and the hop-skip-and-jump of her run, the Scarecrow felt an ache round his heart the likes of which he'd never known.

At moments like this, he wanted to die.

Twenty-One

High in the hills, inside the cave from which the Spring of Prophecy bubbled from the rocks, the Arch Druid Vincentrix paced the floor.

All day he had sat cross-legged in front of his fire, patiently adding his magic herbs to the crackling flames and waiting for his gods to arrive. All day he had sat alone, and then he had sat alone all through the steadily lengthening night. No morsel of food had passed the Druid's lips to contaminate his communion with the Eternal Ones, and the only water he had drunk was that which sprang in purity from the stone. But there was no purity in Vincentrix's heart, only the burning heat of anger, and anger, as he knew full well, was a sin.

Yet he was powerless to stop it.

He watched the first shaft of light brighten the sky over the hills, and his ears opened to the sweet trill of the blackbird, always the first to start the daily chorus.

Years peeled back. Suddenly, he was seventeen again. A besotted, loyal virgin bridegroom contracted to an empty marriage bed. She only married him, she said, because her family kept pressing her to take a husband. What comfort, knowing Vincentrix had been the only youth in Gaul not to see through the bitch!

Warblers, flycatchers and finches joined the chorus.

It was not through inheritance when her aunt had died that his wife acquired the ring. Vincentrix had stolen it from a Roman goldsmith's shop, an act that had liberated him in more ways than he had envisaged, since not only had the ring funded his wife's travels, the theft had demonstrated an innate ability to blend with his surroundings. But the humiliating knowledge that everyone in Santonum knew the truth about his frigid bride still rankled. There was only one solution. By

176

volunteering to become a Druid, he would rise above them – above them all. But even as he had boarded the boat bound for Britain, Vincentrix had no suspicion of the destiny that awaited him.

He had the Gift, the Elders had told him. It was Vincentrix who had been chosen by the gods. He was the Special One. In that cold, far-distant land across the water, where the winter winds whistled down bleak valleys and the snow piled high across the pastures, two decades of his life had been devoted to communing with the gods. As youth passed to manhood, he learned to suppress human emotions. As manhood passed to early middle age, he subjugated bodily desires, because it was his duty, the Druid Elders informed him, to rise above secular passions and channel those energies into a spiritual union with the Divine Ones, so that Vincentrix might lead his people through Darkness and the Hall of Change to Light.

'We are born in blood,' ran the ancient texts. 'Blood gives us life, and it is through blood that the power of the gods is replenished.'

His hand did not falter, nor his eye blink, the day he set torch to his first screaming wicker man.

As a priest, Vincentrix had been taught how to gauge the mood of the gods. Through prayer, through meditation, through his fire and through his herbs he was able to predict when blood was needed, and how much, and from whom. It was this wisdom, coupled with his ability to commune with those he served on the astral plane, that had ensured his election as Head of the Collegiate when he eventually returned to Gaul. Feared and revered in equal measure, his new role guaranteed that the people of Santonum forgot the shame of his past – but old habits die hard. He couldn't resist mingling unobtrusively among the crowds to make sure, one day perhaps a woodsman carrying bundles of faggots or charcoals, another a huntsman, a thatcher, a peasant in hooded leather jerkin. Disguise brought rewards of its own. Snippets of conversation here, secrets overheard there, folk observed doing things they should not. All these Vincentrix stored in his specially trained memory and his power grew.

So what had gone wrong?

Vincentrix held his head under the running spring water,

shuddering at its icy coldness as it pounded his scalp, and washed away the lime that helped him blend with the crowd. The answer was simple. The power of the gods was waning, because the tribes were turning away from the old ways in favour of more earthly – and immediate – pleasures. He lifted his face from the water, wrung out his hair and combed it through with his fingers.

The conquerors did not believe in putting themselves out, he thought bitterly. None of this trekking into the sacred, silent heart of the forests to conduct their religion. Lazy bastards worshipped in the *street*, if you please, where temples of stone soared on marble pillars into the clouds to impress the weak and the gullible, while simple folk were drawn to the feasting that usually followed the sacrifice, to the music and laughter, dancing and singing – and the lure, he had to acknowledge, was strong. But until now, until he had spent a full day and a full night waiting in vain, Vincentrix hadn't realized how strong the pull was, or how harmful.

The anger that he had been trained to suppress boiled up until he could contain it no more. Balling his right hand into a fist, he let out an almighty roar and slammed it against the rock face. As blood oozed down the white limestone, the Druid began to chant, channelling his rage as he had been taught all those years before, until sunlight flooded the cave and the chariot of the Shining One was high in the sky.

The power of the gods was waning, this was true. But tomorrow would see the start of the autumnal equinox . . .

'By the hammer of the Thunderer and the sword of the Piercer of Shields, I will harness the powers of the universe,' he vowed. 'I will strap them to the seasons, yoke them to the moon, drive them between the shafts of the tides.'

Holding his throbbing knuckles beneath the waters of the Spring of Prophecy, he bound flesh with spirit, passion with reason, fire with ice, thus binding the oath for eternity.

'You *will* have your powers restored,' the gods were assured, as Vincentrix solemnly placed his lips against the Ring of Pledge. 'By all that is holy, you *will* have the blood that is owed you.'

Better still, he knew exactly whose blood it would be.

Twenty-Two

The air in the Governor's atrium was kept cool by high, vaulted ceilings and an abundance of marble, and kept fragrant with fountains and roses. Satinwood inlaid with ivory and mother-of-pearl gleamed in the muted, late-morning sunshine, while family shrines embellished with silver offered libations of the very best vintage. Looking at the proud ancestors staring into eternity from their lofty stone pedestals and at the famous victories celebrated in mosaic and paint, Orbilio could have been home.

As slaves washed his feet and massaged the skin with oil of peppermint, serving girls plied him with dates stuffed with almond paste and tiny pancakes dripping with honey. Since he hadn't eaten for over twenty-four hours, his stomach would have preferred something savoury to line it. A thick steak of tender young lamb, for example, or a gravy-filled venison pie, but beggars can't be choosers, and he wolfed down the sweetmeats at a speed not normally associated with the aristocracy.

'Sorry to keep you waiting, m'boy!' The Governor's voice boomed down the hall. 'Needed to tie up the last few strands of paperwork. Nasty old business, what?'

Orbilio gulped down the last pancake before the plate was whisked away. 'Indeed, sir.'

'You've done Rome a great service, lad, ridding us of those scum.' A large paw clapped him on the back. 'And to think my chief scribe was the orchestrator!'

'I noticed he wasn't among the prisoners in the yard,' Orbilio observed smoothly. It didn't take a genius to guess that the chief scribe was the last of the Governor's 'paperwork', no doubt left alone with a sharp sword to fall on, or perhaps that old favourite, a nice cup of hemlock.

'Better this office is kept out of it,' the Governor said,

179

shrugging. 'Shit sticks and we can't afford to have one bad apple contaminate the barrel, can we?'

'No, sir.'

'Must say, m'boy, you handled this whole thing exceptionally well—'

'I hardly think so,' he protested. 'The nightwatchman was butchered, a seven-year-old defiled—'

'Eggs and omelettes, lad. Eggs and omelettes.' The Governor waved his objections away with a massive hand. 'You've cut off the head of a heinous monster. The gang's finished, thanks to you, and now we have the names of the bastards involved—'

Yes, Orbilio had heard the screams ringing out from the prison, and that was the thing, of course. Since none of the gang had opted for Roman citizenship, torture was a legitimate method to extract information. And a satisfying one, judging by the smiles on their inquisitors' faces. A lot of the men in the garrison had children the same age as the girl in that dark, dingy attic . . .

'The credit for this is all Zina's,' he said. 'She went out on a limb for what she believed in, knowing it would tear her family apart.'

'Like to meet this plucky little minx. Where is she?'

'Governor, I have absolutely no idea,' Marcus said, spiking his hands through his hair.

She was at his side when they burst open the attic door. She was at his side when they carried the whimpering child down the stairs. She was at his side when the soldiers burst in and arrested her stepfather. But at some point between rounding up the rest of the gang, finding a caring home for the victim, searching the boatyard and rushing back to the villa to spread the word about the manhunt, Zina had taken herself off.

'That girl is a law unto herself,' he added ruefully.

The Governor leaned forward to whisper in confidence, 'My mistress is a Gaul, so you ain't telling me anything new, lad. Minds of their own, won't do a damn thing you tell 'em. Just as well our Roman gels don't grow up like that, what?'

Marcus thought of Claudia and said nothing.

'What d'you say we give that Zina of yours a commendation?'

'I think, sir, that she'd much prefer a gold bracelet.'

The Governor's laugh echoed round the atrium. 'That can be arranged, but dammit I've a seven-year-old granddaughter meself. Even if Rome don't thank her officially, I'd like to express my personal gratitude, and it's important I get the sequence of events right. Don't suppose you'd mind running through it again, would you, lad?'

'Not at all, sir.'

After the chaos of the last twenty-four hours, he welcomed the chance to put things in order, if only for his own peace of mind.

'As you know, Zina left an anonymous tip-off at the inn where I was staying. For some time, she'd been suspicious of her stepfather's movements, thinking he was cheating on her mother, so she followed him. It was only when she saw him handing over a child tied up in a blanket that she put two and two together about the beggar children who'd gone missing.'

'Those rumours never came to my ears,' the Governor growled. 'Bastard scribe made sure of that.'

Orbilio wasn't going to allow himself to be distracted at this stage. 'From snatches of conversation that she'd over-heard, Zina was convinced someone in authority was behind the child sex ring. That's why she approached me. Fresh from Rome, she hoped I'd be unbiased, but kept an eye on me just to make sure I wasn't part of the operation or about to cut myself a slice of this very lucrative cake.'

The surveillance man under surveillance himself!

'She realized I was serious the night they handed over another small victim, when Rintox the nightwatchman was killed.' He saw no reason to tell anyone, least of all the Governor, that a seventeen-year-old girl knocked him out cold when he'd drawn his dagger, intending to rush the gang single-handed! 'Outnumbered, there was nothing we could do, especially since we didn't know who was masterminding the abductions.'

What they hadn't realized, of course, was that they'd been looking at the whole thing back to front.

'When Zina first saw her stepfather by the river handing over a child, she assumed they were bringing the kid ashore.'

181

This had coloured Orbilio's thinking, too. Her note was so specific – who, what, where and why – that he hadn't thought to question the 'how' side of it, and when he'd heard the muffled whimpers the night Rintox died he, too, had assumed she'd come by boat.

'That's what niggled Zina,' he explained. 'Why didn't we hear any wheels or hooves? Then she realized the girl must already have been imprisoned in her stepfather's yard, and the boat hadn't come to collect her. It had come to take her *away*.'

'To that stinking den upriver with the sign of the Black Boar.' The Governor snorted. 'Knew it was a gambling den, of course, but no matter whether gaming is against the law or not, m'boy, it ain't going to stop. Far better we know where and keep an eye on it than have it disappear underground, where we can't trace it.'

Bear-fights, dog-fights, fist-fights, cock-fights, everything went on at that old shack by the river, because the minute you brand a vice illegal its popularity soars, as everyone wants a bite of the action. Rich man, poor man, beggar man, thief, they were all there, at the sign of the Black Boar. The chief scribe merely saw a business opportunity opening up. Guttersnipes, who'd miss them? Their parents, who should have known better than to keep breeding children like rabbits? Half of them were orphans anyway, the product of drunkards and brawlers who'd dug their own graves with their wine jugs. What loss to society were scum like that?

'Your scribe knew a lot of men who would pay handsomely for tender young flesh.'

Heaven knows how. Orbilio hadn't had a single bite from the perverted requests he'd put out. Perhaps it was some secret club? More likely, he thought, he hadn't been in town long enough to be trusted. Paedophiles operate in stealth, but, more importantly, they never rush what they're doing.

'For him, the boatbuilder and the rest of the gang,' he told the Governor, 'it was purely a business transaction.'

'Be interesting to see how highly they value their profits on the long haul to Rome. How many sesterces being paraded through the streets is worth, when garbage and dog shit are thrown in their faces, and even more interesting to see how far their ill-gotten gains take 'em during a protracted and painful execution, what?'

Did torturing the torturers make it right? Hell, Orbilio didn't have seven-year-old granddaughters. Who was he to judge?

'Thanks to Zina following her stepfather the other night, and seeing coins change hands outside the Black Boar, she was able to sneak in and determine the situation.'

'Bastards.' The Governor all but spat. 'Don't suppose y'know what happened to the poor little sods who had gone before her, do you?'

'No, sir, but we can guess.' He'd seen for himself the ease with which Rintox's throat had been cut. That kind of handi-work didn't come without practice.

'Well, good work anyway. Both of you!' The Governor rubbed his jowls thoughtfully. 'Y'know, we could use a chap of your calibre in Santonum. Seen your record, lad. Nigh on a hundred per cent detection rate, what? I tell you, Aquitania needs men like you.'

'I, um . . .'

'I'm serious, Marcus. The Security Police has no repre-sentation here. Reporting directly to me, you'd pick your own men, set up your own team and run the whole damn shooting match yourself. What d'you say?'

Orbilio drew a deep breath and let it out slowly. Claudia didn't want him. His wife had divorced him for a sea captain in Lusitania. Why go home? Why slog his guts out for a boss who didn't appreciate him, among a family who despised his choice of career?

'I'll certainly give it my serious consideration, sir.'

'Can't imagine why you don't jump at the chance.' The Governor grinned. 'Short winters ain't to be sniffed at, there's excellent hunting to be had in the forests and, take my word for it, lad, these Santon women know how to keep a chap warm at night.'

As Orbilio's fist made a salute he was hardly aware of, he wondered why he wasn't biting the Governor's hand off. Head of the Security Police in the steadily rising province of Aquitania while still a month short of his twenty-eighth birthday was not to be sneezed at. All the same, there were more pressing matters right now.

*　　*　　*

'Zina?' he called up from outside. 'Are you home?'

He was pretty sure she'd taken herself home after her stepfather's arrest. Her poor mother would be riddled with guilt not only for harbouring a monster, but living off the proceeds of his evil trade. But Black Eyes still hadn't grasped that she wasn't Marcus-my-lord's woman, and, sure enough, as he bounded up the stairs, he smelled bacon with lentils cooking on the stove, along with the scent of fresh crusty bread.

'Zina, the Governor wants to—'

It was as far as he got. As he pushed open the door, once again Orbilio's world exploded in a million white stars.

Twenty-Three

'Mummy, why is it you can say something to one person and everyone laughs, then when you say it to someone else, they burst into tears and run off?'

Stella looked down into the puzzled eyes of her middle daughter and cupped her little round face between her hands. 'Luci, Luci, Luci. What horrible mischief have you been making this time?'

'It's not *my* fault,' the child protested. 'Blame Auntie Marcia! I was just handing over my spelling list, when one of her maids came—'

'Why were you giving your spelling list to your aunt?'

'Because she *always* demands to see our letters and numbers, silly! Anyway, this slave comes rushing in to say that the Governor's wife was seen in town wearing an . . .' Her face screwed up in the struggle to remember the long word. '. . . an *identical* robe to the one Auntie Marcia wore to the banquet. The red one.'

Stella sighed. 'I am obviously going to have to have another word with your aunt. She can't keep interfering like this, but go on. The Governor's wife copied her gown and Marcia was furious.'

'No!' Little blonde curls shook vigorously. 'You're not listening, are you? Auntie Marcia wasn't cross. She tipped her head back, like this. "Hardly *identical*," she said, and she sniffed. "Mine's half the size round the hips!" And *that's* when everyone burst out laughing.'

'Luci, where is this leading, please?'

'Well, when I said the same thing to the cupbearer's daughter just now, how her friend was wearing an identical tunic only a lot smaller, she burst into tears.'

'I see.' Stella brushed a wayward strand out of her daughter's eyes. 'I suppose it didn't occur to you that it might be rather cruel to poke fun at that little girl?'

'But she's just as fat as the Governor's wife! *Fatter!*'

'That might well be true.' Mother kneeled down to look daughter in the face. 'But it strikes me that that little girl doesn't like being fat, and that you've made her even more self-conscious about her weight than before.'

'I wondered about that,' Luci said thoughtfully. 'Because when she started to grizzle, it reminded me of something Koros said while they were all laughing about the Governor's wife. That inside every fat person there's a thin one crying to get out, and so that's what I said to that girl just now. I asked her if that's why she was crying.'

'Well, I apologize, darling. That was very sweet of you.' Stella ruffled her daughter's head. 'What did the little girl say to that?'

'She said yes, so I repeated what Auntie Marcia replied to Koros. I said, "Only the one?" And *that's* when she ran off.'

Stella groaned. 'We'll talk about this later,' she said, burying her head in her hands. 'I really don't have the energy right now, Luci. You run back to the villa, there's a good girl, and keep to the path like I told you.'

'All right, but you won't forget you promised to play butter-flies, will you, Mummy?' She picked up the hem of her little pink robe and made wings, which she flapped as she ran round in a circle.

'No, darling, I haven't forgotten.'

'But you forgot to put your wedding band on.'

'Eek, I've spawned a monster!' Stella grabbed her daughter and tickled her ribs. 'She has the face of an angel but, truly, the eyes of a hawk!' Eventually, she released the giggling child and they both collapsed on the grass, panting. 'I didn't forget to wear my wedding band.' She pulled on the leather thong that hung around her neck. 'I'm going to sacrifice it.'

She opened the tiny drawstring sack on the end of the neck-lace and tipped the ring into the palm of her hand. A flurry of fragrant petals fluttered on top of it.

'Is that why you came down here?' Huge blue eyes gazed round the canyon from which a small pool seeped water from a fissure in the rock. Lining the sides of the ravine, red valerian wafted its scent on the sticky autumn breeze as jackdaws cawed and lizards darted in and out of the crevices.

'See this?' Stella picked a small purple flower spike out of the fragrant assortment. 'Hyssop purifies the waters into which I drop the ring. Thyme adds strength to my prayers—'

'Are you praying for Daddy?'

'Yes, darling, I am.'

'But I thought that band was the only precious thing from Daddy that you had left. So why are you throwing it away?'

'Well.' Stella tipped the contents back in the bag and drew the string tight. 'For a start, your father gave me six very precious things, and you, my angel, are one of them.' She planted a kiss on the top of her daughter's blonde head. 'And, for another, since this *is* the only object of value that I can call my own, I'm hoping it will carry some weight with the spirit to whom I entrust it.'

'You're not throwing it away, then?'

'Far from it, darling. Now off you go.' She patted Luci's bottom. 'I'll be along in a couple of minutes, then we'll play butterflies.'

As the little girl skipped and sang her way up the twisting path to the top of the hill, the eyes of the Watcher returned to her mother.

From behind a rock, they watched as she unpinned the bun coiled at the nape of her neck and released a cascade of dark, glossy hair down her back. They watched as she removed a knife from her belt and cut a lock to tie round the ring to bind her life-force to the metal band and breathe her own spirit into it.

There was no doubt about it. Stella had reached the pinnacle of physical perfection. Another few years of living hand-to-mouth as the future grew more uncertain and lines would ravage her beautiful face. Hands that were today long and slender would compact and grow knobbly. The belly that housework kept as taught as a drumskin would quickly turn to ripples of flab.

The Watcher listened as her sweet voice charmed the spirits that flowed through the water and felt nothing but pity that those lovely long tresses, shining with health in the sunlight, would one day become dull and speckled with grey. What a waste. What a terrible, terrible waste . . .

As Stella kneeled on the soft, green moss that covered the stones in front of the spring and raised her hands in supplication, it was inevitable that the Watcher's thoughts turned to the others, who had been so vigilantly followed and observed with such discipline.

The first was the redheaded sister of a man who made millstones. Athletic and spirited, it would have been a tragedy of the most enormous proportions to see such strength and energy become sapped by the tedium of housework or trapped in the prison of poverty. But, lively as she was, even the redhead could not compare to the voluptuous charms of the root-cutter's wife. Passionate, vibrant and kind, the Watcher could almost hear the echo of her laughter as she took men to her bed and left them glowing with warmth, their hearts filled with memories that would last them a lifetime. To stand idly by while those generous breasts sagged would have been criminal, and it was merely a matter of time before the cheese-churner's snub-nosed perfection was disfigured by the rigours of her arduous work. How quickly, too, the ripe curves of the tanner's daughter would have ballooned after childbirth, or the basket-weaver's work would have crippled her, like it had her grandmother, turning dextrous hands into claws.

Young and perfect – so utterly, utterly perfect! – those young women had been spared the rigours of old age and poor health. Never would they be forced to experience physical hardship or endure the long ache of loneliness. Each and every one was set free.

The Watcher's eyes followed Stella as she consigned her ring to the spirit, then strew her petals and herbs over the waters. They watched as she lit a small oil lamp and placed it on a ledge, and they watched as she stood up and brushed the moss off her tunic before backing away.

In fur-lined leather boots, the Watcher's feet made no sound on the floor of the canyon.

Twenty-Four

L ying on her bed with a bowl of juicy plums and a plate of crumbly white local cheese, Claudia stroked Drusilla's ears and congratulated herself on how well the word about tomorrow's manhunt was spreading.

'He might have been rounding up gangs of paedophiles while being heaped with crowns of glory, but there's nothing like an ambitious Security Policeman to make sure no stone remains unturned in the fight against corruption and evil, poppet.'

'Mrrrrw.'

'Exactly.' She raked her fingernails down an ecstatic furry spine. 'When it comes to a seat in the Senate, a chap can't have too many credits to his name.' Indeed, at this rate, Orbilio would be clearing up the imperial crime rate single-handed!

'Brrrrup?'

'Of course he'll drop his investigation into those ridiculous fraud allegations!' The man had honour stamped all over him.

'Frrr.'

'I know.' It was a damned shame he had tenacity, truth and intransigence tattooed on him as well. 'There isn't much that a spot of bribery, coercion or blackmail can't fix, but somehow Marcus Cornelius manages to block the bloody lot.'

Professional that he was, he wouldn't even agree to speak to Marcia about postponing the manhunt until he'd struck a deal.

'You succeed with the Scarecrow where others have failed? This I must see,' he'd chuckled.

Leaning back on her rainbow of pillows, Claudia wriggled her toes on the damask coverlet and checked the sun's march by the shadows on the wall. Unlike certain parties she could mention, she was not remotely sceptical about the Scarecrow

189

rising to her bait, but this would not be before nightfall, and in the end she'd agreed that Orbilio could act as an observer. 'Provided you don't interfere,' she'd insisted.

'I can't promise,' he'd murmured. 'If the poor man calls for help, I'm duty bound to pitch in.'

Very funny.

'He can scoff all he likes that it took Marcia months *not* to track the Scarecrow down,' she told Drusilla, 'but Marcia's been using the wrong methods.' Or, more accurately, the wrong people.

'This business about the Emperor's birthday is bollocks,' Tarbel had growled earlier that morning. He'd been waiting on the landing, looking more than ever like he'd just been hewn out of some ancient oak tree. 'What's going on?'

Claudia had widened her eyes in incredulity. 'I have absolutely no idea.'

'Don't play the innocent,' he retorted, leaning so close she could smell dense, cedary forests through the thick leather breastplate. 'You Romans plan so far ahead you know what you'll be doing the fourth Saturday in August six years from now. Imperial birthday celebrations don't spring up out of the blue.'

'Maybe it's not Rome,' she said sweetly. 'Maybe the postponement is your mistress's idea?'

Chestnut eyes narrowed. 'Bullshit.'

'Do you know what I think, Tarbel? I mean, apart from wishing that I'd taken longer over my bath, so that you'd have had to kick your heels for another hour outside my bedroom.' She swept past him and placed her hand on the latch of the door. 'I think you're sulking.'

There was a rumble from deep in the big Basc's throat, and it wasn't the sort of sound a cat makes when it's purring. 'Why do you do this? Why do you always provoke me?'

'And here's me thinking men liked provocative women.'

'I've never done one bloody thing to offend you. Hell, I even saved your life in the woods—'

'No, you didn't.'

'I bloody well would have.' Colour was flooding his cheeks. 'The only thing you've done since then is insult me.'

'Because I don't like liars,' she said, sweeping into her room and closing the door.

'I am a Basc,' he hissed, almost kicking the door down as he followed her in. 'Bascs do not lie. We stand by our honour and you will apologize.'

'I'm sorry, but I never apologize. Especially,' she added smugly, 'when I'm right.'

Nibbling on another chunk of crumbly white cheese, she remembered that he'd been standing just there, right between the bed frame and the clothes chest, smelling of leather and cedar and deep indignation, his shoulders so broad they practically blocked out the light from the window.

'Rrrrp,' Drusilla purred.

'You want to know what Tarbel replied to that? Something quite unsuitable for cat's ears, I'm afraid.'

But the big Basc wasn't giving up. 'At what point am I supposed to have lied to you?'

'When you told me you enjoyed your job and, before you say anything else, our conversation's just proved it.'

Tracking the Scarecrow was the first 'real' job he'd been given since hiring himself out as Marcia's minder and already his orders were being countermanded. Men who don't care don't get angry.

'Very well, acting bodyguard to a rich bitch *didn't* turn out the way I expected.' Tarbel turned on his heel. 'But I fail to see how my attitude to my work is any of your bloody business, or why it should make you dislike me.'

'Who said I disliked you?'

He stopped in his tracks.

'It works both ways,' Claudia told him. 'If I didn't care, I wouldn't bother about what happened to you, either, but you're no trained bear, Tarbel. That green and gold livery itches your skin.'

'*Sí.*' The big man nodded slowly. 'But I'd still give my life for her.'

'As you would have for Rome. Yes, I know.' The difference is, the Empire would have been grateful. 'You're a man who needs more out of soldiering than covering the occasional body with your own, tagging along with a crowd of simpering flunkies, searching other people's rooms—'

'Maybe I don't like some of the jobs I am tasked with,' he thundered, 'but, by the gods, I do them well.'

191

'Perfection isn't the issue here, Tarbel. Marcia wouldn't have hired you if you weren't a stickler for detail. But you're a soldier. A mercenary. Fighting is what you do, remember?'

'And?'

'And nothing.' She slipped into a new pair of sandals and swept past him into the corridor. 'I just thought you should be reminded, that's all.'

Plumping the pillows, Claudia glanced once more at the sun's progress on her bedroom wall. The shadows had barely moved and, biting into a soft yellow plum as Drusilla stretched languorously over the counterpane, her thoughts drifted. She was glad, for the children's sake, that Orbilio had managed to bust the paedophile ring so quickly. Dammit, though, you'd think a man who was that good at his job would give a grieving widow a break. And although she knew he'd keep his word regarding her fraud, she intended to have a quiet word with that little snake Burto once she got home. (And if that quiet word happened to contain the letters that spelled out 'branding iron', 'pincers', 'thumbscrews' and 'knuckle dusters', then so much the better.)

'He suspected Qeb was involved,' she told Drusilla, but the cat's paws were twitching as she caught mice in her sleep.

Claudia yawned and stretched, too. She could well understand what had aroused Orbilio's suspicions. The doll in the bushes. All those crates coming and going to the menagerie. I mean, who would notice one more whimper or cry? She closed her eyes and snuggled down into the cushions. But it was over and Qeb *wasn't* involved, the gang *wasn't* operating out of the villa and Marcia *hadn't* been inflicting her own pain on— Her eyelids sprang apart. Qeb might not be part of the paedophile ring, but we still have a man who refuses to meet people's eyes, whose younger brother has to take responsibility for him and *He strokes my hair*, Luci had said, as she played with the grey kitten Qeb had given her. *It feels really nice.*

Nausea lurched in Claudia's stomach as she jumped off the bed. Dammit, he was grooming the child, in every sense of the word! She reached in her jewel chest for the thin, narrow dagger and strapped it to her calf. Right, you bald bastard. Let's see how you play with the big girls.

* * *

192

It felt strange, not wearing her wedding band. Her ring finger seemed naked. Vulnerable, somehow. As though something was missing, and yet not. Stella sighed. She would get used to the sensation, she supposed. It would just take time, that was all.

Glancing over her shoulder, she watched the flame of her prayer candle dance in the breeze. Below it, hyssop spikes purified the offering she had made and sprigs of thyme added strength to her prayers. She sighed again. She had sacrificed all that she had. Her fate was in the hands of the sylph of the spring now. There was nothing left to do, except hope – hope with all of her heart – that the gentle spirit would smile upon her.

The cawing of jackdaws echoed in the canyon. High on the wing a buzzard mewed, and a red admiral came to rest on a fallen crab apple. Brushing the white local limestone from the hem of her skirt, Stella suddenly remembered her promise to Luci about playing butterflies and didn't notice the footsteps at first. Startled, she turned. All these stories about missing women . . .

'Hannibal!' Her face relaxed into a smile of relief. 'Didn't anyone warn you about creeping up on people?'

Wedged between the slaves' quarters and the guest accommodation, the rooms Marcia's artisans had been allocated were spacious without being grand, comfortable without verging on luxury. It seemed a pity not to take a peek in the others as Claudia passed, but Hor's room was locked, Paris's was so tidy it could pass for army barracks, while Semir's was a clutter of embroidered robes, combs, depilatories, beads, bangles and slippers, with enough oil to light the Capitol for a year. Not only did his bedroom smell like a Persian brothel, she mused, it bloody well looked like one, too.

Qeb's room was at the far end of the corridor, and he couldn't match Paris for neatness, but then he didn't have to. There was so little in it, even a Spartan would have complained. Still, a mere three pieces of furniture made the search simple. Claudia started with the bed, and found nothing of interest in the thin coverlet and flat pillow. She moved to the clothes chest, but it contained just two linen kilts, some spotlessly clean loincloths and a light, waterproof cloak. Which left the table, as sparsely decorated as the rest of the room. One razor, whose handle was shaped like a dung beetle, although quite why Egyptians imagined a replica dung beetle should protect them was beyond her. One alabaster bowl in which incense burned. And one looking glass with lotus flowers carved into the rim. What looked back at Qeb, she wondered? Was he aware of the slouch of his shoulders, the slow, almost clumsy walk? She replaced the mirror and turned to the only other personal item in his room.

He keeps a cheetah in his bedroom, Luci had whispered. *It's lovely and smooth and has blue lizards round its neck, but Mummy says I'm not allowed in there, so you won't tell her, will you?*

Hor, too, had been astonished when Claudia said she'd seen his brother's cheetah. It was the night of Marcia's banquet, and although the conversation had moved on, Hor deliberately switched back to the topic of the cheetah. She remembered how he'd leaned towards her, his eyes narrow.

You saw it?

And she remembered how he'd relaxed when she explained that she'd heard it, as well.

Heard? Oh. The menagerie, you mean.

At the time, she had merely filed it away in the library of her mind, because two creepy Egyptians was, frankly, one too many. Then Luci mentioned the cheetah, only what she omitted to say was that the cat was completely life-size. Expecting it to be wood, probably holm oak but possibly alder, Claudia was surprised at the echo that sounded when she rapped its side with her knuckles. It was clearly made out of terracotta, then laquered. The lapis lazuli that encircled its neck had been corrupted by a six-year-old's tongue into lizards, but the gems in the collar were authentic, and the cat felt warm to her hand.

'Please don't touch that.'

It was the longest sentence Qeb had probably ever spoken, and, goddammit, she hadn't heard the sneaky bastard approach.

'Why not?' She kneeled down at the cheetah's side. 'It's beautiful.'

'Yes, it is. Perfect. But I'd be obliged if you would respect my privacy, please.'

194

'This artwork has to be your brother's doing. The dark lines of the muscles. Yellow eyes that follow you round the room.' Claudia began to pick at one of the gems with her fingernail. 'And this gorgeous lapis lazuli collar!'

'I must ask you to be careful. That's a very fragile piece.'

'Really?' She slipped off a sandal and was about to bring it crashing down on the cheetah's ear when, to her astonishment, Qeb dived across the room and threw his arm round its encrusted neck.

'Don't!'

It wasn't his ability to move so fast that astonished her. Not even the way he protected the terracotta cat with his body, in much the same way Tarbel threw himself over his mistress. It was the tears that were coursing down his cheeks.

'Don't hurt my baby,' he sobbed. 'Please don't hurt my baby.'

Gooseflesh rippled down Claudia's arms. *Sweet heaven, what had she done?* Watching this big Egyptian blubbing his heart out, she suddenly realized she had totally misread this poor wretch. The incense should have alerted her, but now it made sense that the younger brother was looking after the elder one. Why Qeb shaved his head. Why Stella had forbidden the children to enter his room. And it was not because she was afraid for her brood . . .

The slouch, the refusal to meet other people's eyes, his inability to interact – for heaven's sake, these were the classic symptoms of grief! Add in the Egyptian custom of shaving heads during mourning, the burning of incense, the great dung beetle that rolled the sun across the heavens and everything fell into place. The cheetah was a terracotta sarcophagus.

Replacing her shoe, Claudia had never felt such a bitch – or been so glad she hadn't brought her sandal crashing down. How on *earth* could she have suspected this poor man of molesting a child?

'Your daughter?' she asked softly.

'She was only three.' He sniffed, wiping his eyes with the back of his hand. 'Three years old, can you imagine?'

Little by little the story unfolded, no doubt exactly as he'd confided to Stella, who would have homed in on his pain with the instincts of a magnet to metal. It was to protect Qeb that she'd banned her kids from his room, not the other way round. She'd felt the best way to let his heart heal would be without reminders of healthy, happy children constantly tearing at the open wound – and his story was tragic. Until the birth of their second baby, Qeb and his wife had no problems. They had a daughter, they adored her, she was three years old, her daddy was the keeper of a nobleman's menagerie and her mother was beautiful. But after the second baby arrived, something went horribly wrong. His wife couldn't stop crying. She'd stay in bed all day, wouldn't wash, wouldn't let anybody near her; she wouldn't touch or even feed the new baby. Qeb had been forced to hire a wet nurse.

'I knew she was ill,' Qeb stammered. 'Physicians examined her, but they said she'd get over it . . .'

How can you ever come to terms with walking in and finding your three-year-old daughter in bed with a pillow over her head? There was no sign of his wife or new baby, he said. It was a neighbour who eventually broke the news that she'd hurled herself under a chariot, the infant clutched to her breast . . .

'It's easy to talk to animals,' he said dully. 'If I'd only talked to my wife, got her to talk to me, she might have told me what demons were troubling her. Instead, the torment built up until it finally burst, and I did nothing to stop it.'

Angry and betrayed, feeling useless, impotent and raw, Qeb decided to bury his grief on the other side of the world. Feeding his animals in strict sequence, at set times and to a predetermined schedule – in other words, dominating time itself – was his way of coping, and, for once, Claudia thought, Stella was wrong. Happy healthy children around him was just the tonic this lonely, heartbroken man needed.

Orbilio was dreaming. In his dream, he seemed to be in a clearing in the forest. He saw acorns littered on the ground and, across the way, clusters of bright red berries of the mountain ash were being devoured by blackbirds. A sultry breeze ruffled the browning leaves, making them rustle. He appeared to be standing up, but since this was a dream it was just one more anomaly that his limbs weren't supporting him, something else was, and it was strange that a small fire should make such a disproportionate amount of smoke. Through the choking swirls, he heard voices talking in a dream language he couldn't understand, and the smoke smelled of catmint and clover, ivy and marsh tea – and wasn't that coriander seed and hemp as well?

Strangely, for a dream, there was a pounding in his temples that felt all too real, and a throbbing behind his eyes that meant he could hardly focus, while from somewhere strange music was made on unfamiliar instruments. Haunting, yet strangely rousing.

Orbilio didn't like this particular dream. He wanted to wake up and shake himself out of it. But it was not in his power to change things, only endure.

Above the trees the sun started to set.

Esus the Blood God tossed his horns and pawed at the ground with his hoofs.

His name had been called. His powers had been invoked. The oath that bound him to honour the old woman's plea for vengeance had been sealed by the final breath that passed from her body.

He paced the ground. She had called for retribution on the soul of her granddaughter's killer, and this could only come through hanging then skewering, that the victim's organs and blood might be drained from his body and his corpse left for the ravens to scavenge.

But who was to be hanged? Who was to be skewered, that his soul could never rest?

In frustration and rage, Esus the Blood God bellowed and roared.

High in the hills, in the cave from which the Spring of Prophecy bubbled from the rocks, the Arch Druid Vincentrix sat cross legged on the floor and watched as four tired celestial horses pulled the chariot of the Shining One towards the dusky horizon.

Seated beside him, the Horned One smiled.

Twenty-Five

Claudia, too, was watching the sun set. Every time Marcia instigated a manhunt, the Scarecrow outwitted the trackers, who quickly attributed his ability to send dogs round in circles to supernatural powers. Possibly. But unless Claudia missed her guess, the answer was much more prosaic. If he could outsmart the hounds, it was because he was lacing his trail with a substance that confused them, in which case a certain herb sprang to mind, whose properties regarding canine attraction would be unfamiliar to Gaulish huntsmen. Anise, bless its little white feathery flowers, was a very recent Roman import! However, on the latest manhunt the huntsmen had nearly caught him. It was only beside the banks of the Carent, when the dogs went spectacularly wild, that the Scarecrow's spoor was lost.

The trackers put this down to the gods no longer favouring him. To Claudia, it smacked of a last-ditch attempt of a man in the throes of panic to throw them off the scent, and she pictured him racing down to the river, the crashing of his pursuers growing ever closer, the baying of the hounds ringing louder in his ears. She saw him tossing the last of his precious aniseed water over the river bank, then diving in and swimming like an otter for his life. In fact, she almost felt sorry for him, as he hauled himself on to an overhanging branch and clambered high into a tree. *But only almost.*

With the soft scents of sage and parsley billowing on the breeze, she shifted position and wondered where Orbilio had got to.

'Rome's famous for its spectaculars and the "Scarecrow Special" is one I wouldn't miss for all the ghosts in Hades.' He had laughed, insisting that he be back at the villa by the fourth hour after noon, no later. Yet still he hadn't shown.

'Just make sure you're camouflaged,' she'd snapped back.

A pair of sandalled feet appeared at the end of a row of smallage. The skin was tanned deep olive, and it glistened with fragrant oils.

'The Greeks used thiss herb to crown the winners of the Nemean Games,' Semir said, and if he thought noblewomen dressed in green lying in the herb beds was unusual it didn't register on his expression. 'I grow eet because mixed with cheese and pine kernels it makes tasty stuffing. This batch iss not ripe for harvest, though,' he added, with a sad shake of his braids. 'Germination slow has been this year.'

'You're very good with plants, Semir. Knowledgeable, conscientious, you have a keen eye for the topiary . . .'

'Thank you.'

'It's not the compliment you think. As a plantsman, you can't be faulted, but you're no landscape artist . . .'

The gardens were neatly laid out and perhaps to an untravelled Gaul they were breathtaking in their design, but there was nothing remotely original about the planning, while the paths and water channels were little more than a geometry lesson.

'. . . and you're not a Babylonian, either.'

That night at the banquet had proved he knew an awful lot about Mesopotamia in general, but sod-all about Babylon itself, suggesting he'd boned up, though sadly not well enough. Also, no Babylonian would touch baked bread or meat on a Saturday, yet he'd wolfed them both while he planted Trojan irises as Claudia and Stella took lunch in the garden.

'I see.' He chewed his lip for a while. 'But since you hef not given me away, you are either very discreet or you want to blackmail me.'

A streetwise horticulturalist. Whatever next?

'I only blackmail the aristocracy and civil servants.'

His mouth relaxed into a broad, white smile. 'I am gardener not landscaper, eet iss true, but you know, Lady Clodia, eef I do a good job here, eef I make a really good impression in Gaul, my reputation iss made, no?'

'Why the skimpy loincloth, though? Why the bangles and beads?'

'You not think eet iss good idea that people notice me?'

199

'Fair point.' She laughed back. 'But a word of advice. Go easy on the scented oils.'

'Better to smell like ladyboy than be eaten alive by mosquitoes!'

As he continued his inspection, Claudia was reminded of the Greek king who was killed by a snake concealed among smallage, and shivered. 'Be careful, Semir. Marcia might, just, accept that you're not a landscaper, but she'll never forgive you for ripping her off.'

That wasn't wine the slave was watering her roses with, it was pond water, and that's why Semir avoided discussing the subject with a wine merchant. He was afraid of being found out.

'That woman hef no idea about plants. To Marcia eet's another way of showing off, telling her guests that she waters her gardens with wine. Wine would kill them!' A sly grin escaped from the corner of his mouth as he plucked off any yellowing leaves. 'But she iss happy, and what the slaves do with the wine iss not my problem, though eef you look at the quality of the leather some of them wear on their feet you might be forgiven for thinking that maybe they sell some of eet on the side. Like the fish, eh?'

'Fish?'

'Marcia sends slaves to buy fish at the market, but –' when he shrugged his olive shoulders, the bangles round his wrists jangled melodiously – 'she forgets two rivers and three streams run through her estate!'

Slowly, the sky turned six shades of crimson, bats took to the wing and nightingales trilled. Where are you, Orbilio? It's not like you to be late, and the Scarecrow wouldn't wait until darkness covered the valley. Fearful as he was, he couldn't afford to thrash around aimlessly in search of aniseed. Having heard the manhunt would be starting at dawn, and aware of the numbers involved, he would creep down at dusk, where the risk would far outweigh the consequences. No anise meant no luck. Without it, the Scarecrow stood no chance.

Wriggling on the warm, compacted earth, Claudia brushed the dust from her robe. Now there was a funny thing, she reflected. When she had returned to her room after her visit to Qeb, there was a box on her bed. Just a small wicker box a handspan in width, it wasn't from Orbilio, because it was empty and he would have left her a note. If she remembered, she'd ask one of the maids in the morning, and if she forgot, well, it was hardly the end of the world, was it?

Gradually, field hands filtered back to their quarters and the herb garden settled into quiet and stillness. Something rustled, perhaps a shrew or a snake, and a fox skulked along the hedge by the orchard. Then another pair of feet hove into view, peeping beneath a long, white, floating robe.

'Wrong time of day to be gathering leaves, Koros.'

The old man's lined face creased even further when it sneered. 'Do you presume to know more about herbs than me?'

'My cat knows more about herbs than you,' she retorted. 'She knows you collect them after the dew has evaporated, but before the heat from the sun has allowed the essential oils to escape. She knows you only harvest plants up to flowering time, before their energies are diverted into seed heads. And she knows that any herbalist worth his salt wouldn't dream of collecting more than one variety at a time.'

He snorted in derision. 'If you have any doubts as to the efficacity of my purges and linctuses, you only have to enquire of my patron.'

'And what a recommendation that is! You give Marcia syrup of figs to make her run to the latrines. You grate rhizomes of Basc peony to make her throw up.' Jupiter alone knows what the pepper enemas did. 'You're a fraud, Koros. Nothing but a fraud.'

'I'll have you know I'm a trained physician—'

'You're a fraud and a charlatan, and what's more I don't give a damn.'

His wizened jaw dropped, but it was true. Any woman who relied on quacks and potions, instead of taking responsibility for her own health, deserved every uncomfortable minute. Provided Koros wasn't poisoning the silly bitch – and a search of his room revealed nothing more than incompetence – Claudia had no complaint.

'On the other hand,' she shot him a radiant smile, 'I do object to your mischief-making.'

'This is monstrous!'

201

'Huff and puff all you like, you old fake, but Vincentrix didn't tell Marcia about the missing girls. You overheard Hannibal telling me, then you took the information straight to your mistress, knowing that she'd instigate a manhunt to catch the Scarecrow and claim the credit herself.'

'Why would I do that?'

'You mean apart from wanting to ingratiate yourself with your mistress, boosting your credibility and increasing your power over the other slaves?'

'I will collect my herbs another time.' The white beard jutted forward in anger. 'I don't have to take this from you.'

'Well, that's the funny thing, Koros. Actually, you do.'

Rheumy eyes flashed hatred for perhaps ten seconds, then the shutters came down. Placing his hands together, he pasted on his meaningless smile and bowed so deeply that his long white robes swept the dust. 'Your servant, my lady,' he said, backing away, and she made a note to test any foodstuffs left in her room.

Taking the doll from the folds of her robe, Claudia combed its hair with her fingers. Could Orbilio have sneaked in while she was sparring with Koros? Unlikely. He didn't believe the Scarecrow would come, so he'd want to do his gloating face to face, and maybe that was the answer. Maybe Marcus Cornelius was so sure of himself that he didn't see the point of turning up, full stop!

As the sky began to darken, her thoughts turned to her father. Where he was. What he was doing. Whether there were half-brothers and sisters of hers running around somewhere. Claudia still had absolutely no idea whether he was dead or alive, living in Santonum or even in Gaul. Would she recognize him, after all these years, she wondered? Would she even like him? And what would he make of her? She fingered the quality of her green linen gown, examined the rings on her fingers. Nothing of her old life remained, not even her slum accent, for him to recognize. What would he feel, when she eventually caught up with him? Happiness? Contrition? Guilt? Resentment at being hunted down like a stag? Despite the jitters in her stomach, Claudia was prepared for any, and all, of these things. Emotions didn't matter. All that mattered was the truth, because rich or poor, young or old, everyone reaps what they sow. Twenty-five years ago an army orderly sired a daughter. He made his home with her and her mother, a home that lasted ten years, and, no matter what prompted him to move on, no action is without consequence. A man cannot absolve himself of responsibility and pretend the past didn't happen. Like it or not, he would have to face Nemesis. As, indeed, would his daughter . . .

When the owl flew out of the tree, Claudia gave it no thought. It was the time of day owls set off hunting. Why not? Then she heard footsteps and was glad of the dagger still strapped to her calf. Crouching, the figure emerged from the woods. Keeping low to the ground, he moved cautiously, but unerringly, through the long rows of herbs. So then. He knew where the anise seeds were.

'Looking for this?' she asked.

There were many things a frightened man living rough in the woods might have bargained for, but a woman in green rising up from the tall ferns of fennel and tossing a doll at his feet wasn't one of them. He was literally too stunned to move.

'Who are you?' he whispered. '*What* are you?'

'Who I am doesn't matter. *What* I am is a friend of Luci's. Oh, and, if you're interested, I'm a friend of Stella's, as well.'

'Is . . . is she here?' Troubled eyes searched over her shoulder. 'Is Stella with you?'

'No.' Now he mentioned it, she hadn't seen Stella for several hours, nor Hannibal for that matter. 'And Luci's tucked up in bed.'

You mean Belisana?'

'Luci, Belisana, what's the difference? She's an endearing little thing, isn't she? Full of life and vitality, just like her mother, and with big blue eyes and blonde hair, the spitting image –' Claudia drew a deep breath – 'of her father.'

She hadn't been prepared for the resemblance to be quite so striking. Right down to the fair curls and dimples . . .

'I shouldn't have walked out on them,' he rasped. 'But there were too many children too quickly and I couldn't cope.'

'You were the one who pushed for a large family.'

'I know.' He rubbed his face with weary hands. 'But I was young, such an idealist in those days. I didn't realize babies would be such hard work or make so much noise. From the word go they demanded not just my time, but my energy. They sapped it all, night and day, until there was nothing left.'

Well, poor you.

'I couldn't sleep. One of them was always wanting something – a drink, a cuddle, reassurance after a nightmare. They drained me like a vampire drains blood and I couldn't stand being stifled by their lack of conversation. The sheer bloody repetitiveness of their games was driving me mad. Their endless questions and mindless chatter, I just had to get away.'

Sorry, he'd said in his note. *Sorry*. Never mind Stella. Never mind what she'd had to put up with (and twenty times over once he was gone). Never mind five tiny tots who cried themselves to sleep, waiting for Daddy to come home. Or number six on the way, whose mother would have no support with the birth, no money afterwards and what little strength she had left needing to be diverted into six demanding kids. No, you just feel sorry for yourself, chum.

'By walking out, I was released,' he said. 'Like a bird, I suddenly found I had wings. Without an identity, without a past, without responsibility, I was free! Free to live as I chose, go where I wanted, see places I had only dreamed of.'

'What places?'

Pain clouded his huge blue eyes. 'Well, that was the problem. It didn't take long to realize what I'd done. I honestly believed Stella would manage. She's such a strong, capable woman that it seemed natural that she would simply take over the business. After all, I'd left her the house, the estate, everything!'

'Everything except experience, freedom, the lack of demands of a young family.'

'I know, I know.' Tears made runnels through the grime on his face. 'I didn't get further than Massilia before my stupidity hit me, but it was winter and I fell sick. By the time I was well enough to travel, it was too late. Debt had forced her to sell and she was living here, under Marcia's protection.'

There were serious flaws with his arithmetic, Claudia mused. Stella didn't fall on hard times overnight. But she let him continue.

'I want to come home,' he wailed. 'I am so sorry for what

204

I put them through, dear god, you have no idea how sorry I am, but now I . . . I just want to come home, and I'm scared.' He wiped his eyes. 'I see the children playing. Laughing. Living Roman ways with Roman names. And I don't know how to tell Stella I'm here.'

Oh. Shit.

'I'll do anything she asks, anything! I'll never leave again, I swear. Only . . .' Pleading blue eyes as big as the Aegean turned to Claudia. 'I want us to be a family again. Can you understand that?'

She picked up the broken doll. Smoothed its ragged tunic and ran her hand over its carefully washed hair. Orbilio was right. This *was* a treasured possession. Probably Luci's (she was always leaving things behind). The Scarecrow had cared for it as though it was his own daughter.

'You're asking me to have a word with Stella? You want me to plead your cause, as a husband, a father, a sinner who repents all his sins.'

His face lit up. 'You said you were her friend.'

'I am,' she said softly, 'and that's why I cannot speak for you.' She handed him back the doll. 'There's only one person who can clear up this mess. You. The responsibility of fatherhood never goes away, and you can take my word for that.'

He drew a deep breath and she was surprised how much it was juddering. 'From the moment I moved into these woods, I knew the day would come when I had to stand up and be counted.' The Scarecrow put his head in his hands and waited until they stopped shaking. Finally, he looked up and this time when his eyes locked with Claudia's his gaze was steady. 'Will you help me?'

'I told you, I'm Stella's friend. Of course I'll bloody well help you. Only for heaven's sake let's get out of this field while we can still see where we're going!'

High in the hills, in the cave from which the Spring of Prophecy bubbled from the rocks, the Arch Druid Vincentrix stretched the long night out of his muscles and kicked over the traces of his fire in which his magic herbs still burned. Dawn was breaking in the east. The four horses that had galloped so despondently as they carried the Shining One on the last leg of yesterday's celestial journey had replenished their energies in the Paddocks of Plenty on the far side of the horizon. Now they were itching to be harnessed to the chariot that would light the last day before the autumn equinox, and Vincentrix smiled. Come midnight, the power of the gods would be restored. Come midnight, the blood that was owed them would be theirs.

One by one, the Druid pledged obedience to his gods.

First, he kneeled at the dainty feet of the Silver One, who sees everything from her star-studded chariot of night. Then he turned to face the Gentle One, who heals the sick and brings comfort to the dying, then the Flower Queen, the Horned One and the Thunderer. Finally, he made obeisance at the feet of the Ancient One, from whose tongue hangs fine gold chains from which the Knowledge of the Universe falls in tiny drips. Vincentrix closed his eyes and begged that one of these droplets might fall upon his unworthy head.

Far below, a cockerel crowed.

A cockerel crowed, and Hannibal stared at the figure before him. Mesmerized by the sweet bloom of youth, his eyes travelled over the curve of her breasts, the narrowing of her tight waist, the slenderness of her hips. Was any skin more flawless? Any eye more clear? A tentative hand reached out to touch the texture of her long, heavy hair. Captured at her peak, age would never raddle her internal organs or time brittle her bones, and the sun would never brown and wrinkle her perfect skin.

He placed a shaking hand against her cheek. The sweet bloom of youth was cold to his touch. Cold and stiff and unyielding. Soon, though, the sun would rise to warm this latest study in perfection . . .

As dawn cast her pink mantle over the sky, Hannibal held his head in his hands and wept.

Twenty-Six

A cockerel crowed, dawn cast her pink mantle over the sky and Claudia Seferius yawned.

She'd spent the night thrashing out a plan of campaign with Stella's husband and her head was throbbing from mental and physical exhaustion. All she wanted to do was drop into bed, but what chance of sleep with the slaves on the go and Stella's raucous brood yelling 'Mummy, where are you hiding this time?' at the top of their voices, and would you just listen to the baying of those damned tracking hounds, straining on the leashes in the yard!

Crossing the portico, she pushed her hair out of her face and rubbed the tiredness from her eyes. As the sun began to climb, its rays penetrated the thin veil of white cloud that was stretched over an azure blue sky. This was exactly like the skies over Tuscany this time of year, and if conditions back home were as fair as this then her bailiff would be organizing the workforce with his customary efficiency to gather the vintage. The cellars would have been fumigated well in advance, the treading floor scrubbed, the wine presses ditto, and she could almost hear the army of pickers singing hymns to Bacchus as their sharp knives sliced through the stalks and bunches of black grapes piled up in the baskets.

With Aquitania getting more hours of sunshine than anywhere in Gaul apart from the southernmost coasts, and with limestone soil that retained moisture up to sixty feet underground, wouldn't this area be good for growing vines, too? Claudia blew out her cheeks. Dammit, this was like an itch in the middle of your back that's just out of reach. You want to ignore it, but can't. As the smell of fresh bread coiled its tempting path from the kitchens, she realized there was an answer to itches like that. You get someone to scratch your back for you! There was no harm in bringing her bailiff over for a look. He'd be able to tell straight away whether vines would take to this climate, this soil, and it wasn't as though she was committed to the idea of expanding in Gaul. Hell, no, it hadn't even crossed her mind and—

'Where's Stella?' Marcia demanded. 'Only I will not tolerate children playing leapfrog in my atrium, and, would you believe, the girls actually had their robes tucked into their knicker cloth! It's a disgrace.'

'It sounds like fun.'

'It sounds like they need their bottoms spanked. I say, you! Yes, you with the birthmark!'

A secretary bumbled forward, stylus at the ready.

'Find their tutors. Tell them I didn't hire them to let these little savages run wild and that I've docked a week's pay from their salary. Then tell them to start bloody tutoring or they'll find themselves another week short. Come along!' Marcia snapped her fingers and the lackeys behind her jumped to attention. 'Padi cast his divining rods,' she told Claudia with a self-satisfied smile. 'They confirm the outlook for today's manhunt is good—'

'Indeed, Mistress,' a lisping voice called from the crowd. 'Both rods and stones speak only of success—'

'And Koros has prescribed Tarbel one of his special pick-me-up potions, isn't that correct, Koros?'

The old man shot Claudia a venomous glare from the corner of his rheumy eye. 'I have, my lady. My calamint and bottle-brush tea should prove most invigorating.'

I'll bet, Claudia thought, as the human snake continued on its way, and he must have slipped Marcia a cupful or two, because although Orbilio had persuaded her to postpone the manhunt for a day she obviously intended to follow it every inch of the way, and Claudia wouldn't like to be in Padi's soft sandals when it turned into another wild-goose chase! She smiled. If nothing else, the Scarecrow had ensured his place in Santon legend, because he was in the one place not even Tarbel would think of looking and . . . And . . .

'Croesus!'

If the Scarecrow wasn't killing these girls, then who was?
Every victim was perfect, Hannibal said. Plucked in the

208

bloom of youth. Primordial fear slithered under Claudia's ribs, and turned icy cold as she raced to Orbilio's room. Marcia's philosophy manifested itself in every square inch of this estate. From her painstakingly landscaped gardens to her exotic menagerie, from each piece of glorious statuary to that remarkable tomb destined for posterity, there was one common trait running through.

Perfection.

The killer, dammit, was stealing perfection and he had to be stopped before another innocent victim was sucked into his evil trap. Skidding on the marble outside Orbilio's bedroom, she thrust open the door.

'Marcus, get up! Get up, now!'

But the covers were neat, the pillows plumped, his washing water as clean as when it had been drawn from the well. That's why he wasn't around to witness her meeting with the Scarecrow. Orbilio hadn't come home last night. Claudia's legs turned to jelly. Never more had she needed the strong arm of the law, never more had she felt such a failure. So busy saving her own skin by proving the Scarecrow wasn't killing these girls, she had lost sight of the larger picture. That young women were being abducted by someone they trusted . . .

And Stella was nowhere to be found . . .

Orbilio was not dreaming now. What he'd thought was imagined was real. The forest, the clearing, the fire, the music. Even the chanting was real.

So, too, the throbbing inside his head.

They were waiting inside Zina's apartment. Poor cow, she wouldn't have thought twice about trusting the Druids and he wondered what tale they'd spun her once they'd rendered him unconscious. Whatever it was, he bet it was slick as they carried him out wrapped in a rug like Cleo-bloody-patra and threw him in the waiting cart. But why him? When he first returned to consciousness, it seemed ridiculous. A Roman patrician attached to the Security Police? What on earth would the Druids want with him? Information, he'd supposed, though what use kidnapping him and tying him to a tree in the middle of the forest was likely to be, he had no idea.

But his brain had still been befuddled at that point. A second

209

knock on the head in a fortnight. Hallucinogenic herbs on the fire. Who wouldn't have been confused? As time passed, however, and the pain in his head subsided, he began to realize that the Druids wanted nothing from him.

Nothing, except his life . . .

Suspicion became certainty when Vincentrix arrived in the clearing shortly after daybreak. Dressed in rich robes embroidered with symbols Orbilio didn't recognize, he took his seat on an oak throne at the head of a wooden table round which his fellow priests were already seated, and addressed them in their secret language. Carved keys were passed round from Druid to Druid – the infamous Keys of Wisdom, he supposed – before Vincentrix rose and strolled across to the prisoner bound to the sacred oak.

'You wonder why you have been chosen?' he said. 'The power of the gods has been waning, Marcus Cornelius Orbilio, and they need blood. Your blood is what's needed to restore their authority over our people. Your blood is rich, it is a sacrifice worthy of the Divine Ones, for it is Roman and the blood of our conquerors. Moreover, it is noble in birth and noble in character, and you need have no worry about a search party coming to rescue you. I have concocted a story to cover your absence.'

'Vincentrix, if you are going to kill me, do it quickly. Please don't bore me to death.'

The Arch Druid smiled. 'Courage, as well. This is good, my friend. Very good, and, if it comforts you in any way, I intend to gild your skull for my collection – a privilege, I might add, that is bestowed upon only a few.'

Withdrawing a small, hooked blade from its scabbard, he sliced away at Orbilio's tunic until his prisoner was naked.

'But before you get carried away by notions of bravery, you should know what lies ahead.'

Orbilio had long since recognized the smell of blood seeped into the bark. Knew the damage such a small blade could inflict, and over how much time . . .

He swallowed. 'Why don't you just surprise me?' he said, and there was no quaver in his voice.

'Rest assured, Marcus Cornelius Orbilio, it will surprise you.'

There was no emotion in the Druid's voice as he checked the knots on the prisoner's ropes.

'Tomorrow, the planets align with the seasons. Night with

210

day, earth with fire, wind with water, every element unites with its counterpart. It is the way of the universe, and at midnight tonight, in fact at the very turn of the autumn equinox, the gods will see their powers restored, but –' he shrugged – 'the sacrifice does require a full day's preparation.'

A day. It would take a full day to die . . .

'First comes the scourging. The testing of the threshold of pain. That will commence now –'

The ferocity of the lash arched his back like a bow and sucked the air from his lungs.

'– and lasts for the length of this candle, after which we apply the Forty Sacred Cuts, and do not be afraid to scream, Marcus. Every man does, there is no shame, and in any case no one can hear you.'

The pounding in his ears came not from the cane that was being so expertly applied to his body. It came from the knowledge that he would die when there were still so many mountains to climb. Mother of Tarquin, there were so many places he hadn't seen, so many things left unsaid. The future that had looked, even this morning, rosy and golden was now merely dust at his feet. Failure that he was, he couldn't even boast children to carry his ancestry forward or glorious deeds to make his family proud – and he was glad now that he hadn't told Claudia that he loved her. Drawing a deep, shuddering breath, he counted to three.

'I can hardly wait to hear what you serve for dessert,' he said between gritted teeth.

'Death is not to be embraced hastily, my friend. After the Forty Sacred Cuts comes the Breaking of Fingers, then the Renunciation of Manhood.'

Vincentrix examined the hook of what Orbilio suddenly realized was a castration knife.

'Another marriage of elements. Human seed to fertilize our Mother Earth, and then, only then, Marcus Cornelius Orbilio, do we embark upon our ultimate sacrifice.'

At the flick of his wrist, a huge wicker frame was wheeled into the clearing. The frame had been fashioned in the shape of a man.

'At midnight exactly, when the stars are in perfect alignment, your ash will rise to the gods on the wind, and, yes, of course you will be alive for the burning.'

211

Twenty-Seven

'Did you find him?' Claudia asked, as Junius came striding down Marcia's elegant colonnade.

The young Gaul shook his head. 'At the barracks, they said he'd received an urgent tip-off about a forgery ring in Burdigala and gone straight off.'

'Rubbish. His belongings are still here.'

'Apparently not, my lady. It appears he sent someone to pack his things and send them on.'

'Orbilio?' She blinked. 'Are you sure?'

'His room is empty,' Junius confirmed, 'and I checked the apartment opposite the basilica, as you instructed, but there's nothing of his in there, either.'

In retrospect, Claudia wasn't sure there ever had been. 'What about Curvy Thighs?' she asked. 'What did she say?'

'The girl wasn't home. According to a neighbour, she screamed blue bloody murder when she found that he was gone and was last seen charging off like a horse with its tail on fire.'

Claudia wondered why that should leave her with a warm glow of contentment.

'There was one odd thing I noticed, my lady. I saw what looked like blood on the door jamb.'

Visions of Zina trying to kill Orbilio and throwing a tantrum when she found the 'body' gone flashed through Claudia's mind. Unfortunately, there were several things wrong with that theory, not least the fact that if a strong girl like that had wanted to kill him she wouldn't have bungled the job!

'Orbilio's a big boy.' Claudia dismissed the stain. 'He's perfectly capable of looking after himself. It's Stella I'm worried about.'

'Luci was the last to see her,' Junius said solemnly. 'She said her mother promised to play butterflies with her.'

A knot tightened in Claudia's stomach. 'Find Hannibal,' she said. If Orbilio wasn't around to track down the killer of these missing girls, Hannibal should help. 'He must have been co-opted into the manhunt,' she added. Why else hadn't he been bowling around with the children?

'I fear not,' Junius said. 'I've just come from his quarters and you wouldn't know they'd ever been used.'

The portico started to spin, but she didn't know why. Hannibal said it himself, he couldn't be tied to one person or place, and it wasn't as though the Security Police didn't chase criminals all round the Empire, either. Not just Aquitania. She'd bumped into Orbilio in Sicily, Umbria, Histria, and even the little island of Cressia in the Liburnian archipelago turned out to have investigators round every corner. So what that Marcus took off without saying goodbye? What did it matter that he left without explanation? She clutched at a spinning pillar. That's what men did, wasn't it? Bugger off when you least expected it.

'Then it's down to you and me to find who's responsible for these women disappearing,' she told Junius. 'And if perfection is their stock in trade, it means they're here. On this estate.'

Colour drained from the young Gaul's face. 'And you think Stella is his latest victim?' He made a gesture she hadn't seen before. 'May the Hammer God strike pity on those poor children,' he whispered.

'We don't know for certain that she's dead.' Who knows what the bastard did to them first? 'There's every chance we can save her, Junius.'

'Where do we start looking? This estate is enormous, she could be anywhere. And who, my lady? Who would be responsible for such a terrible crime?'

Who indeed? Padi and Koros were both perfectionists in the art of bullshit, but neither seemed capable of murder. Their aim was more subtle, their ambition more cunning. Each was intent on turning slave into master by making Marcia reliant on them. Padi achieved this through his soothsaying nonsense, telling her whatever she wanted to hear, while Koros was controlling Marcia's health – and how soon before he added an extra irritant in the purge, a stronger narcotic at bedtime, before she was

213

fully dependent on her physician? Slaves they might be, but each had recognized her vulnerability and were exploiting it for all they were worth. Murder was not in their sphere.

'The tomb!' Claudia clicked her fingers. 'We've got to get to the tomb!'

'Why?' Junius asked, as they pelted through the gates, down the hill.

'Because every able-bodied male has been assigned to tracking the Scarecrow today, and that's the one place privacy can be assured.'

Not in the forest, with teams of hunters criss-crossing backwards and forwards. Not in the house. (Never in the house!) It could only be Marcia's tomb the killer had taken her to.

As they crashed down the path past the herb beds, it seemed to Claudia that it was surely a million years ago that she had hidden herself in the fennel to wait for the misfit who lived in the woods. What is it about lonely people that drives them to destroy the one thing that could have made them happy? A man has everything he could wish for. A loving wife, a thriving business, children who adore him, yet he tosses them aside because he feels stifled.

Marcia was the same. It was loneliness that had driven her to become so ruthless in her business dealings that grown men feared her, so pitiless to her staff that they trembled at the sight of her shadow. Being sold into prostitution at the age of twelve taught her to be manipulative and devious, the need to survive outweighing everything else, until it reached the point where, hardened by her experiences, she was incapable of normal emotions. Control was her substitute for love, and sure she was happy to bleed Claudia dry when it came to finding out whether vines would thrive on Aquitanian hillsides, but that wasn't the reason she'd invited her to stay at the villa.

At the time, Claudia had hoped to pick up a few tips from the richest woman in Santonum, but in practice it was the other way around. Marcia had no idea that Claudia wasn't the wealthy, successful wine merchant she purported to be, and by surrounding herself with people on whom Fortune smiled Marcia hoped that happiness would rub off on her. And that by offering lavish hospitality, they would stay . . .

214

How sad that she constantly threw away her real chance of happiness. A succession of young studs lined up to bed her, but, since sex alone wasn't enough for a sophisticated and educated woman, she threw them out because they bored her. Yet, if she'd only been patient (and not looked down her nose because they were Gauls), she might well have ended up with a devoted young husband who worshipped the ground she walked on, eternally grateful for the wealth and education he'd been given.

'It has to be the tomb,' Claudia said, as they reached the stream. 'Because the killer has to be someone who can come and go without arousing the suspicion of the professionals.'

'Whilst taking advantage of the deserted work huts for his grisly task,' Junius added grimly.

Mighty Jupiter, don't let Stella be dead! Let us find her laughing. Shaking that cascade of dark, glossy hair down her back. Let her be calling her children monsters when her tone implied angels, or playing barrels as she rolled the littlest one down the garden path. For pity's sake, please. Just let us find her alive . . .

The little bridge blurred beneath Claudia's feet. Too late, too late, too late, her sandals rumbled. Too late, too late, too late, the timbers echoed back.

She scrubbed the tears from her eyes. Marcia's vulnerability had left so many cracks for maggots to crawl through that the villa was infested, for the rot ran far deeper than Koros and Padi. Tarbel, too, was living a lie, even if it took someone else to make him see it, and Semir, of course, went without saying. How he'd sold Marcia the idea that he could recreate the famous Hanging Gardens she had no idea. Nebuchadnezzar died, what, five centuries ago? He couldn't possibly have any idea how to replicate the famous gardens, never mind that the conditions for planting in Gaul weren't remotely similar to Babylonia, even allowing that such flowers could survive the climate or the long journey! Yet such was Marcia's ego that she'd swallowed his sales pitch hook, line and sinker, and whatever kind of garden Semir ended up giving her she would have no doubts that it was a genuine replica. To question his authenticity was to question her own, and reality had long since slipped off Marcia's agenda. The estate, the villa, the

215

gardens, the tomb – together these things combined to create a world of their own. A world so isolated from reality that it was almost a fantasy, where a lonely, damaged woman could feel safe, without knowing she had also created a perfect breeding ground for other, more destructive fantasies.

'You search those huts!' Claudia shouted. 'I'll check these.'

Every man Marcia had hired was a perfectionist, yet each was a worm in the apple of her integrity. Hor might be famous throughout Alexandria, but a man who only painted scenes that showed his patron in a flattering light? Exquisitely executed or not, no artist worth his reputation would lower himself to that level, even for his brother's sake, while Paris sculpted faces on figures carved by others. Talented, undoubtedly, but hardly what Marcia was paying such exorbitantly high prices for.

'Nothing?' She couldn't believe it. 'Are you sure?'

'I've checked and double-checked,' Junius said. 'There's nothing here.'

How *could* she have been so wrong? Claudia slumped down on a half-chiselled plinth. In the forests, mournful hounds sneered at her stupidity and the lump in her stomach was lead. Silly bitch. If you'd only thought things through – talked it over with someone – with Orbilio – you wouldn't have wasted so much time.

Time Stella didn't have . . .

Sagged against the ropes that bound him so tightly to the oak, Orbilio felt as though every inch of his skin was on fire. What a ridiculous way to discover the secrets of the Druids, he thought. What a ridiculous time to learn the ways of their torture.

At first, he truly believed he could take it. A candle burns while he is flogged. His blood runs out in Forty Sacred Cuts. His fingers are snapped. By the time he's dragged into the wicker frame, he'd probably be grateful.

How wrong could he be?

It wasn't that he'd underestimated the excruciating pain of the lash. It was the way the cane was designed to inflict maximum pain for minimal damage and, as Vincentrix so calmly pointed out, determine a man's threshold for pain.

216

The other surprise was that his life – or more accurately his death – was to be measured in a series of candles. He couldn't see how many were left, but they'd used the second to pour refreshing water down their victim's throat and lay soothing compresses on his lash marks. The bastards, goddammit, were reviving him.

The Druids wanted their sacrifice very much screaming and kicking when the flame to the wicker man was finally lit.

'Dammit, Junius, I was *certain* the killer brought his victims here.'

Claudia wanted to move, but her limbs were as heavy as the marble blocks that surrounded her, and the lead in her stomach had turned cold. Despite the warm autumn sun, she was shivering, but there was no comfort in this haven of eternal tranquillity. Not in the soft, swirling particles of white dust, nor the chip-chip-chip of Paris's chisel, nor the flicker of Hor's oil lamp as he worked on his frescoes, his body almost as white as the linen of his kilt as he stretched on tiptoe to apply the finishing touches to his latest scene.

'My lady?' There was a strange expression on her bodyguard's face as he tugged at her sleeve. 'I think maybe the killer did bring the girls down here.'

His dagger was drawn, she noticed. And the grip round the handle was tight.

'Look over there.'

The lead in her stomach flipped over. 'I—'

'Look at the caryatids, my lady.'

'I've seen them.'

Pretty girls in floaty robes holding up Marcia's tomb for posterity, they were brilliantly sculpted, considering the man was a fraud. He might be Greek, he might well come from Myceanae and, hell, Paris might even be the sculptor's real name – but he wasn't 'the' Paris. That's why he'd avoided meeting prominent people at the banquet. Rome, at least wealthy, influential Rome, was a relatively small world, and word would quickly spread that he was too young/too blond/ too heaven-knows-what to be the genuine article. Which wasn't to deny Paris his talent. That fourth nymph along he'd given deep dimples, another one had been assigned a cute little

217

snub nose, while the caryatid he was working on now, the one with the huge eyes, he'd endowed with arguably the most curvaceous legs any woman could hope to put on show for eternity . . . *Oh, sweet Janus.* Claudia turned a bloodless face to her bodyguard's.

'Those aren't imaginary women holding up the roof, are they?'

'No, my lady.' His face was ashen as well. 'They're real.'

She hadn't known the root-cutter's flighty young wife or met the young basket-weaver or known the girl who'd churned cheeses. But Brigetia, the tanner's daughter, had deep dimples, had she not? And didn't the sister of the man who made millstones have a snub nose? Of course, they could be coincidence. Features that any brilliant sculptor might add to give his caryatids the individuality that lifted his work above the average.

But the girl Paris was chipping away at now, the girl with the big black eyes and the curvy thighs, was no coincidence. That was Zina. And all Claudia could think of was how Marcus would take the news that the boatbuilder's daughter was dead.

The third candle had burned two-thirds of the way down, and Orbilio had learned something new.

The Forty Sacred Cuts was not a ritual the Druids liked rushed.

He forced his mind to go to another place. Another time. Anywhere, please god, except here . . .

The blade was gleaming in the sunlight, as the bastards intended, but ignore it. Rise above them. Think about something else. Anything. Herbs. Think of the herbs. In those quantities, the combination of catmint, clover, marsh tea and bay heaped on the smoking fire could conjure the very egg that hatched from Chaos at the dawn of the world. Once you mixed them with hemp and coriander seeds, as was happening here, the effect was hardly surprising, and had they been Roman priests it would be the Olympians the Druids would be talking to in the forest. The Egyptians, of course, would be welcoming Isis and Osiris to their table, the Assyrians would be paying homage to Mylitta and Asshur, and no doubt the

Sabaean Arabs would be bringing down the sun, the moon and the stars. Indeed, such herbs had kept the Delphic Oracle in gold, so for Orbilio to see his own family massed in the clearing was hardly surprising.

His mother, wincing as each slash of the knife burned his body. *I love you, son.*

His brother, shaking his head with that same degree of told-you-so smugness he'd worn from early childhood. *Didn't I warn you about joining the Security Police?*

His father. *For Croesus' sake, if you couldn't be a lawyer or continue the family name, couldn't you at least have died honourably on the fucking battlefield?*

Uncles, cousins, aunts and siblings clustered closer, some of them living, some of them dead, but every one of them censuring him. Marcus shook the runnels of blood from his eyes. He forced his mind away from the pain to concentrate on what little understanding he had of hallucinogenic herbs. How people see not so much what they want to see, but what they have been conditioned to expect. Which probably explained why the one face he longed for wasn't in the crowd.

As the point of the knife danced under his skin, it was Claudia's name that went round in Orbilio's head.

But the word he screamed out was as primeval as the dark, silent forest.

When confronted by absolute perfection, trivia such as the noise of the tracker dogs and the relentless glare of the sun was blocked out. Concentrating on the chisel that was an extension of his own hand, the Watcher transformed straight Gaulish locks into tight Roman curls, which he tied up in a neat Roman ribbon. Just the one. Only married women, like the second caryatid in the line, were permitted to wear the double band.

Chipping away as he decided the ribbon should be painted the same vibrant green as her gown, Paris reflected on the improvement that long, flowing robes made compared to the short Santon skirt. They lent an air of maturity and elegance that had been stifled by the garish colours and deep fringe, yet retained every ounce of her feminine vibrancy.

'You are lovely,' he whispered, glancing along the line. 'You are all lovely, Women of Caryae. You are the most beautiful women in the world and nothing can taint you now.'

'Immortal and immortalized,' a woman's voice said. 'Plucked in the rosebud of life.'

For a moment, Paris was confused. The voice. Had it come from inside his head? Surely his caryatids were not so alive that they could speak? Then he realized there was someone standing beneath his ladder, and his pulse raced at the sight of this specimen of physical perfection.

'You guessed,' he said sadly, descending the ladder. 'What a pity. Such a terrible waste.'

'Why? Aren't I good enough to join the line-up?'

'Not good enough?' Paris laughed. 'With those flashing eyes and wayward curls you are perfect. You have no idea how often I've imagined sculpting your perfect cheekbones and sensual lips.'

'But?'

The chisel turned in his hand.

'But,' the Watcher sighed, 'I could not place you among my Women of Caryae, any more than I could risk the slave girls from the villa being recognized, or Stella, or—'

'Stella's *alive*?'

Paris shrugged. 'Why wouldn't she be? To have her face smiling proudly from Marcia's tomb would be to undermine a whole lifetime's work—'

'There have been others before this?'

'You sound shocked.'

As his foot touched the ground, he employed the same reas-suring smile he'd used on the others when he'd chosen his moment. So easy, too. All it needed was a charcoal and parch-ment. *Would you think it an awful liberty if I sketched you?* Everyone knew Paris – *the* Paris, no less – created statues in human likeness. Who could resist the ultimate in flattery?

'Yes, Claudia, there have been others.'

Without charcoals or paper he would have to rely on the sex appeal he deliberately cultivated. Tossing his head, he waited for the hair to flop back into place. Sun-bleached hair that accentuated his bronzed skin and solid muscles. Muscles that could so easily wrap round a girl's chin, lifting her body clear of the ground . . .

220

'Beauty is all around us and, thanks to me, it remains timeless.'

He tossed down the chisel and enjoyed the surprise that flared up in her eyes. *What a waste*, he had said, and he meant it. Not to have donated such perfection to posterity was nothing short of a crime, and there was no chance of using her in Marcia's garden now, either, where her beauty could have been sustained through the centuries. All the same, he could not bring himself to tarnish perfection. That was the job of rats and maggots. For a man whose life had been dedicated to female excellence, Paris was determined not to keep to his usual methods. Hand round chin to cover her mouth and then, while the body was off the ground, thus powerless to scream or leave traces of struggle, the fingers of his other hand were free to ram up her nostrils. As always, though, death takes its time. Each caryatid fought like a wildcat, but a sculptor's hands are strong, his patience legendary. He ensured they died without blemish or flaw.

'Worry cannot shrivel their unlined faces,' he told her. 'The pains of growing old and enduring hardship has been removed, and in their place I have given them perpetual peace, whilst ensuring their beauty remains eternal.'

'You – excuse me, but I need to make quite sure I've got this right. In killing these girls you've done them a *favour*?'

'You seem surprised.'

'Actually, Paris, I think you're the one in for a surprise. Ready, boys?'

For a man who spent so much time watching, it astonished him how three men – the Gaul bodyguard, Qeb and Hor – could spring out of nowhere without him even having been aware of their presence.

'You bitch!' he screamed, as rough hands tied him up. 'You dirty, double-dealing, distracting bitch!'

'I will accept that as the perfect compliment,' she replied.

As more herbs were tossed on the Druids' fire, so the hallucinations increased. There was the Governor of Aquitania standing alongside his boss from the Security Police, both bemoaning the lack of stamina in employees these days. Even Orbilio's old nurse had appeared, and, hell, she'd died before he'd turned eight.

I told you to eat your parsley, Marcus. It makes your blood strong.

He wanted to take issue with that. It seemed to him that his blood was strong enough, judging from its copious donation.

'The gods take heart from your courage, Marcus Cornelius Orbilio.'

Vincentrix's sepulchral tones overrode the stridency of the long-dead nurse and Orbilio tasted blood and sweat on his tongue as another exhausted candle was removed from the spike. Once a new one was lit, soft cloths began blotting at his wounds and his brow was sprinkled with water.

'The Horned One is especially pleased with the sacrifice you are making—'

'Go to hell.'

'Defiance is good. It shows spirit and guts, and the gods commend me for the choice of sacrifice.'

'Tell me, Vincentrix, is it art you're making on my body, or are you merely marking me out for a chessboard?'

The Arch Druid's lips pursed as the candle flame guttered and died.

'What a shame I have to deny you reincarnation,' he said, as the priests withdrew their bloodied cloths and bowls of sweet water. 'You have a warrior's soul that deserves more, but rest assured you will not depart without honour, for I intend your skull to become my libation bowl.'

'Unfortunately for you, I've never had a head for drink.'

The Druid laughed as he lit another candle.

'I admire a man who makes jokes through his pain, because I know how much you are hurting, my friend. I know exactly how much you are hurting.'

Did he? Orbilio thought. Did he really? Did he have any idea of the nausea that accompanied it? The burning, the throbbing, the white flashing lights? The noises inside his head? Did he have any concept at all of how it felt, knowing your life was measured by the wick of a set of candles that never seemed to burn fast enough? Of being completely and utterly helpless? *Of the shame of not being able to die?* Why bother castrating the victim, he wondered dully, when he'd emasculated himself?

222

'No, you don't,' he sighed. 'You don't know what pain is, Vincentrix, because you don't know love.'

Emotion flickered behind the Druid's green eyes as he applied the twenty-first sacred cut.

'I know love, Marcus Cornelius Orbilio, and because of it – twenty-two – I know pain.'

'Wrong.'

Twenty-three. He gasped for breath.

'You only know the obsession, rejection and humiliation of unrequited love.'

Why was he doing this? Why was he taunting his torturer, the man who could only prolong his death agonies?

Vincentrix frowned as number twenty-four exploded under Marcus's armpit. 'Why do you smile?'

He couldn't answer until twenty-five stopped slicing his inner thigh.

'You wouldn't understand,' Marcus wheezed, as twenty-six brought a torrent of sweat down his face.

The joke was not that he was taunting Vincentrix. That business about obsession, rejection, unrequited love, that was himself he was talking about, and what irony! Bound, whipped, blood pouring from his wounds and with castration and burning to follow . . . yet he can't resist torturing himself alongside!

'Pain affects people differently,' Vincentrix said kindly, as twenty-seven and twenty-eight went in crosswise. 'For some, humour is their defence mechanism.'

As twenty-nine slid under his fingernail, Orbilio forced himself to focus on his ever-swelling audience. Family and colleagues had been joined by several of the slimeballs he'd tracked down over the years. He noticed a vicious Armenian rapist among the crowd. The baby-faced child killer who'd stalked the city of Rome. The wealthy patrician woman who'd poisoned her family for the simple reason they bored her.

As more herbs were heaped on the fire, the hallucinations changed. Now a unicorn – a white unicorn, to be precise, with a gold horn – came charging into the clearing. With a whinny, it rose up on its hind legs before galloping off in a thunder of hooves. As the cloud of dust settled, a woman was standing where the unicorn had reared up. The woman was dressed from head to foot in white.

223

Orbilio suddenly became aware of a sense of weightlessness descending over his body. Having conjured up the world and his wife from inhaling the drugs, it was only fair that he conjured up her. Sweet Juno, it was all he had wanted.

To see her face before he died.

'For heaven's sake, Vincentrix, don't pretend you haven't seen me shapeshift before.'

Despite the blood and the pain, Orbilio laughed. Trust Claudia Seferius to induce a better class of hallucination!

The Arch Druid picked up the knife that had slipped from his hand and wiped the blade on his robes. She could read the uncertainty in his piercing green eyes. Unicorns were a myth, he was thinking. They did not exist. Yet he had seen one with his very own eyes, white with a single gold horn, and now the woman who had left him tied and bound to his own chair stood in its place. There was something else glittering in those piercing green eyes, too, she noticed. And that something else was not very pleasant.

'You honour us, Claudia Seferius.'

He bowed.

'Your arrival is impressive by any standards. But to what do we owe this pleasure?'

'Isn't it obvious?'

She forced herself to look at him. Not at the bloodied lump of meat tied to the oak. That only made her legs weaker.

'I've come for a word with Orbilio.'

'A . . . word?'

'Well, a couple really. It's just that we go back a long way, Marcus and me, and I didn't want us to part on bad terms.'

'You realize you cannot save him, don't you? He is our sacrifice to the gods, and since you are surrounded by Druids and the families of Druids you must understand that there is no escape for this man.'

He didn't wait for her answer.

'I know you are alone here, Claudia Seferius. Your bodyguard is a Gaul and he is terrified of our powers, and your only other ally, Hannibal I think they called him, has gone.'

All the way from the villa she kept telling herself that Vincentrix had been manipulated every bit as much as he

224

manipulated his people today. The minute this lovelorn dupe had stepped ashore in Britain, the Collegiate had seized upon the opportunity of turning a vulnerable youth into an obedient puppet by construing his enforced celibacy as a 'special gift' and twisting his turbulent emotions until he was sucked so thoroughly into the vortex that was Druidism that he couldn't see any other life. Using the same cheap smoke and mirrors tricks he would later employ on his own subjects, they'd taken him on a road he had no desire to travel and brainwashed him so completely that, all these years on, he still didn't realize he'd started the journey. Vincentrix was a victim just as much as his fellow Santons, kept in mental subjugation by his 'superiors' and imprisoned in his religious beliefs. But it did not give him the right to take life for no reason. *Especially not in this way.*

'Never trust your own eyes, Vincentrix.' She thought of the box left on her bed. 'But that isn't the point.'

Her mind flew back to the short time ago (was it really only a couple of hours?) when Junius, Hor and Qeb were manhandling a struggling Paris up to the villa and the box fell out of the folds of her robe.

'W-where did you get that?' Junius rasped.

'Hannibal left it as a farewell gift,' she laughed, shaking the empty box. 'A pun on the salary I didn't pay him.'

'Go on without me,' Junius instructed the others. 'Lock Paris in the cellar and keep guard.' When he'd turned to face Claudia, his face was grey. 'Hannibal didn't leave this, my lady.' The young Gaul's voice was barely audible in the stillness. 'And the box isn't empty. If you open it –' his hand was shaking as he lifted the lid – 'You'll find it contains a small pinch of ash.'

'Ash?'

'From the last wicker man sacrifice.'

Her knees had given way. The callous, evil, cold-hearted bastard had left her a message, in the sure and certain knowledge that she'd never find the place where the wicker man burned, in punishment for what she'd done to him in his own house . . .

'I knew I shouldn't have sheathed that bloody knife. I should have slit his bastard throat there and then.'

There are places in this forest, Hannibal had said, *a full*

225

day's march from here where the soil is black from scorching and where the stains against the oak are suspiciously sticky.

If only she had demanded proof! If only she'd insisted that he show her, take her to that dreadful place, she could have saved him!

The wicker man is not dead, madam, I assure you. The Collegiate has not given up its ways.

'Hannibal's the only person who knows where the Druids make their vile sacrifice,' she said hollowly, 'and now Hannibal's gone, and even if we could find the place a day's march is too late.'

'And when I said a day's march,' a fruity voice droned in her ear, 'I was referring to the Druids' processional pace. On a fast horse, we can be there in two hours. Oh, and madam –' he clicked his tongue in castigation – 'I told you before, Hannibal never leaves without saying goodbye.'

A fast horse, he said – plus a bit of fast thinking on her part. All it needed was a change of clothing and a gold trumpet and it was Find the Pea all over again. Oh, Vincentrix, Vincentrix. When will you learn!

'And what *is* the point, Claudia Seferius?' The Arch Druid's eyes mocked her. 'What exactly is the point of your visit?'

'I want you to spare your prisoner—'

'Impossible.'

'Until that candle butt burns down.'

Sacrifice was one thing. She glanced at the huge wicker frame. But she'd imagined he would be in one piece when they strapped him in. *Oh, Marcus, Marcus. What have they done to you?* She drew a deep breath. Held it until the shuddering subsided.

'Two fingerfuls,' she said, and if the Druid noticed her too-even tone it didn't show on his face. 'Two fingerfuls of a candle is all that I'm asking.' She forced a bright smile. 'Surely that's not an unreasonable request?'

Green eyes travelled round his fellow priests gathered in the clearing. Eager faces that demanded leadership and most of all direction.

'Very well.' Vincentrix nodded. 'The Roman's life is spared for the rest of that candle butt.'

226

'You give me your word as a priest and a Druid?'

He bowed. 'You have my word as a priest and a Druid.'

Claudia snipped Orbilio's cords.

'Good,' she said crisply, blowing out the candle and dropping the stub down her cleavage. A pity Vincentix hadn't thought to ask whether she intended to keep it alight. 'Now do hurry up, Marcus. This chanting is really starting to grate on my nerves.'

Twenty-Eight

The autumn equinox dawned soft and golden, the air heavy with the drowsy calls of wood pigeons and pungent with the scent of ripe mushrooms. Deep in the forests, the sharp tusks of boar turned up beechmast under leaves that rustled in the warm breeze and hawfinches cracked open the stones of fallen damsons. A sense of change was everywhere. In the massing of swallows. In the shrivelling of brackens and ferns. In the dulling of the roe deer's coat to a darker greyish-brown.

Nowhere was the sense of change more prevalent than at the villa.

Claudia watched from the gallery as cases and trunks piled up in the atrium below. For the people of Santonum, as with Gauls everywhere, the equinox was sacred. A time of reflection and prayer as the Demon Star rose bluish-white in the east and the battle for winter commenced at last. But here at the villa the observances were Roman, and thus it was business as usual as slaves lugged crates and chests into the courtyard.

'If you expect me to pay you for walking out on your contracts, think again!' Marcia barked. 'I have every intention to sue you.'

'Your lawyer will find us in Alexandria,' Hor said, wrapping the lacquered cheetah in blankets. 'My regret is not that we haven't been paid, Marcia, only that we ever left.'

The brothers had explained to Claudia yesterday, as they hauled Paris away from the tomb, that the only reason Hor had accepted this commission was to help Qeb overcome his grief. It didn't matter one iota, Hor added, that the paintings were twisted exaggerations of the truth. As far as he was concerned, Gaul was the back of beyond and he didn't expect anyone to see the damn things, anyway. Qeb's well-being

228

was all that concerned him. Pride and money were never an issue.

'And who's supposed to look after the menagerie?'

'I am taking the king cobra back to Egypt,' Qeb replied politely, and Claudia noticed the first hint of dark hair growing back on his skull. 'She is too dangerous to leave, but you should have no trouble finding a competent keeper for the rest.'

'Where the hell do you think *you're* going?' This time Marcia rounded on Tarbel. 'Did I give you permission to leave?'

'I gave myself permission.'

'If this is because the manhunt ended in failure, don't blame yourself. The Scarecrow obviously uses some kind of substance to put the hounds off the track, we just need to identify what, and in any case it was Paris killing those poor girls, not the woodsman.'

'My resignation has nothing to do with the manhunt,' Tarbel rumbled. 'The reasons . . .' Chestnut eyes flashed up to the woman leaning with her elbows on the rail overhead. 'The reasons are personal.'

Marcia snorted as they trooped out one by one. 'Rats deserting the sinking ship,' she said dismissively. 'Who needs scum like that, anyway?'

Claudia smiled to herself as she descended the stairs. Marcia's ship wasn't in any danger of sinking. Another rocky sea to cross, maybe. But this woman – painted and pointed, and with her beauty fading – was too much of a survivor for the boat to capsize.

'They're not rats,' she said, 'but they have no choice. To work on a site where mass murder took place is to have their reputations tarnished for ever.'

She'd misjudged Hor. He obviously *was* famous throughout the whole of Alexandria, so there was no question of his not finding another commission. Qeb's role as menagerie-keeper came through inheritance, so he wouldn't have trouble either, and such was Semir's love of horticulture that this would only be a small setback in his fragrantly oiled, braided career.

'Provided you water the rosses twice a week with white wine, they'll be fine,' he'd told Marcia, slipping Claudia a

229

sly wink as he kissed his patron's hand in farewell. 'And don't forget to give your fruit trees a gallon of red every month.'

Alone once more, Marcia was as close to tears as she would ever be as a dozen legionaries wielding sledgehammers tramped past in metallic precision.

'You realize those bastards are about to dismantle my tomb?'

Claudia goggled. 'You can't seriously want the caryatids to stay?'

'Why not? To smash the statues is to have the girls die for nothing.'

Strangely, she had a point. 'Have they found where Paris buried the bodies?'

'Not yet, but no doubt it'll be Semir's landscaping they ruin next.'

Definitely, Claudia decided. That ship is definitely unsinkable!

'I'm sorry you're leaving as well, Claudia, but with the seas closing in a couple of weeks, I quite understand.' Marcia paused. 'One thing before you go, though.'

She glanced at her soothsayer, whose cheek looked suspiciously red and puffy. As though it might have been slapped.

'Those soil tests of yours. You . . . might want to rethink some of the advice.'

Claudia smiled. It was the closest Marcia would ever get to emotional generosity. 'You might, too,' she replied.

Out in the garden, the heat warmed the shrubs, wafting aromas of bay and citrons around the peristyle, and the fountains gurgled and sang. Who would clip the topiaried cockerel now Semir was gone? How quickly would his 'rosses' die, with wine poisoning their roots, and what would become of the flamingoes, the lovebirds, the chattering monkeys? Without Tarbel, who would take Marcia's arrows for her? Surely it was the slant of the sun, but already the villa seemed to have an air of decay about it.

Down in the herb garden, a man in a freshly laundered blue tunic was digging a hole with a trowel.

'Let me guess, it's a grave for a mole.'

'Close, madam, very close. This is indeed a grave, but one to hold a dead canary, not a rodent.' Hannibal laid his cluster of feathers in the hole with reverence. 'I found this to be a grand talking point in inns and taverns on my travels, and I cannot deny that it helped me strike many a robust relationship with the ladies. But there comes a point when all noble creatures reach the end of their allotted span.'

Claudia watched as he covered the feathers with earth.

'The gesture is purely symbolic, of course, but it is my opinion that it's not always enough to say goodbye to the past. Sometimes burial is the only answer.'

She nodded in understanding. 'No more roving.'

'My travels, like my purple-striped tunic and this good-luck charm, have reached the end of their lifespan.'

She owed him an apology. When he had sloped off from the Forum, leaving Junius alone while Claudia went to meet with his so-called informant (and how could Hannibal possibly have known it was Vincentrix?), the reason she couldn't find him at the villa was because he'd been in bed with Stella. Waiting behind the shrubbery, she'd despised him for the sorrow she'd believed he was sowing, fully expecting him to move on, when Stella clearly deserved so much better.

'What about your aversion to orange blossom? You said it made your nose run something wicked?'

'Ah, but there's the rub, madam, there's the rub. My bright little star has a husband she can neither divorce nor declare dead, but even were she free such are the scars he bequeathed that she is in no hurry to replace him.' He straightened up and ran a leathery hand over his face. 'No fetters, dear lady, are often stronger than those that bind.'

Pollen in the air, Claudia presumed. What else would make her eyes water? And suddenly Stella's absence became less of a mystery, too. 'You know who the Scarecrow is, don't you?'

'It seemed a strange coincidence that birds mostly fluttered from the trees when Stella or the children were in the vicinity, so I put my theory to the test, using a meadow in a bend by the river as bait. When I was certain, I confronted her with the knowledge, and, frankly, until I took that walk in the canyon I had not considered myself a coward. I would rather walk barefoot over hot spikes while being beaten with clubs than repeat that experience. However,' Hannibal patted the soil over the grave, 'my little star is adamant that she does

231

not want the scoundrel back and, call me biased, I believe she is right.'

So did Claudia. It just took her all bloody night to convince the Scarecrow that the best thing he could do for his family was keep right on walking . . .

'I'm assuming you whisked her away to talk things through on neutral territory?'

Something approaching pain tightened his jaw. 'I whisked her away, certainly. To an inn you are yourself familiar with, close to the river in Santonum, though before you ask, you saucebox, it was nothing like that. You see, it wasn't until I saw the relief that swept over her when she recognized me that I began to comprehend the terror that women in these parts experienced. And, since Stella is at her peak of physical perfection, I felt it my duty not only to protect her, but hunt down the killer.'

'The children were worried sick.'

'An exaggeration, madam, an exaggeration. The children were curious, as all children are. Their routine had been disrupted. But they were safe with their aunt.' He slanted her a wry glance. 'Miserable, I grant you. But safe.'

'You couldn't possibly have known it was Paris!'

'Yesterday morning before dawn, I took a walk round Marcia's tomb and saw that a new caryatid had been carved. One so young and so perfect and with such an air of authenticity that her perfection made me weep with fear. I hadn't heard of another girl reported missing, but this statue was so real that I set out to make enquiries.' He cracked his knuckles. 'You know, between us, madam, we are not a bad team.'

No, Hannibal, we are not, and Stella was wise to seize her chance to escape, though the sad part was Marcia was so busy haranguing deserting rats that she hadn't actually noticed the trunks stacking up outside her own cousin's quarters.

'Where will you go?' Claudia asked. 'How will you manage?'

'Any place where eight free spirits can breathe freely and, as I told you before, hard work doesn't scare me. Though if the day dawns when it does, I plan to sell the children off one at a time. There are so many, their mother won't notice.'

232

Yes, and he'd cut off his own leg before he'd harm them.

'May you find equal happiness,' he said, embracing her. 'But what's this?'

'Back pay.'

He scratched a puzzled head. 'There must be something to those Druids' herbs. I thought I was in your employ for a fortnight, not a couple of centuries, and, besides. I am not your father.'

'Of course you're not! For a start, you're too old—'

'Thank you.' The sarcasm in his voice was heavy. 'But that, madam, is not what I meant. Do you imagine I don't know why you engaged my services at one measly sestertius a day? You hoped such dismal pay would drive me away—'

'Bollocks! I employed you specifically to *find* my damned father. Now take it,' she said, thrusting the purse back. 'If not for yourself, take the money for Stella. With that many free spirits, you'll need something to start off with.'

'You hoped such dismal pay would drive me away, proving the inconstancy of men everywhere,' Hannibal persisted. 'Your father abandoned you and since it is your belief that we're all cast from the same mould, you set out to prove it. But some day, young lady, you will have to place your trust in a man.' He glanced at the cripple limping down the path on crutches. 'I'm sure there are a few half-decent ones left.'

As he ambled back to the house, she watched as he stopped to shake hands with Orbilio and then, to her surprise, salute him, and something bucked inside her ribcage. What if she hadn't stuffed that wicker box into her robe yesterday? What if Hannibal hadn't appeared on the scene? *What if she hadn't been able to save him?*

'Aren't you supposed to be in bed?' she remarked, as he approached.

'Doctor threw me out,' Marcus replied. 'Told me I was scaring the werewolves.'

She studied the patchwork of bruises and swellings. 'More likely you set off on a speedy recovery then took a turn for the nurse.'

But there were hollows round his eyes whose origins did not arise from any physical ordeal at the hands of the Druids . . .

233

'I'm sorry about Zina.'

'It seems so unfair,' he said quietly. 'She was willing to forfeit her family, her culture, everything, to bring her step-father to justice, yet at the very moment she's branded a national heroine, some sick bastard comes along and –' he clicked his fingers – 'she's gone. Just like that.'

There was nothing Claudia could say.

'I'm going to miss her ridiculous misinterpretations, you know that?' A sad smile twisted the scabs in his cheeks. 'Those big black eyes and bossy ways. Heaven help the Empire if all Gaulish women are like her!'

'From the few that I've met' – Marcia, Stella, Zina, the landlady – 'they're not the sort who turn their faces to the wall. What will happen to Vincentrix?'

A muscle twitched in his jaw. 'We have two options,' he said evenly. 'One, let the full retribution of Rome descend upon the Druids.'

By that he meant drag them through Gaul in chains, that everyone might see what happens to those who practise human sacrifice, before executing them in the arena.

'The danger there is that we unleash a backlash as the Gauls side with their spiritual guides. After all,' he shrugged, 'to make martyrs of the Druids is to raise them up to become judges, philosophers and gods rolled into one again.'

'I'm guessing you favour option two?'

'As much as I'd like to see Vincentrix toppled from his pedestal, the sword of Vengeance is still capable of striking a fatal blow.'

Far better, he argued, that Rome clamp down quietly on the Druids' practices to ensure that no more wicker men were sacrificed, then let human nature take its course.

'Their power is already reduced to little more than the settlement of boundary disputes and the odd inheritance issue,' he explained. 'Let's keep it that way.'

'And have the beast die slowly?'

He smiled. 'Delicious, isn't it?'

Above the smell of mouldy bread poultices and vinegar antiseptic wash, she caught a whiff of sandalwood unguent, overlaid with a hint of the rosemary in which his long patrician tunic had been rinsed. She watched as he swiped his

234

fringe out of his eyes. Followed the line of crisp, dark hairs on the back of his hand as they disappeared up his forearm.

Let it go, the landlady had said. *Let it go.*

As bees searched the last flowers of the oregano and butterflies explored the massive thistleheads of purple cardoons, Claudia thought back to that day in the tavern.

I'm sorry for you, honest I am, because you wouldn't have come all this way if it wasn't important.

At the time, though, it was . . .

It's never just one man, she had said. *It's always somebody's father and somebody's son, a brother, a lover, a friend.*

Yes, but whilst a woman might have several brothers or sons, lovers or friends, she will only have one father . . .

The way I see it, love, if the man you're looking for's dead, then he's dead, and if he's alive – well, I reckon he don't want to be found.

The Merry Widow was right. Of course the wretched woman was right. And, in her heart, Claudia had known all along that it was stupid to waste time and effort on a man who hadn't thought his daughter worth so much as a note. It was the future that mattered, not the past – but what was the future? It was so easy to manage the past. The past was a known entity, something you could deal with because it was familiar, where the future was no more than a gamble that relied on the toss of dice by an unknown hand.

Or was it?

Was it really coincidence that the Security Police had turned up in Sicily, Umbria, Gaul? Was it really coincidence that Marcus Cornelius could crack paedophile rings and thwart assassination attempts on the Emperor's life, yet was incapable of clapping widows in irons for paltry misdemeanours? It wasn't until she had cut him down from the tree yesterday that she had realized. As he slumped on to her shoulder, he didn't thank her or let out a sigh of relief. He'd said *I love you* before he collapsed.

'That four letter word you muttered in the forest.'

'Yes, I apologize about that. It was just that Vincentrix—'

'Not that one.'

'Oh? You have to remember I'd inhaled a lot of drugs by the time you arrived. I was seeing people who'd been dead twenty years. Can you be a little more specific?'

Dammit, he wasn't making this easy. 'Like it or not, Orbilio, you're worse than a rash—'

'I hate it when you flatter me.'

'But since there's no cure for this rash, I . . .' She cleared her throat. 'Orbilio, there's something I have to tell you.'

'Now there's a coincidence.' He moved closer and his voice was little more than a rasp. 'I came down here with something to tell you, too.'

He might not have remembered that moment in the clearing, but there was a dark, intense glint in his eye that she didn't recognize. With a skittering inside, the likes of which she'd never known, Claudia resisted the urge to wrap her arms round his battered, bruised body and heal his cut, swollen lips with her kisses.

'You first.' She wasn't sure she could get it out in one breath anyway. Treacherous lungs had stopped pumping air. 'There's ample time for me to say my bit on the journey home.'

'Well, that's the thing,' Marcus rasped. 'I need to move on with my life, Claudia.' He paused. Shifted his crutches. 'I won't be returning to Rome this time round. I've made other plans for my future.'